Un
Journey

Unintended
Bride

Michael J. Leamy

ISBN: **9798878103763**

DEDICATION

This work of fiction is dedicated to the glory of God.

Ecclesiastes 12:12 says,"Of making many books there is no end, and much study is a weariness of the flesh." The author sees this as the student's life verse. But, he chooses to take part in the making of books for those who enjoy the printed page, and dedicates these thoughts to cluttering the minds of readers with characters who have inhabited the caverns of his mind, acting out the drama recorded in these pages. Enjoy!

Then they cried to the LORD in their trouble, and he delivered them from their distress. He made the storm be still, and the waves of the sea were hushed. Then they were glad that the waters were quiet, and he brought them to their desired haven. (Psalm 107:28-30)

CONTENTS

ACKNOWLEDGMENTS

My dear wife, Lynda, has read these pages, catching typos and random punctuation marks, proofreading as she enjoys the chapters. The characters in the book are imaginary. The historical characters, settings and events are real, and are part of the stage where the characters interact. The conversations with historical characters are fictional.

I would also like to extend heart-felt thanks to Brittany, Justina and Brianna for their pre-publication critical analysis and suggestions as they read a romance written from a masculine viewpoint.

Part One

Ohio

June, 1851

Chapter 1

BUDDY WILSON looped the reins over the handles of the single bottom plow. Flexing stiff fingers, he surveyed the flood-ravaged bottom land that held such promise just two months ago. In mid-April, the acreage had been green with thriving corn. Heavy rains of May had ballooned Brush Creek into the biggest flood locals could recall. Indeed, every stream in the Ohio Valley sent such volumes of water that the Ohio River itself ran at a rampaging depth of over sixty feet.

The sprouted crop that had held so much potential was now sealed beneath more than a foot of sand and silt. The low field of the Wilson farm languished in a morass of ruin, along with the other low-land farms along the creek. The downpours that had continued throughout May had moved to the south and west, but the runoff that had overflowed the streams of Ohio had washed away hope of productivity for the year, and threatened the payments that would come due after the harvest that would not come.

Humming to himself, Buddy pulled a muddy boot out of the silt, and picked his way forward, checking the harness and traces. Benny was old, and his skin was quick to show wear wherever the gear rubbed against him.

Humming changed to snatches of the hymn as he examined the contact points.

When I survey the wondrous cross
on which the Prince of glory died,
my richest gain I count but loss,
and pour contempt on all my pride.

The hymn was broken by his effort to walk through the mud.

"I'm not sure this is the time for such work, even if you're willing." The young farmer scritched the base of the mule's ears, and checked the halter. "I'm not going to push you this time. You just might turn traitor on me again. But, one of these days, we will have to get this done. For us, it isn't a matter of money. We have a stewardship. It's a point of honor."

Buddy turned, staring with exasperated eyes at the length of the furrow he had just plowed, now half filled with water. The hoof prints of Benedict Arnold, the old mule, were goblets that held the seepage of the bottom sogginess. The mule's hooves, like his own boots, had made slurping sounds as they struggled to make progress down the length of the field. Four days without rain had not been enough time for the water to drain out of the soil. The field was exposed, but Brush Creek still ran bank full.

Throughout May, Buddy had watched the creek.

The deluge had come, and almost overnight the spring planting had disappeared beneath the muddy flow that spread nearly to the road that ran between the house and the lower forty. Downstream, the road and the bridge over No Name Creek had also disappeared beneath the swirling flood. With the falling flood water, the road and bridge had emerged unscathed. If the road was undamaged upstream, the isolation of May would be ended.

Buddy popped the sled from between the handles of the plow and set it beside the muddy blade. Flexing his fingers again, he seized the grips and lifted the plow out of the furrow and set it on the skid, and buckled the sled straps to the harness. Grabbing the halter by the cheek strap, he said, "Come along, Benny. No use wasting our time here. Let's get you back to your stall."

The plow slid easily over the smooth silt. Buddy followed the furrow, then turned up the slope toward the gate. Above the silt-covered lower field, the plow skid pressed a path through the grass that had not been buried. The bruised grass perfumed the air like the new-mowed hay he hoped late July would bring.

When they reached the gate, Buddy released the cheek strap and reached for the latch. Old Benny cocked his long ears southward, and snorted. Distant hoof beats and the rattle of wheels grew gradually louder, and a doctor's buggy, top down, topped the rise. The portly driver, who had slouched loosely on the seat, gathered himself into a more dignified posture.

Buddy grinned. "Jackson Wiggins, Esquire. I wonder what he... Oh, yeah. I was supposed to stop and see him a couple of weeks ago."

Swinging the gate out across the road, Buddy led the mule to the other side. He got the gate closed again just as the buggy clattered to a stop.

"Well, son, looks like old Brush Creek got a bit wild. Lose any ground?" The merry face above the white whiskers tried to look serious, but failed.

"No, Mr. Wiggins, I think I gained some. Trouble is, I didn't gain any acreage. What I got was piled on top of what I already had." Buddy shook his head, and sighed. "The new stuff is too new. I tried plowing it, but all I did was to plow a river. Benedict Arnold did his best, but his footsteps and my own were wells."

Holding a dignified posture was too demanding, and Mr. Wiggins sagged back down on the seat. "Young man, by now I should be Jack."

Buddy reached into his jacket pocket and pulled out one of old Benny's carrots. "Yes, sir. Can Penelope have one of these? I keep a supply to bribe the mule to work a little, Mr. Wiggins...Jack. Grandma Wilson always told me to honor my elders, so you've always been Mr.

Wiggins. I am a little older, but it seems I haven't caught up enough to be on a first name basis with you."

The shaggy brows drew down, but the eyes below them twinkled. "Listen, you young whipper snapper. I decided you are old enough. Sure, give the girl a carrot. And I like a treat now and then. Call me Jack."

Buddy frowned, and shook his head. "Grandma Wilson would turn over in her grave. How about Uncle Jack? She sometimes called you that."

The old man laughed. "Well, now. That's family. It'll do."

Buddy held the carrot out to the mare. Groping lips brushed his hand, and the morsel vanished, to be slowly crushed to release all of the hidden flavor.

Old eyes surveyed the devastated field. "Kinda late for a crop this year. The creek was a bit hard on your field. Are you going to be all right? You have money on account, you know."

Looking over the mare's neck, Buddy locked eyes with his visitor. His expression was resolute. "Uncle Jack, you know better. That field is not mine. The money is not mine." Buddy's hand trembled a bit as he scratched behind the mare's ear. "Sure, I did the work, but, since the fire took the Wilsons, and since Sarah disappeared, this has been a stewardship. Nothing is mine. I can't even say the name I use is mine. Grandma Wilson gave it to me. I don't know who I really am."

Jackson Wiggins shook his head. "No, Son, I don't know that any of us knows who or what we are, until our character reveals that to us and to others. A name doesn't make a man. But that is why I came by. You were going to drop by my office before this little shower we had. I need to chat with you."

"Well, I headed your way, but when the water reached my knees, old Ben and I turned back. I guess I should say, Ben turned back. He didn't want to go to New Orleans."

Uncle Jack laughed. "I guess I'd have had some choice things to call you if you had showed up. As bad as it was, we just got the top edge of it. Guess it's worse the farther down the river you go. As it is, I still saw trees spinning down the Ohio as I drove up. We even had that fool river tickling the sides of Rome. Lost a couple of shacks early on. They were down close to the shore. The river picked 'em up whole, took them out in the middle, and tore them apart. No idea if all the folks down in the bottoms made it out."

Silence hung between them for a moment. Then, "What are you going to do with that field? It's a mite late for planting any kind of grain."

Buddy turned, and surveyed the fruitless work of

the morning. "I don't know. I had to try something. That sand and silt likely would not produce anything. Besides, I used up my seed."

Uncle Jack snorted. "No, I'd say all the value in that dirt has made it past Saint Louie by now." He pushed his shapeless hat to one side, and scratched the fringe of hair above his left ear. "Tell you what I'd do, if that was my field. The grocer in Rome has three barrels of potatoes that are wrinkly and sprouty. He can't sell them, and nobody would eat them anyway. Hitch old Benedict Arnold to your buckboard, drive into town, and I'll tell him to give them to you. Most of them should make seed potatoes. You will likely lose some of them. The ones at the bottom of the barrels might be rotten and stinky."

Buddy looked at the stretch of silt the creek had left, and asked, "You think that mess will grow potatoes?"

"Might. Taters do all right in poor soil. Seems I recall they like sandy stuff." Uncle Jack paused, thinking. Then, "Save yourself some time, too. I think that may be the only money crop you could get, with the year half gone."

Looking over the muddy bottom land, the old man traced the shape of the field on the leather seat of the buggy. Running a finger back and forth along the imaginary map, he said, "Once the water settles out of that muck, take your plow down and run the length of the field up here just below the road. Leave the furrow open. Then turn around and plow another furrow about three feet closer to the creek. If you get water in the furrows, lay off for a day or so. Working toward the creek, you'll chase the water down hill as you work, not that you have that much slope."

Buddy ran his fingers through his unruly brown hair, then settled his battered hat back in place. He turned from the field, looking to where the mule stood dozing, his muzzle hanging near the ground. "I guess it won't hurt to try. I can go tomorrow and be back by evening."

Wiggins threw up his hand. "No, wait a bit. I have to be in West Union all day tomorrow. I'll get back to Rome the next day, and talk to the grocer." Uncle Jack scritched his whiskers, then said, "Come down in three days. I'll have a couple of men ready to help you load those barrels. Get an early start, and then when you are loaded, I can get a couple of hours to pick your brain. So far, I hit a bunch of dead ends on you and Sarah. But, you might have another clue hiding in that empty head of yours."

Both men grinned at the last part. Buddy laughed and said, "If there's anything more up there, I have not found it. But then, I was a bit younger when all that happened. I might have lost it."

Uncle Jack chuckled. "You would be surprised what all is hiding between your ears. We just have to shake it loose. Maybe I should grab a stick of fire wood..." His belly shook with silent laughter.

Buddy laughed out loud. "That might help! Couldn't hurt. Grandpa Wilson used to say, 'Where there's no sense, there's no feel.' That would sure fit in my case. How far apart should I plant those potatoes?"

Uncle Jack's eyes twinkled. Crow's feet above his white whiskers showed the kindness behind his banter. "It can't be all vacant up there. Any youngster like you who can squeeze a profit out of this patch of ground year after year has to have something between his ears." He gazed at the low field for a moment. "Tell you what I'd do. Walk the furrows, and drop a tater every three feet. Cut the bigger ones in half. That'll give each one plenty of room to store the new crop. They won't starve each other that way. Even spacing will look kinda good, too."

"Three feet each way. Got it. Guess we all need a bit of space to grow. Sarah's been gone, what, seven years? Would I even know her now?" Buddy paused. "No, it's more like eight years. She was four years younger than me. She'd be seventeen, now. I can't even remember what I was like at seventeen."

Uncle Jack roared with laughter. "I do. You were an old man, like you are now. You've been older than your years since you took up the reins of this place. You fixed up that log cabin after the fire, and planted and harvested since before you could make that plow bite into the dirt. You could have lived in Rome with any of half a dozen families. Why did you insist on staying here?"

Buddy sighed. "The Wilsons were the first folks that really wanted me. My mother and father died somehow, before I can remember. Sarah was here, and I owed it to the Wilsons to take care of her stuff. It was a point of honor."

Uncle Jack gathered the reins, and said, "Point of honor. We'll discuss that when you get those taters. Today's Wednesday. I'll be back in town on Friday. If you drive in on Saturday, we can talk a bit without anyone interrupting. Checkers and a cuppa?"

Buddy grinned. "Gonna beat me again? The tea sounds good, though. Better move along. The way that mare of yours moves, it'll be dark before you get to where you're going. It's what...eight miles? It could take her until tomorrow, with the load she has to pull."

Uncle Jack drew himself up, harumphed, and slapped the reins on the mare' caboose. "Just for that, you get molasses in your tea. Git along, girl. We know when we've been insulted. We'll think of some smart come back as we go."

Over his shoulder, he shouted, "Put that mule away. And don't forget to clean the plow!"

Chapter 2

JACKSON WIGGINS set his cup of tea on the chair beside him, leaned back and propped his heels on the scarred table that served as his desk. Buddy Wilson leaned his elbows on the opposite side. He held the heavy mug with both hands wrapped around it, soaking up the heat. He stared at the worn soles of Uncle Jacks boots.

Shifting his gaze to the old face of his friend, he said, "Those boots have a few miles on them. Why don't you get some new ones?"

Uncle Jack didn't open his eyes. "Young man," he said, "These boots have walked different men about this country. They've carried a farmer, a soldier, a green grocer, a U. S. Marshall, an attorney and a justice of the peace. They have been resoled about as often as I have. The tops are still good, and I can't tell you which of us has more miles left in us. What's left is in the Lord's hands. If I wear out first, you can have what's left of these boots. You might get too big for your britches, but your feet should stay the same size for a while, and I think these would fit you."

Buddy drained his tea, and savored the slug of honey in the bottom of the mug.

Without opening his eyes, Uncle Jack said, "There's more in the pot. Fill your mug. You might want to add a bit of hot water out of the kettle there on the pot belly. The pot might be getting a bit rich. While you are at it, toss another spoon of tea leaves in the teapot, and fill it with some of the hot water. We might be a while, depending on what you can recall.

"Paul Revere made that teapot. Kinda special."

Buddy picked up the silver teapot, and turned it about. "Looks like the one Grandma Wilson had. She said George Washington gave it to Grandpa Wilson's great grandfather. I think it was a Revere, too. I use it, but I never thought of its history."

Buddy added honey from the chipped honey pot, and tasted the tea. "Yeah, it's getting a bit strong. Got any milk?"

"There in the ice box. Put it here on the table when you're done."

"You still have ice?"

"No, but cold water holds the milk for a while. I just sink a bottle up to the neck in a bucket. The ice box keeps it cool."

Buddy hummed a little, then softly sang the

words of the hymn.

> **At the cross, at the cross,**
> **Where I first saw the light,**
> **And the burden of my heart rolled away,**
> **It was there by faith I received my sight,**
> **And now I am happy all the day!**

"Isaac Watts." Wiggins fumbled for his own tea mug. "Love his songs. Can't sing at all, but I like good words when I hear them. Sing it again, Buddy."

He did.

Wiggins said, "I recall hearing a bit about Watts having a part in the war. Seems the Colonials were fussing with the Redcoats, and ran out of waddin' for the cannons. Minister came running out of the church with songbooks. Said, 'Give 'em Watts! Lord knows they need it!"

When Buddy sat staring into the mug, Uncle Jack asked, "Got your taters loaded all right?"

"Yeah. And I think I have more than enough for that lower field."

"Got a way to unload them?"

"There's a block and tackle in the barn. I can hoist a barrel, drive the wagon out from under it, and lower it to the floor. I cobbled a cart together that will hold all three barrels, so I can move it out of the way. And, by the way, I did not thank you for the idea and the influence with the grocer. The thing is worth trying. Thanks."

Uncle Jack waved the thanks aside. He said, "It was an excuse to get you in here. Now, spin me a tale. Start as early as you can remember, and throw in all the details you can recall, even if they seem unimportant. There may be a clue we missed."

Buddy shook his head. "I told you everything I recalled. I haven't come up with anything else."

"Well, tell me again. I might have missed something while I was napping. I might ask a question here and there. Now, get started. What is the first thing you remember? Where were you born?"

Buddy ran his fingers through his hair, and hooked his fingers on the back of his neck. He heard the ticking of Uncle Jack's old grandfather clock as it stretched the seconds into minutes. With a whir, the mallet struck once. One o'clock? Something thirty? With a sigh, he started the narrative again.

"I'm not sure where it was. I recall a log home, smaller than the Wilson one. There was a stream or a pond or a lake nearby. I remember...'Stay away from the water!'" Here Buddy's voice rose to a high pitch.

Uncle Jack grunted. "That would have been your mother. Go on."

Buddy didn't notice the interruption. "I don't remember how old I was, but there was a bunch of people who came. After they left, my father never came home again. I remember going with my mother to the church. We would go up behind the building, and there was a place where she would sit down and cry."

"He had died." Uncle Jack said. "Your father's grave was behind the church."

"I don't know what I was doing, but she would always say, 'Don't shame us.' I guess that was the start of my 'point of honor' thing. I didn't want to shame them. Sometimes she said it twice: 'Don't shame us, shame us.'"

The tired eyes flew open, and the boots crashed to the floor. "What was that? Say that again!"

"She would say it twice. 'Don't shame us, shame us.'"

Uncle Jack repeated what Buddy had said. "That is a clue. You were Irish. You never mentioned that part before."

Buddy had jolted out of his reverie when Uncle Jack's feet hit the floor.

"I had forgotten that part. But as I was telling you, it was as if I could hear the voice saying it in my head. But, what do you mean, Irish?"

"She was not saying it twice. S-E-A-M-A-S.

Sounds like shame us. Seamas is Irish for James. So that is your first name. Seamas. James. Don't shame us, James. You must have been playing on the graves, not showing what your mother thought would be the proper respect."

"How can you be sure of that?" Buddy asked. "I mean, could that really be my name? James?"

The old man frowned. "No, I can't be sure. I'm guessing, but I can tell you it is a good guess. You can be James, or Jim, or Jimmy or Jimbo. You can be Irish and call yourself Seamas. Or you can hold on to Buddy. That means friend, and sounds friendly. Not that any form of James doesn't."

"I think I'll hold off on changing my name. I got kind of used to Buddy. A new name would take some getting used to."

"All right. Now go on with your story." Uncle Jack resumed his former position. "See if you can make me jump again."

Buddy leaned back, balancing his chair on two legs. Looking at the ceiling, he went on. "There was a time later when my mother cried out, and then told me to run to the neighbors, and tell the lady it was time. I didn't know what it was time for, and the neighbors were over a hill, down above a hollow. The lady carried me back home. She sent her husband for another neighbor lady farther from our house. When they got to our house, the man took me out to the barn."

"Um-hmmm." Uncle Jack let Buddy know he was listening.

"The neighbor lady and her husband took me home with them. The next day, we went up behind the church again. There was a hole beside my father's grave, and they put a big box in it. The neighbors took me home with them again. I never saw my mother after that. I know now that they both had died. The neighbors told me to call them Aunt Sarah and Uncle Hank."

Uncle Jack mumbled, "Childbirth."

Buddy looked up. "What did you say?"

Uncle Jack cleared his throat. "I said, childbirth. Your mother died giving birth to the baby she was carrying when your father died."

"Oh. Anyway, Aunt Sarah and Uncle Hank called me Sonny. Then, one week, they loaded all they could into a big wagon, and put me on the seat between them. They headed down river. I asked where we were going, and they said, 'We are going to Nebraska.' They emphasized the word we. I found out later that I wasn't included in their plans. We got to Brush Creek, and they drove up to No Name Creek. They turned the wagon around at the bottom of the road that headed up that little creek, and then set me down on the ground. They said, 'We did all we could for you, Sonny. Now it is Grandma Wilson's turn.' Then they drove back down Brush Creek, and disappeared. I waited to see if they would come back for me. They didn't.

"It was hot, so I started up No Name. I came to a long pool that looked inviting. I left my clothes on a rock, and went wading. They were the only clothes I had. I saw a fish go under a cut bank, and was trying to see where it went, when I heard a kid's voice ask, 'What are you doing?' I said, 'I'm cooling off.' There was a little girl on the bank. 'Can I come in? It's too hot.' I told her she could, and went back looking for my fish. Then she splashed into the pool. Her clothes were on the rock by mine. She helped me look for the fish. Neither one of us was wearing anything, but at that age, it did not matter. We were just cooling off."

"Ahem!" Uncle Jack chuckled.

"What?"

"Oh, nothing. I was just remembering skinny dipping in the Ohio when I was a kid. But, it was just us boys. Go on."

"Our legs got cold, so we climbed out and sat on a rock in the sun. That dried us off, and we got our clothes back on. A woman's voice called, 'Sarah, where are you? Get in the house, right now!' The little girl was another Sarah.

"She asked me, 'Where do you live?' I thought about Aunt Sarah and Uncle Hank driving away without me. 'No place,' I said.

"She said, 'I'll take you to Grandma Wilson. Her name is Edna, but she said to call her Grandma. And Grandpa is Joe.' I said, 'I can't get something for nothing. That's a point of honor.' She latched onto that last part, and forever after, when she wanted me to do something, she would say, 'Point of honor!' I had to do her bidding."

Uncle Jack shook with laughter. "A girl can do that to us! Just imagine if you had been married to her! Go on, though."

Buddy rocked his chair back down on all four legs, and leaned his elbows on the table again. "There's not much more. Sarah told Grandma Wilson I had been wading in the creek, and didn't have any place to live. She said I didn't want to take something for nothing. She told Grandma Wilson maybe I could work in the barn. Grandma Wilson looked me over, and said I might, but I was kind of puny. She thought maybe they could fix an empty stall up for me to sleep in. Imagine that! Here Sarah and I had been wading naked in the same pool, but we couldn't sleep in the same loft!"

Uncle Jack murmured, "Point of honor!"

Buddy finished, "That was the way it was until the fire. I worked with Grandpa Wilson as I was able, and learned how to farm. They called me Buddy. So, I went from Son to Sonny to Buddy, and somewhere between Logan's Crossing and Brush Creek, I lost my name."

Uncle Jack's feet crashed to the floor. "There you have done it again. That's the first I've heard of Logan's Crossing. That may be another clue! Where did Logan's Crossing come in?"

Buddy looked puzzled, then slowly said, "Some man stopped by the farm on his way to West Union. Looking at me, he said to Grandpa Wilson, 'He's older and bigger, but he reminds me of the kid usta be over at Logan's Crossing.' And Grandpa Wilson said, 'Might be.'"

Uncle Jack grabbed a stub of a pencil and a scrap of paper. He wrote: *Seamas –James?? Logan's Crossing??*

"Now, go back to the fire. That was eight years ago. You were thirteen, maybe fourteen then. What happened. It was at night, wasn't it?"

Buddy shuddered, remembering. "I was in the barn when I heard Sarah screaming. I got the door open in time to see her running from the house. Her night dress was in flames. The loft was above the cook stove, and that is where the fire started. The logs behind the cook stove were the worst burned in the fire. I put a sheet iron shield behind the stove when I fixed things. With all that smoke, she should have been dead. She made it down the ladder, but her dress caught fire. She ran out the door, and her running toward the barn fanned the flames. I tore what was left of her night dress off of her, and dunked it in the trough. Then I spread it on the ground, and put her face down on it. She couldn't lie still. Her back was all blistered, and a bunch of the blisters were popped. I told her to stay there, and ran to the spring house. There was a basket of eggs there, and I took them and broke them over her back. I held the yolks in my fingers, and threw the shells and yolks aside, then spread the whites all over the blistered parts of her."

Uncle Jack shook his head. "Where in the world did you learn that trick? That's the one thing that would keep her from having scars all over her back!"

Buddy's eyebrows shot up, showing his surprise. "Aunt Sarah was a 'Kaintucky yarb wummin', as Uncle Hank put it. He said she knew all sorts of medicine tricks like that. Once he broke an oil lamp, and burning oil covered his arm. She broke eggs over the burns, and his arm healed up as good as new. Uncle Hank said he was just like Naaman in the Bible. His skin was like that of a baby. I just hope Sarah healed the same way."

"Hmmmm." Uncle Jack shook his head, and made a clucking sound. "So she was naked again."

Buddy blushed. He muttered, "Yeah, but I pretended not to notice. So did she."

Uncle Jack mixed hot water and cold tea in his

cup, sipped it, and set it aside. "What about the old folks?"

"The smoke killed them. They are buried up above the orchard. It took me two days to dig their graves. I didn't make any boxes for them. I wrapped them in their blankets, and Benedict Arnold carried them up the hill.

"I started cleaning and fixing things up in the cabin. I think it was a week later when I got back to the house from working in the barn, Sarah was not there. I checked the loft, and her stuff was gone. There was a note on her pillow."

Buddy pulled a folded, tattered paper out of his pocket, and handed it to Uncle Jack. "I knew I had this, but I had forgotten where I put it."

The older man took the letter, and read it aloud: "Buddy, I'm leaving. The man says he is my Uncle George, and he is supposed to take me. He said he is the guardian of me and my estate. I don't know what an estate is. I don't know him. He says if you try to follow, he will kill you, and then me." The two men stared at the paper. Uncle Jack said, "You have read this. Do you still want me to try to find the trail? It has been eight years. A seventeen-year-old girl is in more danger from such a man than a ten-year-old."

Buddy bowed his head, then said, "We have to. Point of honor."

Uncle Jack thought a moment, then said, "If I can

follow your back trail, I might find something of her front trail. I think I'll try to track down Logan's Crossing."

Chapter 3

THE MULE Benedict Arnold drove himself home after the interview in Rome. Buddy contemplated the importance of names. Mr. Stout had insisted on naming the settlement after the city in Italy. Some folks called it Stout, after the founder, but gradually Stout's choice stuck. It was Rome. The town occupied only a quarter section, but in spite of its diminutive size, the grandiose name labeled its rag tag collection of buildings. So, he wondered, which of his names should he choose? Seamas sounded a little exotic, and a lot foreign. James was aristocratic, even royal sounding. There had been kings named James, and an apostle. Jim or Jimmy was down-to-Earth, friendly sounding. But then, so was Buddy.

"What about your name?" For want of better company, Buddy talked to the mule. "Benedict Arnold was a traitor. What did you do in your younger days? You've always been somewhat settled while I knew you. I think I like Ben or Benny better. Maybe as a youngster you rebelled against Grandpa Wilson's work plan. Was that it?"

Old Ben just plodded on. The wagon wheels

squished through the mud and silt in the low patches, and crunched the gravel on higher ground. Buddy settled back into his reverie.

His mind wandered to Sarah. Was that even her name? Could she have been assigned that name? Was she a Wilson? Grandma and Grandpa Wilson seemed a little old to have a girl Sarah's age. If she was not theirs, who was she? She had mentioned an estate. Was she somebody's heir?

Without thinking or noticing, he turned up Brush Creek. Above the clouds, geese encouraged one another on their northward flight. The mule crossed No Name Creek, labored up the slope and stopped in front of the barn. Buddy sat a moment, and then realized the wagon wasn't moving. Down toward the creek, a chorus of frogs sang in the damp residue of the flood. The musty scent of mud clung to the earth.

"We're home?" He stretched, kicked the stiffness out of his legs, and jumped down to open the barn doors. "We still have a couple of hours of daylight. Let's get the wagon under cover, and you in your stall. I owe you for getting us home. How about an extra measure of oats?"

Buddy drove the wagon into the barn, unharnessed the mule, and led him to the trough. Water dripped from old Ben's muzzle as he was shut in his stall. His head drooped as Buddy rubbed him down with a handful of straw, humming as he worked.

He gave voice to the words.

Alas, and did my Savior bleed,
And did my Sov'reign die?
Would He devote that sacred head
For such a worm as I?

As Buddy latched the stall door, Ben was eye-deep in the grain bucket. The warm animal smell perfumed the air in the barn. "You smell better than all that mud!"

Buddy glanced at the barrels in the wagon. "Tomorrow. I'll unload tomorrow."

Outside, Buddy surveyed the sky. Clouds sagged toward the horizon, threatening more rain. He shook his head. "If that furrow has water in it, there won't be any plowing for a few days." He called back to the mule, "Looks like you get a bit of rest, my friend. But, maybe the clouds are just fooling. We'll see what tomorrow brings."

"No more rain!"

Buddy spun around, and saw a man swinging down from a piebald horse. He recognized the mare of his neighbor from down the river from Brush Creek.

Joe Simmons looped the mare's reins over the hitching rail. "Things drying out any, Buddy?"

"Not that you'd notice, Mr. Simmons. I tried a furrow, and came up with a long lake. Every footstep was a well. I can get you a cuppa in a few minutes, if you have the time. I just got back from Rome."

"If it's tea, I could use a warm up. I think we have about half an hour. I've got to ask a favor of you."

The two men climbed the three steps to the wide porch. Buddy pulled the latch string, and led his neighbor into the front room. With one match, he lit the two kerosene lamps. He kindled a fire in the Monarch cook stove, and set the kettle to boil.

"Milk? Honey?

Simmons nodded. "Yes on both."

Buddy got the milk from the ice box, where, like Wiggins, he kept it in a bucket of cold water. He took the jar of honey from the cupboard, and set two mugs on the table. "I'll hotten the pot." After he set the silver teapot on the stove, he pulled out his Barlow pocket knife, and whittled some tea from the tea brick. "Grandpa Wilson had this knife. He said it was made in England before the Revolution. One of his ancestors got it from a redcoat. Good knife."

Pulling two chairs out from the table, Buddy said, "Sit. We can use the boiling time to talk. What do you need?"

"Your upper forty. My lower forty looks like yours.

I used mine for pasture. I can't put my cows and horses on my upper forty. I need that for hay, or they will starve this winter. They are going through the last of last year's hay. I'll run out the middle of next week."

"Well, that flood was hard on all of us along the creeks and the river. I lost my crop on the lower forty. It's under a foot or more of sand and silt. Jackson Wiggins said I should plant potatoes in that dirt this late in the year. He even arranged for me to get a load of sprouted potatoes for seed from the grocer in Rome. That's where I was today. I was just putting my old mule away when you came."

Buddy walked to the stove, and moved the hot teapot to the cooler part of the hot iron top. He poured the boiling water, and spooned the shaved tea into the teapot, a spoonful for each of the men and one for the pot. "Five minutes."

Joe Simmons pulled a mug to his end of the table. He spooned honey into it, and added a splash of milk. "Name your price. I can't argue. I need the pasture."

Buddy carried the teapot to the table, and wrapped a towel over it. "I won't hold you up." He prepared his mug, and went to the rack to get the tea strainer. Pouring the two mugs of tea, he asked, "Could you help me run the fence up there?"

Simmons waved him off. "I'll do that myself. You'll be busy planting taters."

Buddy sipped his tea, and said, "Only if the water goes down. That bottom land may not drain any time soon, and then only if it doesn't rain any more. Two can run that fence and secure it faster than one. I'll help."

Simmons stirred his tea, gazing at a stray tea leaf that circled, chasing the spoon handle. "All right, and then I'll help you plant taters. You're going to plow open furrows, right?"

"Exactly. That is what Uncle Jack suggested."

"Uncle Jack?"

"Mr. Wiggins, I mean. He said I should open furrows three feet apart, and drop the seed potatoes three feet apart in the rows."

Simmons laughed. "He sounds like a farmer. That will give your field a pretty pattern. Anyway, I'll help. You drop the taters, and I'll rake the dirt back into the ditch. But, what do you want for the rent of the upper forty?"

Buddy laughed in turn. "I don't want anything. But old Ben wants a ton of hay for his winter feed. Maybe a ton and a half. If your critters graze the upper forty, I won't get any hay from it."

Simmons frowned. "That's not enough." He

slurped tea and gulped it. "Tell you what I'll do. I'm going to kill a yearling, and I'll split it with you. I can even salt your half, if you like. I'll bring it to you in a brine barrel."

Buddy finished his tea. "I think you are trying to give too much. But, if you insist, I'll not refuse. A bit of beef will sure help this table! Thanks."

Simmons shook his head. "No, I don't think it's too much. Without your upper forty for pasture, my stock will starve. Without the income from the stock, I can't pay the bills. You are keeping me afloat."

Buddy waved the thanks aside. "I'll be busy Monday. Come over Tuesday, and we'll get to work on that fence. If we can get it finished in a day, I'll help you get the stock over here on Wednesday. That might leave you a bit of hay for that mare of yours.

Simmons rose and held out his hand. "You're an easy mark, Buddy. You could have held me up for a king's ransom, and here you are giving the store away. How come?"

Buddy took the offered hand. The grip of the two farmers would have made town men cry out, but for the two who labored in the fields, it was a solid bond of friendship. He said, "It seems I read somewhere, 'If a man has two coats, and sees his neighbor has none...' I've got a forty that is lying fallow. You have hungry stock. I think we each get a blessing. I can't just say, 'Be warm, be fed.' If I turned you away, as Grandma Wilson used to say, 'How dwells the love of God in him?'"

Simmons smiled. "You're a believer, then?"

"By God's grace and the Wilsons' prayers and teaching, I am."

Simmons clapped Buddy on the shoulder, and said, "Bless you, my friend. The Lord will get us through this. Maybe He allowed this trouble to get us to encourage one another. The Book is full of those one-another teachings." Heading for the door, he said, "I've stayed longer than I planned, but Snip knows the way home. She will just follow the smell of oats. I'll see you early Tuesday."

As the door closed behind Joe Simmons, Buddy picked up the mugs and put them on the sideboard. He turned and ran to the door. Pulling it open, he called, "Wait a minute!"

Simmons had the reins in his hand and was just swinging up onto the mare. "Did I forget something?"

Standing at the porch rail, Buddy spoke into the gathering gloom. "No. I just thought of a question you maybe could answer. Does the name Logan's Crossing ring a bell?"

Simmons thought a moment, then said, "No.

There were a lot of crossings along the Ohio. Most of them were named for a settlement, or for the guy in charge. I don't recall a town named Logan on the Ohio side, or over in Kentucky, for that matter. Maybe it was somebody's name."

Buddy laughed. "I'm too young to remember local history. You've been here a few years longer than I have, so I thought I'd ask."

"Well, there are a couple of old time settlers downstream from my place. If I remember, I'll ask them next time our trails cross. Now, I'd better head this old girl toward the barn. I'll be back on Tuesday." Simmons turned the horse, and faded into the gathering darkness.

Buddy listened as Snip's hoof beats faded into the sound of Brush Creek and the still-roaring Ohio River. In the barn, old Ben snorted as he settled in for the night. Overhead, a rift appeared in the drifting clouds, briefly revealing a crescent moon.

Looking as the moon vanished, Buddy prayed, "Lord, that was just a bit of light. Today held just enough for me to see the step I'm on. You know where this journey leads. Potatoes instead of grain, and You even provided the seed for the crop. Wherever Sarah is, or whoever she is, could You give her grace for her circumstances? And could You help me find her?"

Buddy's prayer was left suspended, as his was an

on-going conversation with the Lord. He crossed the porch, pulled the latch string, and entered the lamp-lighted front room. "Suppertime. I still have some bread, and soup won't take long. Thank You, Lord."

Chapter 4

Light rains, but persistent, returned to the Ohio valley on Sunday. Earlier heavy rain had been supplemented by snow melt, causing the flooding. With the snow gone, Sunday's rain only brought a three-inch rise to Brush Creek, but by evening, the single furrow in the lower forty was brim full.

Buddy led Ben out to the trough. When the mule had enough, and was back in his stall, he shook himself like a dog. His fur was left in tiny peaks.

"Yeah, you have to dry off. I can just take my coat off and hang it on a chair to dry." Buddy measured out oats, and forked hay into the mule's manger. Addressing the mule, he said, "I was just reading in Psalm 135, 'Whatever the LORD pleases, he does, in heaven and on earth, in the seas and all deeps. He it is who makes the clouds rise at the end of the earth, who makes lightnings for the rain and brings forth the wind from his storehouses.' We did not get the wind and lightning, but we sure got the clouds and rain! He must think you need more rest. I was going to try the plow again tomorrow, but I guess I'll sort taters instead."

On the way back to the house, Buddy looked up

at the sullen clouds that blanketed the sky. "Lord," he said, "You order our steps and shape our days. Sometimes You use circumstances, and You give peace in spite of what goes on around us. Sometimes I want to argue with You about what You are doing. Maybe You could help me rest in Your wise watching over me."

Tuesday dawned cloudy, but dry. Buddy had just finished a breakfast porridge of boiled cracked wheat, when he heard Joe Simmons' mare nicker in the yard as Simmons tied her to the rail. He opened the door as Simmons stomped mud off his boots on the bottom step.

"Good morning, Buddy. I figured after all that rain, I'd have to drag you out of bed. You ready, or do you want me to tackle that fence while you do other stuff?"

Buddy frowned at his neighbor. "No, I'll help. I got the potatoes sorted yesterday while I waited for the clouds to finish watering the place. With all that watering, you'd think my eighty would have grown to a quarter section. I only lost about a bushel and a half out of those three barrels. They won't plant the whole lower forty, but that will be about all the crop I'll be able to harvest."

Simmons tried to put on a serious face. "I'd use your stall fork. Potatoes are about the same size as what you dig out when you clean up after that mule."

Buddy chuckled. "You're right. And anything smaller can stay in the ground, and I'll have the new crop already planted come spring!" He ran to the barn, and came back with an ax and tool bag.

Simmons asked, "Why the chopper?"

"It's a snake fence. I might have to cut poles to replace any that are rotten." Buddy handed the ax and tool bag to Joe Simmons. "That reminds me. I may need a saw and sledge hammer in case we need to replace any of the posts that lock the corners." Hurrying to the barn, he returned with the additional tools.

The men trudged up behind the barn, following the wagon ruts to the upper gate. Buddy said, "I call this the upper forty, but it is a bit less. I've got about five acres in trees above the fence on the other side, and the buildings take out another five acres. I guess calling it the upper forty and the lower forty just puts a label on the parts of the farm."

Simmons nodded. "Mine is the same, but my buildings are on a bench at the upper end of my eighty. I've got trees above the house, but part of that patch is taken up by my orchard. But I know what you mean."

At the gate, the two turned to the right. Wading through wet, knee-high grass, they came to the first angle in the fence. The locking post was broken, and the poles had toppled down the hill, to be covered by the growing grass.

Simmons said, "I'll dig these poles out and weave them. You go cut a new post."

Taking the ax, Buddy skirted the field, counting the joints that would need repair, humming as he went. Entering the stand of trees, he chose one that had a gently tapering trunk t hat would make half a dozen posts. He kept the ax sharp and oiled, and chips flew as he worked both sides of the tree. A final swing of the ax caused the tree to hop off the stump, and alternately snagging and releasing branches of other trees, it fell.

Buddy measured two ax handle lengths, and notched the pole. Another two lengths, and another notch. When he had marked half a dozen posts, he chopped through the trunk. Then, lifting and balancing the trunk on his shoulder, he walked to the fence and tossed it to the ground on the other side. Reaching over the fence, he leaned the ax on the other side, and clambered over into the field. He could tromp through the field, because it would be pasture instead of its usual hay field.

Buddy picked up the pole and ax, and carried them down to the gate on the lower side of the field. Swapping the ax for the saw, he cut the trunk into the six posts.

Simmons had the collapsed corner rebuilt. Buddy

said, "I'll point these, and we can lock that into place. I saw six more that need fixing between here and the upper corner. By the time we get up there, I'll need to cut another tree for posts. But, these will get us almost there, unless we find more posts that we have to replace. Some of them might be bad, but the corners might still be good."

Joe Simmons reached for the ax. "Here, let me do that. I've put more points on posts than I can remember. You fetched and cut them. I can chop the points, and then you can hold the post while I pound this one, at least."

Twelve posts and six corner repairs later, they reached the upper corner. Buddy had cut five long poles to replace rotten ones. The men had worked silently, putting their energy into the work instead of talk. They stopped to flex tired arms and shoulders. Buddy said, "I'm going to knock down another couple of trees for posts along the top, here. No need to cut them into posts yet. We'll go down for a cuppa, and then see if maybe we can finish this job this afternoon."

Simmons said, "I'll go around the rest of the field and see how much more we need to fix. I'll meet you at the gate. A cuppa sure sounds good about now."

Buddy whistled as he cut across the field and reached the gate ahead of Joe Simmons. He watched as his neighbor leaned two more broken posts against corners that had not yet fallen apart. When he reached the gate, Simmons said, "Two dozen posts and twelve corners. You'll need to cut another couple of trees. I think we'll make it before dark."

Over tea, Buddy asked, "How do you plan to get the stock over here? Will you need help?"

Simmons set his mug down. "I've been thinking about that. I'll need you to be down at the foot of Brush Creek to turn them up this way. Then, somehow, you'll have to get ahead of them to turn them up toward the barn. They'll be interested in the grass along the side of the road, so they won't move too fast. Once some of them get turned, the rest will follow. Maybe you could run along below the road above your lower field to head them off."

Buddy nodded. "That should work. A third person would sure help, but I think the two of us could handle it."

Simmons pursed his lips, and wiggled his mouth from side to side. Swallowing his tea, he said, "Well, I could have the missus stand at the foot of Brush Creek. She's handled that chore more than once. That way, you could be in place up here." He paused. "That might be a better plan. The beasties don't know you. Yeah. Let's plan it that way. My wife will flag them up Brush Creek, and you can turn them in at your place. We'll leave the gate open, and once they are headed toward the barn we can close in on three points to get them up the hill and through to the gate."

At the top of the field, they gathered their tools, and moved to the next repair point. While Simmons rebuilt the corner, Buddy measured and marked the two trees he had cut before tea, and carried them out of the grove. Cut and pointed, he carried them along the upper fence, dropping them where Simmons had leaned the broken posts.

Back in the grove, Buddy sang as he worked. The lyrics were broken by the efforts of chopping, the ax supplying the percussion to give rhythm to hymn.

How firm (chop) a founda- (chop) -tion, O saints (chop) of the Lord, (chop)
Is laid (chop) for your faith (chop) in his ex- (chop) -cellent word! (chop)

He cut two more trees, measured and marked them and carried them out to the field.

"I heard you caterwaulerin' back in the timber." Simmons stopped to mop his brow.

While Simmons cut the posts, Buddy cut another three replacement poles, and carried them out. Trading off on the various parts of the task, the two used up the afternoon. The light was fading as they carried the tools back to the barn.

Simmons led his mare over to the trough to drink, then walked with Buddy into the barn. While Buddy tended to the mule, Simmons said, "I've been thinking about your question about Logan's Crossing. I remembered someone talking about a flood years ago. It was not as wild as this one, but they said it washed away a couple of flatboat ferries. Some of the first ferries were flatboats that were pulled back and forth across the Ohio with cables. When they weren't in use, they let the cables sink, so folks floating down the river would not catch on the cables.

"For flatboats on the river, it was a one-way trip. They floated down stream. When they got where they were going, they were usually taken apart, and the lumber was used for something else. Some folks built their houses out of flatboat boards. I think someone salvaged the cables from the ones that washed away, and somebody got the boards after the water went down. The flatboats were sprung, but the river left them high on an island. But, one of those might have come from Logan's."

Buddy pondered that information. Then, "If that happened years ago, and the ferry was not replaced, would they still call it Logan's Crossing?"

Simmons chuckled. "They might. Names are kind of sticky. My guess is that the home of the ferryman was not washed away. So, if it had been Logan's Crossing, they would not likely drop the crossing part, even if nobody crossed the river there any more. But, with the Ohio on a rampage, there's no telling where it picked up the flatboats. I'd say, though, that it was above Raccoon Creek. The ferries usually crossed at a narrow point in the river. That took less cable.

"Later, there were those ferries that crossed the slow moving pools, no matter how wide they were. Those were animal powered. They put a horse or mule on a treadmill that turned a paddle wheel. Sounds crazy, but it worked. Maybe Logan had one of those."

Buddy muttered, "Anything to muddy things for me."

As if he had not heard, Simmons went on. "Another twist now. Steamboats have started moving upstream, so traffic on the river is two way. The crossings are turning into landings. The steamboats nose in to the landing with a gangplank out front. Folks and stuff go ashore at the oddest spots along the river's edge. If there is no landing, the gangplank plops down on the river bank. So now, it could be a town of Logan, or a spot known as Logan's Landing, or just Logan's. Have I got you confused?"

"Yeah." Buddy frowned. "It is as clear as that barn wall. But thanks. Maybe I'll bounce all of that off of Jackson Wiggins. He's trying to figure some things out for me."

Simmons nodded. "He's a good man, and good at all he does. He might fool you, to look at him. He might look like he's not all there, but he's sharp as your Barlow."

Buddy changed the subject as they walked out of the barn. Closing the door, he asked, "What time tomorrow?"

Simmons scratched his chin, calculating. "Let's aim for mid morning. Say, nine o'clock. I should have all the chores done by then. You don't mind a couple of horses in with the cows, do you? If you don't mind, I can come up and care for them. I have a couple of mares in foal. They won't be jumpers. And maybe I can run a line from your windmill to a trough in the upper field so the stock can get water."

Buddy raised one eyebrow. "No need to do that. There's a spring in the trees yonder. It runs into No Name Creek. We can put a weir up there, and then it will be a short run to the fence. You could put the trough up there."

Simmons nodded. "That's even better. Critters like spring water better than well water. Don't know why. They'll drink from the groundwater, but they would rather have water from the spring. It comes out of the ground, just like the well water, so I have no idea what the difference might be. Tastes the same to me!"

Buddy laughed. "I've never noticed any difference,

either. But, we'll spoil them."

Simmons mounted, and turned the mare homeward. "Nine o'clock, then."

Chapter 5

Buddy Wilson tied his mule at the rail. He peeled off Grandpa Wilson's great coat, and shook the rain from it. He stomped the mud from his boots on the step up to the boardwalk in front of Jackson Wiggins' office.

Before he could knock, Wiggins opened the door. Welcome warmth spilled out from the room.

"I was wondering when you might get here." Wiggins stepped aside. "Come in and close the door. Sure is chilly for the middle of June! Had to light a fire this morning!"

Buddy hung his coat on the peg beside the door. "I've been busy. But now that it's raining again, I thought I'd get some supplies, and stop here to swap news. Heard anything?" He declined the chair Uncle Jack offered. "I've been sitting for miles. Old Ben needs a bit more padding. I'll stand a bit." A hint of wood smoke hung in the air. "I feel warmer already. I can listen while I stand."

Uncle Jack laughed. "Well, I won't. I've been standing for years. Time for me to sit. You need to get yourself a saddle. That mule is just going to get bonier as he gets older. If you keep riding bareback, don't tell me about your backside."

Buddy sighed. "He's never been a rocking chair. I feel every step all the way up my back. Grandpa Wilson didn't put money into a horse. He figured the mule was a multi-purpose animal. Ride, plow, pull, whatever."

A comfortable silence settled between the two friends. Finally, Wiggins asked, "Did you think of anything? What have you been up to this past couple of weeks? Get those potatoes planted?"

"Finally." Buddy stood at the window, his hands clasped behind his back. The raindrops were large, but not close together. Overlapping circles rippled across the puddles in the muddy street. "We got a break in the rain, enough for me to tear open those furrows. Joe Simmons helped me. His stock is in my upper forty. The flood took his pasture."

"You rent it to him?"

"No. He is going to give me a ton or more of hay off his upper forty. I don't need any money for it. He followed me with a rake, and covered the seed potatoes as I dropped them. Oh, and he helped me restore that fence around the upper field so his stock would stay put. We put a weir in the spring back in the woods to make a bit of a pond, and ran a pipe to the top of the field to fill a trough for his stock."

Wiggins snorted. "Been a bit lazy, haven't you? That sounds like a month's work and you got all that done in those few days when it didn't rain? Learn anything from Joe?"

Buddy recounted the conversation about the ferries, especially Logan's Crossing. He turned from the window, and settled in the chair Wiggins had offered. "He said Logan's Crossing might be something else now, but he could not remember such a place. That part about me looking like the kid over at the crossing was interesting, though. Over could mean upstream, or even across the river. Not much territory to explore there. Just Kentucky and West Virginia." On the table, Buddy traced the area with his finger, then jabbed at the areas of the two states.

Uncle Jack rubbed his chin. "Or, it could be downstream. Maybe on the Ohio side. Could even be in Indiana.

"I've been digging into the history of the area a bit, looking for Logan's Crossing. When this country was first being settled, the trails led to the river. The first folks to arrive built cabins at the end of the trails, and then went into business. Canoes or row boats served as ferries for people. For a fee, they crossed the river without having to swim.

"Those on horseback, well, that was a different

proposition. Horses didn't fit in a canoe, and it was too dangerous to have the beasts swim along behind the small boats. But, the crossing usually got the name of the settler who ran the ferry.

"When the trails widened to roads, and wagons started showing up, the ferryman had to build a bigger craft. That led to the flatboat ferries that could carry people, livestock, wagons and goods."

Buddy interrupted the narrative. "Simmons mentioned those flatboats. Maybe one of the ones that landed on an island downstream was from Logan's."

Uncle Jack opened one eye, and scowled at Buddy. "I have the floor, so don't stop me."

Buddy hushed.

"I found out there's an abandoned cabin just inside Raccoon Creek. It's roof is falling in, but I'll have to poke around to see if there might be anything left there that could tell us whose it was. That would be a good place for a crossing, and the ferry could be parked in the mouth of Raccoon, and be out of the way of floods on the Ohio, and protected from ice during the spring break up.

"Trouble with some of these early crossings is that when the ferryman dies or moves on, the crossing and the name gets lost. And then, the folks who knew the man and the place move to the church yard, or to another state, and there are no brains to pick.

"If these rains ever stop, my plan is to visit around on both sides of the river to see if I can scare up an old timer who can remember something about the early day crossings."

Wiggins lowered his feet to the floor, then lurched up out of the chair. "Your turn, now. Tell me about the tater planting. How much did you get put in? I'll get us some tea."

Buddy stood, then walked back to the window. The raindrops were closer together. "When the water settled out, we started with the furrow I had already plowed. I spaced the seed potatoes in that one, but I left it open for a marker when I plowed the next furrows. The rain held off for four days, and I was able to open furrows on eight acres.

"Once I had those ready, Joe Simmons came over, and it took us a day and a half to finish planting. The stuff I got in those barrels planted seven acres, so I had another acre of furrows opened that we didn't plant. I just left them."

Wiggins poured the two mugs of tea and brought them to the table. Buddy resumed his seat. Restless, he took his tea, and went back to the window.

The fragrance of the tea blended with the wood

smoke, giving the room a companionable feeling. Wiggins said, "I'd have done the same thing. Sounds like you had a profitable few days. Harvest those potatoes, and it should get you a little more profit."

Buddy dug in his pocket. "I might have already harvested." He walked to the table, and laid his fist beside Uncle Jack's mug. "The plow went through a clay jar the flood picked up somewhere. Here's what it had in it."

Buddy opened his hand, and pulled it back. On the table lay a handful of gold and silver coins. He pulled out two more handfuls. "Two hundred thirty-five dollars in gold. The silver is mostly foreign and some of it is cut up in pieces. What do I do with it? I don't know where it came from, or whose it is."

With his finger, Uncle Jack sorted the pile. "Even some Spanish milled dollars, and some cut into bits." He turned some of the coins over. "The latest date is in the thirties. Here. Here's a coin made in 1834. That's what...seventeen years ago? You were four years old then.

"Seems all that weight would have kept the jar out in the channel. Was there anything around in the furrow that would float?"

Buddy thought a moment, then said slowly, "Not right there. Just a big rock. But there was some wood and what looked like a hinge about a hundred feet back. The plow threw it up to one side with the dirt out of the furrow. We found that when Joe was raking the stuff in to cover the potatoes."

Uncle Jack studied the scattered coins. "In a box, this would have floated. But the box must have been letting water in. An eddy carried it into your field, where it sank and got buried. Your plow tore the box, and dragged the jar until it smashed it against a rock. Hmmm. Mostly small denominations. Like a ferryman would collect over time. My guess? The flood destroyed an old cabin or shed, or somewhere a ferryman hid his savings back in the thirties.

"My guess is this is the way the good Lord chose to pay you for the crop the flood destroyed. So, as Justice of the Peace, I'll tell you to take it home. I declare it to be yours, unless I hear from somebody claiming it within, say, thirty days. Anybody else know about it?"

"Joe Simmons. He helped me sift through the dirt to make sure I got all of those little silver wedges."

"Bits. Pieces of Eight."

"Bits?"

"Yeah. The Spanish milled dollar was cut into eight pieces, see?" Uncle Jack pulled eight of the wedges aside, and fitted them into a whole coin. Then he picked out an uncut Spanish dollar and set it beside the assembled one. "Two of these wedges was a quarter of a dollar. Four was a half dollar. Two bits. Four bits. Even with the American coins, they still use the Spanish dollar, and still cut it up for change.

"Just a quick count here, I'd say you have about three hundred dollars, with the silver stuff. Take it home, and find something to store it in."

Buddy laughed. "Three hundred dollars? That's a really good day's wages!" As he gathered the coins, he said, "I was going to give half of it to Joe Simmons."

Uncle Jack shook his head. "No, Not yet. Not for another thirty days. You would give Joe the whole eighty!"

Buddy shook his head in turn. "Nope. That farm is held as a stewardship for Sarah. It's hers. I'll use it while we try to find her, but the farm and its profit belong to her. That note mentioned her estate. Since the Wilsons died, the farm has to be her inheritance. I'm just taking care of it for her. Joe can have half the flood fortune, but the farm is not mine to give."

Uncle Jack raised one eyebrow. "Well, young man, you go on back to that farm and watch the potatoes grow. That field just might produce a bit more gold for you, and for Sarah. Now, I've got some hunting to do, but it can wait until the rain stops. You have a slicker, so you can go ahead and brave the storm. Keep that mule dry!"

Wiggins watched through the window as Buddy swung up on the mule, and started him at a walk through the rain on the way out of town. When he was beyond the last house, a tuneless verse from Isaac Watts burst from the old man:

There's not a plant or flow'r below, but makes Thy glories known,
And clouds arise, and tempests blow, by order from Thy throne;
While all that borrows life from Thee is ever in Thy care;
And everywhere that we can be, Thou, God, art present there.

Looking up, he said, "If I could ask, maybe we could do with a little less of the tempests."

Wiggins turned to the bookshelf, and running his finger along the spines of the volumes, found an atlas of the Ohio Valley. He put that book on the table, and took the teapot and mugs, washed them and put them away. Then, resuming his chair, he started paging through the maps, looking for any point along the Ohio with the name Logan attached.

Chapter 6

Unseen behind thick clouds, the sun had set. Buddy had been standing on the porch, leaning against the rail, watching the potatoes grow. The circles of green were already a foot across, in neat order, row after row. Twilight shrouded the lower field. He was comfortable in the cabin, but he decided it was time to banish one of the ghosts that lodged there. Since the fire that took the Wilsons while they slept, he had not kindled a fire in the fireplace. He could still see the flames licking the wall behind the cook stove. He had run in, holding his breath, with bucket after bucket of water from the trough.

The flames had been subdued, but he had kept sloshing water on the hot logs, until they stopped steaming. Then, tying a wet handkerchief over his face, he had gone in through the smoke-filled room to the back bedroom and dragged the Wilsons out onto the porch, then coughing, he had fallen on his hands and knees. He had crawled to each of the old folks, and found that neither one breathed. To a boy of fourteen, it was a traumatic discovery.

He had taken Sarah to the stall in the barn where

he slept. He had walked with her, supporting her arm. She had cried, partly from pain and partly from the shame of her nakedness. He had had her lie down on his cot, face down, and then he had applied the last of the egg whites to her burns. Stringing a rope across the stall, he had tented a blanket above her, since she could bear no contact with her burns.

Tonight, he decided to light a fire in the fireplace for the first time in eight years. It was not that he feared the fire, but distrusted the memories it would call to mind. Tonight, he would let the flickering tongues evoke the ghosts of the past, and banish them if he could.

In the lean-to off the back of the house, he set the lantern on its shelf, chopped kindling, and gathered enough wood for a small fire. The weather was not cold, but the dampness brought its own chill.

He knelt on the hearth and whittled a pile of shavings. Placing two short pieces of wood between the andirons, he scooped the shavings between them, then built a log cabin of kindling above the shavings.

Grandpa Wilson had forged the andirons so they sloped toward the back of the fireplace. Pieces of firewood could be stacked up the sloping ends, so they would slide down as the lower pieces burned. The fire would feed itself.

Buddy cut a long splint from the kindling and stuck it down the chimney of the oil lamp to light it. He drew a deep breath, sighed, and touched the tiny flame to the shavings. Flames licked up the shavings, ignited the kindling and soon had larger flames dancing on the lowest log.

He pulled a chair over and sat gazing into the fire. The movement of the blaze was hypnotic. His mind started to play past images which he saw, now vividly, then in blurred motion. Sarah ran in her blazing night dress through the flames, then vanished. He threw bucket after bucket of water on the burning wall, but it kept burning. Grandma and Grandpa Wilson called to him through the leaping tongues of fire. He could hear Grandpa's voice in the distance.

"Hello, the house!"

Buddy shook his head. The voice seemed so real, so present. He shut his eyes to close out the vision in the fireplace.

"Hello, the house!"

Buddy jumped. The call came from outside. It was not his imagination.

"Hello! Anybody there?"

It was a man's voice, but not Grandpa Wilson. Nor was it Joe Simmons.

Buddy got up and went out through the lean-to.

Staying in the shadows, he slipped silently to where he could see around the corner to the front of the house. There was a figure of a man, dimly lit by the glow through the window.

"Hey! Anybody home?"

The man stood back, waiting. He appeared harmless enough. Buddy answered, "There is. Looking for someone in particular? Or do you need some help?"

The man started, his hand dropping to his hip. "I'm trying to locate Buddy Wilson. Know him?"

"You've found him," Buddy answered. "What do you need?"

"A chance to talk. I've come a couple thousand miles with a message. Do I holler out here, or can I come in?"

Buddy said in a kinder tone, "Just a minute. I'll get the door." He went back in through the lean-to, and lifted the latch, pulling the front door open. He held the oil lamp to light the steps and the porch. He had never seen the man who entered.

Buddy held out his hand. "I'm Buddy Wilson. At least, that's the name I use."

"Tom Flannagan."

The two surveyed each other, measuring their manhood as well as their stature. They could have been looking in a mirror. Both stood six feet, with muscles hardened by the challenges of work. Their handshake had been firm, and would have been crushing for lesser men. Their eyes met and probed, each plumbing the character of the other.

"Hungry?" Buddy set the kettle on a rack on one of the andirons.

"No. I cooked a bite down the shore a few miles."

Buddy stared. "You walked here?" he asked.

"No. Paddled. I beached my canoe down at the mouth of the creek. I saw the light in your window, and thought I'd ask to see if anyone knew the place I was supposed to find. Guess I found it."

Buddy's face showed his amazement. "You paddled a canoe against that flood? You're a better man than I am!" He kicked the other chair over by the fireplace. "Sit down."

Flannagan waved the comment aside. "You stay close to shore, and between the eddies and the slack water, you don't have to fight so much. The struggle is mostly out in the middle. You take the cautious approach. Always take the cautious approach." He lowered himself slowly onto the chair Buddy had occupied. "You get a bit stiff after hours in a canoe."

"Right. So you are taking the cautious approach

with me. Cup of tea?"

Tom nodded. "I'm checking you out. Sure, I haven't had a good cup of tea in, let's see, five years?"

Buddy fished out his Barlow, and shaved tea from the brick, humming as he worked.

Tom watched, and said, "I could just gnaw a corner off that thing. You've got the good stuff. I'm obliged."

"You sound educated. What were you doing two thousand miles away?"

Tom laughed, relaxing. "Educated? It's worse than that. I'm ordained. I went to California when the stampede began. I thought there might be some work among that heathen mob. I was in several mining camps. Set up a church tent among the liquor tents. I could not draw a crowd of one. The lust for gold was only a tiny bit stronger than the lust for alcohol and for the camp-following women, if you can honor them with that word. I'm heading for New York to make my report.

"I stopped and saw the folks at the Lee Mission, and went up to pray at the mission where Marcus Whitman was killed."

Buddy poured two mugs of tea, and handed one to Flannagan. Taking the other chair, he asked, "So, what was your message?"

Flannagan sipped, closed his eyes, and swallowed. "It's been a long time." He turned to Buddy. "You live here by yourself? No wife?"

"No, no wife. Just me. Why?"

"I came here to see what I should tell you. I'll say you are worthy. Let me ask you this. What is Sarah Wilson to you?"

Buddy could not have been more surprised if Sarah herself had stepped from the fireplace. "Sarah? I haven't seen her in eight years. If you are asking about the same Sarah. I've been searching for some trace of her since her Uncle George left with her."

Flannagan snorted. "Uncle George, my foot. She sent me to ask you to head west, point of honor, as she put it."

Buddy jumped to his feet. "Point of honor? It's my Sarah, all right. That's the line she used when she really wanted me to do something."

"The guy who has her is Elmer Gilson, and he is as crooked as a snake. He has a hash house in Dalles City in the Oregon Territory. I ate there. The food is good because Sarah cooks it. She is making money for that...I can't call him a man. He treats her like a dog. The girl is seventeen now, and he has this hold on her. She tried to call you from the barn when Gilson took her. He figures there is some emotional tie between the two of you. I think he told her he plans to come here and kill you if she does not stay. She said he told her when she turns eighteen either she marries him, or he will sell her to someone up in Cayuse country. Someone who is not too particular about marrying.

"She told me where to find you, and said I was to give you the point of honor message.

"I told her I would marry her myself. She said she is safe until she is eighteen. She's underage, and that keeps Gilson at bay. He needs someone's permission to marry her before her eighteenth birthday. He's after her estate, or fortune. He figures if he marries her, it is his. Know anything about it?"

Buddy pulled out the tattered note from Sarah, and handed it to Flannagan. "That's all I know. Grandma Wilson had taught Sarah to read and write, and she could communicate beyond her years. But, I can't fabricate any estate beyond this farm. She was here when I got here, and with the Wilsons both gone the same night, this patch of ground and what it has produced over eight years I've been guarding it for her is all she's got, unless I can find out more of her past."

Buddy recounted his arrival at the Wilson farm, his work, and the night of the fire. "I buried the Wilsons a couple of days later, up above the orchard. I put two big rocks out of No Name Creek up there to mark their graves. Sarah didn't even have time to heal from her burns before he took her away. They left no trace. Nobody saw them headed anywhere."

Flannagan filled in the blank spaces in the disappearance. "She said they drifted in a flatboat down to New Orleans, sailed down to Panama, and crossed the isthmus. They sailed up the Pacific coast, and ended up in Dalles City. Actually, they are a bit down the Columbia River from the city itself. They are down toward the Cascades of the Columbia. Boat traffic stops there."

The two men lapsed into silence, each lost in his own thoughts. One by one, the logs on the andirons burned, and the next one up caught, sustaining the dancing flames.

Tom Flannagan broke the quietness when he asked again, "What is Sarah to you? Would you marry her?"

In the fireplace, another log broke, and a tower of sparks swirled up the chimney. Attracted by the light of the lamp, a large moth bumped against the window.

Buddy said, "I don't know. She was a sweet kid. I treasured her. Ever since we were wading that hot day, I just saw her as Sarah. She was more like a sister to me. Marriage has to be based on so much more than knowing she is a girl. When we were in that pool on No Name Creek, I did not even notice she was a girl, except for the beauty of her eyes and hair. I knew she was a girl when I rubbed egg whites all over her back, but for her comfort, I pretended not to notice. Do I love her? Probably not. At least, not as I should in order to have her as my wife. I could learn to. The sacrificial love as Christ bestows on us, though? I don't think I'm there. To save her from those threats, yes. I would marry her, and pray the Lord would give me that sacrificial love."

It was Tom Flannagan's turn to stretch the silence into lingering minutes. Then he said, "Well, if you are not smack in the middle of true manhood, you are well inside the border, with that evaluation. That love of Christ's consistently and actively seeks the best interest of the object of His love, and that is us. That is the love we are to have for each other, and the love a man is supposed to have for his wife. I'm with you, though. I would marry her, and pray that I would be enabled to give her that kind of love.

"But, tell me honestly. Would you travel over a couple thousand miles of dangerous trail for her? It's late in the season, and you would travel alone. You would have to be on guard the whole trip. The Oregon Trail is well marked by the wagons that have already gone that way. But, between here and there, the tribes have been a bit stirred up. Traveling alone, you could be an easy target. Would you be prepared to undertake such a risk, leaving everything and everyone here, for such a prospect?

"Once you got there, you could claim twice the land you have here. If you marry Sarah, you could make that four times this farm."

Buddy pondered that question. He walked to the window, and looked out into the darkness. Out there, the potato crop was growing, promising a harvest that would sustain the account that was slowly growing. Leave it? Would he? Could he leave everything here? Uncle Jack would take charge of the farm, he was sure. But leaving Ohio, he would leave behind the only chance of finding out who he really was. He prayed silently for light for what lay ahead. Then, "I would, I think. I would have to do some thinking and preparation. And praying."

Flannagan straightened in his chair. "Sit back down, then, and I'll tell you what I have been thinking about. I think you are an honorable fellow. I developed an affection for the girl that seems to be about the same as yours. I don't know her well enough to call it love. I did determine, though that she is a girl of faith. She attributed her knowledge of salvation and of the Savior to the woman she called Grandma Wilson."

Buddy put in, "So do I. She was a godly woman."

Flannagan continued, "You are a believer, too, then. This is my proposal. I have to make my report. I have to see a couple of friends about joining me in the Territory. Then, I will have to attend to some financial business. After that, I will start back along the trail. On my way, I'll swing back here to see what you decided. We will agree that whichever one of us gets there first will see if Sarah will agree to marry."

Buddy stared in uncertainty. "Would that honor the Lord? He holds marriage a holy thing. Would that be like casting lots for the girl? I'm just thinking out loud. But it's as if we were mindlessly dividing up the last slice of pie."

"Well, she would have the final word. I understand what you are saying, though. She's not like you last saw her. She's a woman now. She smiled a couple of times while I was there, and her smile would light up a room. She will make some man a precious bride, if she can ever shed that garment of fear she is forced to wear. That'll be a job for one of us." Flannagan surreptitiously rubbed tears away. "That guy is a brute. I could sure almost lose my sanctification just looking at him."

Silence settled again between the two young men. The breeze over the chimney stirred the embers that were all that remained of the fire to a brighter orange. A single tongue of flame danced momentarily, then flickered out.

Buddy broke the quiet, asking, "What stirred the tribes up?"

Tom sighed. "What sets the prairie afire? A bolt

of lightning, maybe. The wind that sweeps the prairie grass into waves pokes around an abandoned campfire, and finds a single live coal. It teases a tiny flame out of it, and touches it to a blade of dry grass. Before you know it, the tiny flame grows to a roaring monster that creates its own wind that sweeps it to the horizon and beyond, destroying everything in its path.

"The tribes? All it takes is one fearful man headed west whose first thought when he sees an Indian is to shoot him. That death has to be avenged.

"Or, some pioneer outrages a girl from the tribe. That has to be avenged.

"I think it was four years ago that some knothead told the Cayuse that Doctor Whitman had a bottle of disease he would open and afflict them. I don't know what he wanted from the tribe, but when the White Man's disease, I think it was measles, started killing the Cayuse, a bunch of the men went to Whitman's mission pretending friendship, and then killed just about everybody there. Men, women, children, it didn't matter. They all got tomahawked.

"Right now, the government is trying to force all of the tribes onto reservations. They chose the poorest land for the tribes, and set aside the best land for the emigrants. To make dependents of the tribes, the government is cutting them off from their food supply. The fish eaters have harvested their food supply from the Columbia at the Cascades and at the falls. The tribes are stirred up by the changes being forced upon them. They are desperate. If you go, you will be in danger all the way."

Buddy stood up and paced the length of the room half a dozen times. "I'll go. Uncle Jack can look out for things here. Stop by on your way west, and talk with Jackson Wiggins in Rome. Stay here tonight, and I will want to pick your brain in the morning. You know more about the trip than I do. To travel fast, I'll have to travel light. You can tell me what to take." He pointed to the ladder leading to the loft. "You can take the bed up there. I'll stretch out on the floor."

Flannagan shook his head. "I've been sleeping on the ground, or in the bottom of the canoe. The floor suits me. Or better yet, is there hay in the barn? I'd rather nestle down in sweet-smelling hay. You take the bed. Just toss down a blanket, and I'll see you in the morning. Don't spend all the night in prayer. He answers quick ones as well as long ones."

Chapter 7

Tom Flannagan entered the house as Buddy descended the ladder. "I took care of your mule. He's a bit old for the trip west. I'd get a younger one if I were you. But you want a mule. The tribes make horses disappear, but they don't want mules. Mules don't increase the herd."

Buddy groaned. "I'd rather walk if all mules ride like old Ben. Would you use a saddle, or go without?"

"You might have to test a few mules until you find one with a gentle gait. I sit on a folded blanket over a pack when I travel by canoe. Miles and miles sitting on my heels or on a hard thwart gets old fast, and when I come ashore, I can hardly move. My guess is that that mule of yours would do the same thing to you. But I think mules would outlast horses on the trail, anyway. Yeah, I'd use a saddle."

Buddy set the cracked wheat on to simmer. He sprinkled a pinch of salt into the pan, and stirred it in.

"Be sure to take a bunch of that salt with you,"

Tom said. "It makes all the trail food taste a whole lot better. You'll want to take a gun, and some fishing stuff. You'll find meat all along the way. You will follow rivers most of the way, and if you have done any fishing, you can't starve. But you will want salt."

Buddy nodded. "I've fished the streams here. Some of the fish are better than others, but they are all food. You can always keep your belly button away from your backbone."

Tom laughed. "That's a good way to put it. There may be times when you go a day or two without food between here and there, but if you do, it will be your own fault. When you need something to eat, go slow, and look sharp."

Buddy laid slices of bread on the stove top to toast. "With rivers and streams, there will be plenty of water, too."

"True, but don't drink any surface water without boiling it. Coffee and tea will keep you healthy. The surface water might look clean and tempting, but it can turn you inside out. You can drink spring water, but don't drink any from rivers or puddles, no matter how thirsty you are. Boil it first. Take a canteen, and carry good water with you. If you camp by a spring, fill it. If not, fill it with boiled water."

Buddy turned the toast, heated the skillet, and cut thick slices of bacon, laying them in the hot cast iron to fry. He prepared a pot of tea, pulled the chairs back from the cold fireplace, and kicked them under the table. Turning the bacon, he asked, "Is the trail obvious? Is there any place I could get lost?"

Flannagan shook his head. "As long as you stay on the wagon tracks, you will be all right. There are some places where people tried to find shortcuts. There's the California cutoff the gold rush crowd took in the gold rush. You do not want to take that. There are a couple of places people turned off and got into real trouble. They lead to places where the river runs through a deep cut, where the cliff is straight up and down, and the river winds like a serpent." Tom pulled a paper out of his pocket. "Here. I drew you a map, as best I could recall. It shows the rivers you have to follow, and the locations of the springs and forts. I even tried to draw some of the landmarks. I'm not much of an artist, but you will get the idea."

Buddy took the map, glanced at it, and laid it on the table. Gathering the breakfast, he joined Tom for the bite to eat.

"I'll pray. You're a pastor, and I'm just a sheep, but you are my guest."

Tom laughed. "None of that, now. The ground is even at the foot of the cross. The Lord loves each of us the same. But, go ahead."

Buddy prayed for wisdom for the two of them, and clear leading in the journey ahead. "Guide our steps. You know the path You have chosen, and the grace You have prepared for each of us. We do ask that You would guard Sarah. You know her circumstances, and Your purpose for her. Protect her, and keep her by Your power. We ask that by Your Spirit You would focus our hearts on the things above, so we do not get all bound up in the things down here."

After thanking the Lord for His provision for their daily needs, they finished off the food Buddy had prepared.

Tom Flannagan took a sip of tea, and said, "You rustle a pretty satisfying breakfast. You might practice roasting things over there in the fireplace. Build a small fire, though, just enough to cook what you are going to eat. On the trail, that's all you can do. A small fire, and then put it out. You do not want smoke telling anybody where you are."

Buddy asked, "What if I do get lost?"

Tom answered, "Well, you are headed west. You can always find the way west on a sunny day. Poke a stick in the ground, and put a pebble at the end of its shadow. Do that every hour. You will have a straight line pointing east and west.

"On a starry night, you can find north. Do you know your stars?"

Buddy said, "I know the big dipper."

Tom smiled. "Good. It's a pan. The two stars at the end of the pan point to the north star. That is at the end of the handle of the little dipper. Once you spot the north star, take a stick and hold its end on the ground. Get down and sight along the stick. When it is pointed at the north star, stick it in the dirt. In daylight, it will still lean to the north. Face that way, and west will be on your left. Look for a distant landmark, and keep it in view.

"Remember, as you travel, stay below the horizon. If you are outlined against the sky, you can be seen from far away. A low profile works to your advantage. A fellow I know met a charging bear on the trail. He dropped to the ground, and the bear lost him. Bears don't see very well, and they can't stop immediately when they are running. Works with people, too. If somebody tries to bull rush you, fall flat. They'll miss. So on the trail, stay low.

"And don't wear white. Most of the land will be tan or brown now. Try to blend in. What about a gun? Don't take a Kentucky long rifle. Got something shorter?"

Buddy nodded. "Grandpa Wilson had a couple of Colts. He had a revolving carbine from the forties, and a Colt revolver. They are the same caliber, and he made up a lot of bullets for them. I'll have to get some fresh powder, though."

Buddy tried to catalog all these bits of information in his mind. Some would be practiced all along the journey. Some would be for emergency use.

Tom thought a minute, then said, "Don't take a tent. Put together a bed roll. You will need a good piece of canvas big enough to lie on and wrap over you. That will keep the rain off. Have it long enough to fold up and over your head. Set it up before you leave. Lay it on the floor, and lay your blanket down the middle of it. Fold the two side flaps over the blanket, then start at the foot, rolling it up until the top flap wraps the whole thing up. Tie a couple of boot laces around it, and it will be ready. When you find a place to camp, just unroll it. Don't unroll it in a hollow, or you will be in a puddle if it rains. Don't sleep in a trail, or you might get trampled in the night.

Tom continued. "Camp well off the trail if you can. In the morning, before you get back into the tracks, survey the area, ahead and behind. You want to know if there is anyone else in the area.

"This time of year, the tribes send out small groups of teenagers who hope to be warriors. It's like old time knights going on a quest. The teens are supposed to sustain themselves away from their people, and look for adventures that will make stories to share around the campfire. The daring deeds may not be much, but the stories are important. That's the entertainment for the village. The more excitement they can pack into the retelling, the better.

"You would make a great story, if they could catch you and dispatch you in some extraordinary way. So see everything about your surroundings. Always move with caution. They might take you home as a captive, to make you a slave. But there would be more entertainment in recounting how they killed you."

Buddy shuddered. "Are there any particular places I should avoid?"

Tom pulled the map across the table. "They are nomadic, to a degree. They follow their food. The meat hunters follow the buffalo herds. They will stay long enough to smoke and dry the meat. When they have enough for the winter and spring, they move to their winter quarters. You'll have to be watchful for those villages. Go well around them. Try to circle down wind. They have dogs with sharp noses."

He pointed at one spot on the map. "Here is where you will have to cross the Snake River. Three Island Crossing. That will be tricky. There is a village set up there right now. Those are fish eaters. They will stay encamped there until the fish are gone on upstream. They may let you cross, but it will cost you everything you have. Toll charges, you know.

"I heard there was a man who did not even make it much past the Missouri River this year. They had three wagons, and a bunch of livestock. Job Ross, the man was. They were surrounded, and held captive for nearly two weeks. Had to cook for their captors. Then they were let go, but without anything. They were sent back the way they came. Ross is trying to get the government to pay him for what their captors took. Government calls it 'Indian depredations.' In any encounter, do not show fear. They respect courage above everything. Don't use weapons unless you absolutely have to. Be watchful. Be clever. If necessary, be daring. Be resourceful."

Buddy studied the map. "So. Up the Platte River, then the Sweetwater, pick up the Snake to Three Island Crossing."

"Right." Tom pointed again to the crossing. "Cross at night. In the middle of the night. Pray for moonlight. Sneak across. Avoid that village."

He slapped his hand down on the eastern part of the map. "You can't get through here. When I came, it was all under water. The rain has been worse the farther west and south you go. This has been the worst rain year in decades, I'm told. You would do best to angle north through Ohio and Indiana and Illinois. Cross the Mississippi and the upper Missouri, and then angle south and west to the upper Platte.

"Once you get across at Three Island Crossing and across again at Fort Boise, you will go through the Blue Mountains, and down to the high desert. Go through the mountains instead of trying to follow the Snake River. It goes to the Columbia, but it is too rugged. Once you are through the Blues, you will pick up the Umatilla River. You can follow that. It will hit the Columbia just above Dalles City. But it is dry country. Down the Columbia, you'll come to the Deschutes River. There's a guy who has a ferry to get you across. Tell him I said not to skin you.

"The John Day was named for a fellow in the Astor party headed for the mouth of the Columbia. He was captured and held as a slave to one of the tribes. He escaped, and was found on a gravel bar at the mouth of the river that has his name. They say that after that, he wasn't right in his head. So be careful."

Buddy traced the route across the map. "South Pass. I see the rivers go different ways on the other side."

"Yes. That is the high point of the journey. The first part of the trip is mostly flat, but you climb as you go. Then you hit the mountains. Once you are there, the west is almost all hills and mountains. Even the desert is not flat."

Buddy searched out a paper and pencil. "What is most important to take? I can't take a wagon. What is the minimum that I can pack?"

Tom did not hesitate. "Good boots. There are stretches of cut rock that can shred whatever you have on your feet. You will need tough soles on your boots. Once you get out of the Blue Mountains, you run into goat heads. Those are worse than thistles. They have thorns that stab in, and as you walk, they keep digging deeper.

"A good knife, and a belt ax if you can find one that is not too heavy. But a good knife will do almost as much as an ax.

"A flint and steel, and a tinder box. Practice starting fires with that before you leave. Matches are all right, but they get wet with all of the crossings you have to do. Your flint and steel can be soaked, and still start a fire.

"Take a small pail, or a kettle with a handle like a bucket. You can cook about anything in that, and dip water from a river. Oh, and be sure to take a long rope, say, fifty feet. If you get caught along one of those deep ravines above the river, you can still get water. Tie the pail on the rope and toss it down into the stream, and pull it up. But be sure to boil it. Be sure the rope is stout."

Buddy finished the list, and asked, "What about food? Can I survive on just meat and fish?"

"You can." Tom smiled, and shook his head. "You won't find a greengrocer anywhere along the way. If you find berries, eat them. Black or blue will be fine. Don't eat any white ones. Red ones are maybe. If you don't know them, leave them alone.

"Check around the springs for cress or miner's moss. That will balance the meat. Take some of that cracked wheat. You won't be able to carry enough to get you to Dalles City, but some here and there along the trail will be good for you.

"You'll find willows along most of the waterways. The inner bark has nourishment in it. White pine needles guard against scurvy. You can even eat the leaves and fruit of the prickly pear cactus, but don't eat too much of it. It will add variety to your diet, but a little goes a long way. Along the streams, you'll find currants and service berries. In the Blue Mountains you'll find huckleberries. All of those are good.

"Take a slingshot. Practice with it. You can kill rabbits and marmots with it, and it is quieter than a gun. Shoot only when you need to, and use a half-powder load. A gunshot attracts attention. If you have to shoot, grab your game and move along. Anybody who hears the shot will climb to a high point and look for who fired it. They will be looking in the direction where it was, and you don't want to be there."

Chapter 8

Jackson Wiggins sat on his chair on the boardwalk in front of his office, with his feet propped up on the rail. Ominous clouds clogged the sky, and a wall of rain seeped toward Rome. Scattered drops began sending circles across the puddles in the main street of the town. Coming at a lope ahead of the approaching squall, Wiggins saw long ears that identified Buddy's old mule. The attorney laughed as the younger man slid to the ground and hurriedly tied the reins to the rail and jumped up the steps, gaining the shelter of the overhanging roof just as the torrent all but obliterated the view of the street.

"In a hurry, are you?" Uncle Jack lowered his feet, tipped his chair forward, and lurched up to greet Buddy. "I don't recall setting an appointment for you today. But then, I don't have any either. Come on in and dry out."

Buddy struggled out of his slicker. "I thought I might need this before I got here, from the look of those clouds. Guess we got here just in time. Old Ben wasn't interested in anything over a walk, until those drops started. Any chance of a hot cuppa?"

Uncle Jack held the door open for Buddy, then, grabbing his chair, he followed and shut the door against the rising wind. "Water's hot. I'll have it in a few minutes. Remember something?"

"No. But I can tell you that Sarah is out in the Oregon Territory. Near a place called Dalles City."

"You sure?" Uncle Jack's eyebrows could not have risen higher. Wisdom lines made a washboard of his brow. "How did you hear that?" The older man plopped down on the chair he was carrying with a force that threatened its structure.

Buddy sat opposite Uncle Jack, and recounted the visit from Tom Flannagan.

Uncle Jack strode to the door, opened it, and dumped the teapot out in the street. Returning, he slammed the door. "Steeped too long. That would have cleaned the rust off a barn pump." As he prepared a fresh pot, he said, "So you are going west. Yeah, I know. 'Point of honor.' Let's talk about all that means."

He poured out two mugs of tea, and resumed his seat. "Know where you are going?"

"Tom says I can't get lost. Just follow the wagon tracks."

Uncle Jack gazed into his mug, stirring and watching the swirling liquid. "It has been too wet for much traffic on the trail this year, although I did hear of one middling train headed west earlier. There was a young ne'er-do-well from over West Union way headed out with them. Weston was his name. Rube Weston. Rumored to have robbed an old man, but the old codger was too scared of Rube's knife to identify him. The young rascal disappeared, but his trail was pretty obvious. Yeah, there should be tracks fresh enough to follow."

Buddy leaned back in his chair. "Tom warned me of some of the dangers. He said the tribes are stirred up right now. I think, though, that one man alone should be able to get there. With no wagons out, there should not be many eyes on the trail, I would think."

Uncle Jack snorted. "If you think that, you are in trouble before you start. Without emigrants on the trail, the tribes may well use it themselves, being a bit nomadic. What is it the apostle Paul said? Walk circumspectly. That means being aware of everything going on around you. Looking all around. At all times.

"Be especially watchful if you see big herds of buffalo. Where the herd is, there are bound to be hunters. There's little difference between a hunter and a warrior. Drop your guard, and they'll get you."

Buddy nodded. "Now, what about things on this end? Can I just drop everything and take off across the country? What about the potato crop? I don't have any livestock, but will the place be safe with nobody there?"

Uncle Jack slurped the last of his tea, and set the mug gently on the table. Gripping the handle between his thumb and forefinger, he turned it so the handle pointed straight toward the door. "I think I can find a renter for the house. I have a couple of men in mind who are honest. One has a wife, but no children yet. I would favor them. Maybe Joe Simmons could help them get started. He will still have his stock on the upper forty. Maybe you should leave old Ben with the place.

"As for the taters, we can wait and see how the crop does. If it is as productive as I think it will be, I have an idea. I have a contact in the Army. If I can interest them in the potatoes, you won't have to be concerned about them."

Uncle Jack pondered a moment, then asked, "How are you fixed for money? You've got that mixed batch you found in the flood debris. You might have to take some of that crop money we've stashed away."

Buddy started to speak, shaking his head.

Uncle Jack brushed his protest aside. "Oh, I know, point of honor. You see it as hers, but you are doing the trip for her. Remember the wise men that went to Bethlehem with those gifts? That was God's way of financing the trip to Egypt Mary and Joseph were about to make. They weren't rich. They would be gone for a long stretch, and the Lord had already planned for the expense. Look at the crop money the same way. God has already provided. You have a little over two thousand dollars. Take, let's see, five or six hundred? That should set you up for the journey, and for any expenses on the other end."

Buddy frowned. "I have a couple hundred in gold from that broken jar. Won't that do?"

Uncle Jack pursed his lips, and waggled them back and forth. "You have to understand something. The farther west you go, the farther you will get from supplies and service. That means prices will be higher. Maybe three or four times what you would pay here. Take your small gold, but it would not hurt to have, say, six hundred in twenties. That would weigh less than two pounds.

"Another thought. Once you get to Dalles City, you might have expenses for Sarah."

Buddy sighed. "And when I get there, what do I do? I don't know this guy that took her. My thought right now would be to shoot him and be done with it. But that would be murder." Looking up, he said, "Lord, forgive that thought. Please give me light for the journey, one step at a time."

"That's better," Uncle Jack said with a smile. "Let me think about the other end a bit. I have an idea, but I need to look around the edges and underneath. I think it would work, but I'll let you know. It would give you some authority there.

"Now, back to this end of the journey. What is your deal with Joe Simmons? Has it changed? Is he renting your upper forty?"

Buddy shook his head. "No. It was barter, for the most part. He helped plant the potatoes, and mend the fence around the upper forty. He's to give me a ton and a half of hay from his upper field to feed old Ben. And, he said he was going to brine half a yearling when he butchers."

Uncle Jack nodded. "Sounds fair to me. He has no claim on part of the taters?"

"No." Buddy smiled. "He thought he was cheating me with the exchange. He did not want a single tater, he said."

"Good. The crop is all yours, then, whatever it produces. The grocer here did not want anything, either." Uncle Jack fished a paper and pencil out of his pocket. "Now, what did this Tom say you would need?"

Buddy reached across and scratched his elbow. "Well, a younger mule, for one thing. He stressed that I should ride a mule. He said the tribes would not want a mule, because mules don't increase their herd."

Uncle Jack guffawed and slapped the table. "He sure pegged that one! When your status depends on your number of rides, and when your herd will pay a bride price, mules would indeed be at the bottom of the list of acquisitions. What else?"

Buddy's finger traced lines on the table. "A bed roll, canvas on the outside, blankets inside. Salt. A good knife. A belt ax. Some kind of cooking pot. A length of cord. A length of stout rope. Fishing gear."

"What about clothes? Did he say anything about what you should wear?"

Buddy looked up and grinned. "He did. He said I should look drab, because everything else will be this time of year. I think he said I should not wear white. Oh, and good boots. He talked about cut rock and goat heads."

"Thorns and thistles. Part of Adam's penalty. The rest of us inherit his consequences," Uncle Jack muttered as he wrote. "And all of this has to take up as little space as possible. How about a gun? Did he mention that?"

Buddy took a deep breath, and said, "He did, but he advised me not to use it, unless I had to. I could shoot game, but he said to grab my kill and move on, because someone might come looking for whoever was shooting. I've got Grandpa Wilson's Colt cylinder rifle. There's a revolver that takes the same caliber bullets, and a bag of bullets already cast. There's a horn of powder, but I will probably need some new powder, after eight years. I want it to go bang, not sizzle."

Uncle Jack smiled. "Right you are. Nothing worse than a sizzle when you have your sights on a nice yearling doe." He surveyed his paper. "Tell you what. I've got a trip to West Union in a couple of days, and maybe beyond. You won't find some of this stuff here in Rome, and maybe not in West Union, for that matter. I know a fellow out that way who has been over the trail, both ways. I may drop in on him, and see what he has to add to your information. He might even have some of his outfit stashed away somewhere, in case he ever gets a notion to go back. But then, he was eighty-something his last birthday.

"I'll stop by and chat with you on my way back. Matter of fact, I'll stop by and take some of that 'furrin money' from you, and see if I can't turn it either into stuff or into gold. It's still good, but who knows how long folks will trust it as money? Any thought about when you might leave?"

Buddy shook his head. "No. It would have to be soon. I'm not sure when Sarah's birthday is, but Tom said I should get beyond South Pass as soon as possible. Snow could fly as early as September, and some on the trail have seen snow in late August. We are already in July. This is, what, the tenth? You'll be gone four, maybe five days? That's the fifteenth. Maybe I'll aim for between the fifteenth and the twentieth. I think the twentieth should be the latest. Two thousand miles. If I can make fifty miles a day, I should make it by the first of September."

"Not so fast, Buddy," Uncle Jack interrupted. "Just speaking from experience on those long marches. The Lord worked six days, and then rested. For the sake of your beast, and for yourself, you should do the same thing. You can push for fifty miles a day, or even more. If it is flat, you can walk three or four miles in an hour. But you will come to hills. Even if you are riding, you cannot gallop for twelve hours, day after day. Mules have good durability, but that would kill even a young mule. No, take a day of rest along the way now and again. Find a spring, and camp somewhere near it, but not beside it. Others will know where it is. It will have feed around it for your mule. Let him graze and rest. Before he eats all the greenery, look for some salad for yourself. Days of rest will put you there in the middle of September, and the last part of the trip is not through high mountains. Trust me on this. I've done a couple of long marches, back when I was your age. I know, I don't look like it now. But, I did. The Army was fond of forced marches."

Buddy reached for his slicker, and stared out the window at the driving rain. "That new saddle is sure gonna soak my britches. I'll sort out the money when I get home, and have it ready for you. I'll need a cuppa when I get there, and likely a fire in the fireplace and the cook stove to drive the dampness out."

"Just wait a bit before you rush off." Uncle Jack got a loaf out of the bread box and sliced enough for a couple of sandwiches. From the larder he took butter and a half-used ham, and deftly constructed a quick lunch. "You might as well have a bite to eat before you tackle that eight-mile trip. And once you get home, see what you can gather for your journey. We'll mix that with whatever I can round up.

"Tom told you you should have a slingshot. Make one if you can, and practice so you can hit what you are aiming for. Close won't get you any supper."

Buddy laughed. "I might as well join the hunters along the trail and use a bow and arrow!"

Wiggins did not laugh. He nodded, saying, "That might not be a bad idea. It would be quieter than your rifle. But then, you would have to practice with that as well. Did Tom show you how to set the trigger on a snare?"

Buddy smiled. "No, but Grandpa Wilson did. We used to snare rabbits and squirrels back of the upper forty. Some of the snares worked without a figure-four. I've got that part learned."

Buddy brushed the crumbs of bread from the table. "I'd better head home. You've got my news. Think I'm foolish to take off like this?"

Uncle Jack shook his head. "No. I'd go myself if it wasn't so far, and if I was not so old and fat. You go, and God bless and keep you in your going. Now, get along with you!"

After Buddy left, Wiggins gazed blankly at the closed door. "Dalles City," he murmured. "Yeah, I'd go..."

Chapter 9

Buddy stared at the array of take-alongs on the table. Was that enough salt? The bed roll looked too big. Maybe three blankets would be too many. He spread the roll on the floor, took out one blanket, and added a sheet. When he rolled it up again, it was not much smaller. He muttered, "Maybe only one blanket. I could roll up in it."

Unrolling it again, he took out another blanket and tossed it aside. He doubled the remaining blanket around the sheet, folded the canvas flaps over each other, and folded the canvas under at the foot end. Opening the flaps and blanket, he crawled in and closed the flaps. "It'll work, but I sure hope the ground is softer than this floor!"

When he rolled it up again, it was smaller, and appeared to be manageable. As he put it back on the table, he heard the rattle of wheels outside, followed by a drawn-out groan.

Buddy opened the door as Uncle Jack labored up the stairs. "I didn't expect you for a couple of days. You must have hurried back. What's the rush?"

"You have to be in Cincinnati by Saturday. There's a steamer that comes up that far. The captain won't try to come any farther upstream. He says he will be heading back downriver early Saturday, and he goes as far as Columbus, but you can go ashore at Cairo. From there, you can catch a little local steamer that will run you up to Alton at the mouth of the Missouri. The river is still spread out so you can't see the channel, but that little steamer is shallow draft, and the captain says he finds his way by landmarks sticking out of the water. He knows that stretch of the river, and finds his way by flooded barns and orchards.

"Once you get to Alton, you will catch a steamer to Independence. That is the jumping-off point for the Emigrant Road to San Francisco. I used some of your 'furrin money' for the tickets. Here." Uncle Jack slapped an envelope on the table beside the gear Buddy had arranged.

Scooting his chair back, Buddy threw his arms out, his hands flailing. Then, leaping to his feet, he yelled, "I can't be in Cincinnati by Saturday! I'm not ready. I haven't found the stuff I need for the trip. I don't have time to get stuff and get there."

Uncle Jack stood, and shook his head at the antics of the younger man. "Calm down and listen. I have an appointment in Cincinnati on Friday. I'm taking you and your stuff in the buggy."

"But, I don't have all the stuff I'll need. I don't even know what all to take. I have some ideas, but some things aren't working. Look at that bed roll. It's too big, and I don't think it will be warm enough in the mountains. Only one blanket..."

Uncle Jack headed for the door. "Come give me a hand out here."

Outside, Wiggins reached behind the seat and dragged a bulky bundle over the back. Handing it to Buddy, he said, "Here. Carry this inside."

As Buddy headed up the steps, Uncle Jack pulled out one more bundle, then eased his bulk back down to the ground. Inside, Buddy stared at the contraption he had set on the floor.

"That's a cross between saddle bags and panniers," Uncle Jack said. He set his bundle on the table. "It's already been to the Territory and back a couple of times. Old Rufus Walker said it has most everything you will need. It hangs behind your saddle, with a bag over each hip of your mule. There are straps to fasten it to your saddle, and straps to hold your bed roll. Rufus said it's waterproof, which is good, because you'll have to swim some rivers. He said you'll have to cross the Platte several times. You'll cross the Sweetwater nine times, but he doubts you'll have to swim it."

"Rufus Walker." Buddy lifted straps, and separated the two saddlebags. "He's the man who is eighty-something?"

Uncle Jack said, "Yes. He said he was glad to give you this stuff. He won't be needing it again, and he figures it misses the trail. Said you might as well get some use out of it. Unpack it one bag at a time, see what's in it, and pack it up again. There's some room on each side for food packets. He said to balance the load, a little on each side. If you have some that won't fit, you can roll some in your bed roll, or tie a bundle on behind your soogan, as he called his bed."

Buddy unpacked and repacked each side. It took three tries to get everything back in the same compact order old Rufus had accomplished. Some of the things in the pack surprised him.

"A spy glass?"

Uncle Jack laughed. "When you are on a high perch, you might notice something moving. That'll show you just what it is. Or, you can study a hillside or valley to see if you have company, or maybe spot something for your dinner."

Buddy nodded. "It comes with its own case, too."

"Yeah. Don't bust it. Rufus said that if you see somebody coming, get out of the way. Hide. It'll get lonesome out there, but there's some company you don't want. Tribes or bandits. When you climb a hill to look around, don't go clear to the top. You don't want to be the thing seen moving, and you sure don't want to be the only thing sticking up against the sky for all to see."

Buddy smiled. "Yeah, that's what Tom said. He sketched me a map along the way."

"All right, let's see that map."

Buddy moved some of his gear on the table, clearing an end, where he spread the map.

Uncle Jack studied it, then pointed at South Pass. "When you get here, you'll be nine hundred miles from Independence. Your first stopping place will be here at Fort Laramie. It's an Army fort. It is in the middle of land occupied by plains Indians. South, here, is Sioux country. They are divided into several sub-tribes. Down here, the Arapaho. Up here, the Pawnees. There's going to be a meeting between the tribes and the Army and government representatives come September. They are going to get together here at Fort Laramie. They are planning to negotiate safe passage for folks headed west through the tribal land. But right now, with no treaty in place, it's back and forth reprisals."

Buddy tapped the fort location on the map. "Who is in charge here at the fort? Do they know anything, really?"

"Ever hear of Thomas Fitzpatrick? He was a fur trader, trapper, mountain man explorer type who has been all over the West. He's the Indian agent to the Sioux tribes. They prefer to call themselves the Lakota, but they get stuck with the name the white man gave them. So, yeah, you'll find somebody there who knows stuff. Pick his brain. Fitzpatrick says the plains tribes want peace. That's why they are coming to the pow-wow come September. Army is in charge. Don't know who the commander is. Probably some captain or some lieutenant. They likely couldn't get a general to take such a remote post, unless he was in trouble. Never know, though. With negotiations for a treaty, they might send a general with whatever big hat they send to do the talking.

"Once you leave Fort Laramie, you'll go up the Platte to the mouth of the Sweetwater River. The river runs through a series of gorges. Don't try to follow the river too closely. One, some of those gorges pinch the river to where there is no trail. Two, it is subject to flash floods. Watch out for the same thing on the Platte. At the crossings, if you hear thunder in the distance, get away from the river. Even if it is sunny where you are, you can be hit with a sudden wall of water. Folks have lost wagons when they were trying to cross. Some have lost their lives. Rufus Walker says one of his friends got caught in one of those flash floods, and got so tumbled about that he arrived at the pearly gates wearing the saddle, and with the mule wearing the spurs. He said the mule was showing his friend what the spurs felt like. Said old Saint Pete turned them both away."

Buddy looked puzzled. "Is that stretch along the Sweetwater flat?"

Uncle Jack shook his head. "Yes and no. The mountains dabble their toes in the river, so the land has its ups and downs. That's why you have your gorges and crossings. It's like life. The Lord gives us quiet stretches, and times of testing. He grows us through both of them. Think of the twelfth of Hebrews, and verse two. When it talks about our Lord, it says that for the joy that was set before Him, He endured the cross, despising the shame. The joy was on the other side of the trial. Sometimes it's like that for us. The Lord is taking us somewhere, and there is good waiting, but first there is a dark valley. We don't like those places, but we can go through them, because He has said that He will never leave us or forsake us. He doesn't say that we are on our own, that He will meet us on the other side of the valley. He goes with us, and sometimes He carries us through."

Buddy nodded. "We can't avoid the hard places. Like the fire that took the Wilsons, or the long stretch looking for Sarah. I remember the apostle Paul asking the Lord to remove a trial for him, and the Lord told him that His grace was sufficient for Paul. In the hard times, I guess we just have to trust that the Lord knows what He is doing."

Uncle Jack chuckled. "Good insight, there. It was Paul who wrote that we could have confidence that the Lord who started His good work in us would be faithful to finish it.

"But, back to your trip. You will leave the Sweetwater where the mountains meet each other, and angle a bit southish. You'll cross South Pass, and probably won't notice, except you'll start downhill. It won't be much of a slope at first, but you will notice the next stream you see is flowing south and westward instead of north and eastward."

Buddy studied that portion of the map. "So Fort Laramie is the first stopping place?"

"Right. And you can resupply there. It's an Army fort, and the sutler there gets supplies out of Independence. If you need something, he just might have it. Get some dried meat from him. He gets that from the tribes. Buffalo is a bit tough, but if you pound it between a couple of stones, and then boil it, it makes a pretty good beef broth."

Looking at the map, Buddy mumbled, "Nine hundred miles to South Pass. Fort Laramie is about six hundred miles out." Looking to Uncle Jack he asked, "What is the next supply station, if I need something?"

Wiggins pointed to a jumble of mountains and valleys beyond South Pass. "You get two choices. If you take the main route after the pass, you will swing south and pick up two headwaters of the Green River. On Black's Fork, you will find a ramshackle collection of buildings of Jim Bridger's trading post. It has been called Fort Bridger, but it is more a trading post than a fort. It will give you a place to rest up, and lighten your load of money. Jim Bridger is always looking for the next pigeon to pluck, and if that happens to be you, you'll be lucky if you have any feathers left by the time you leave his place."

Uncle Jack traced back to a fork in the road on the map. "This is the Greenwood cutoff. Some call it Sublette's cutoff. But it was first traveled by a man named Greenwood. It is a shortcut. It will save you about eighty miles, or a little more. But it has fifty miles with no water. You will want your canteen full to start, and you will have to give most of that to your mule. Once you are across that dry stretch, you will come to Fort Hall. It was sold to the Hudson's Bay Company. But now, it is in Army hands. There's a contingent of soldiers sent up from the Oregon Country to guard the way to Dalles City and on down the Columbia. They spend the summer there. Good folks. The sutler there will sell you what you need, if they have it. They've even been known to give away emergency supplies to those who were flat broke."

Buddy smiled. "That won't be me. I have some money for stuff. That is a long way to haul supplies to the fort, though. What all do they have?"

Uncle Jack snorted. "They have a bunch of broken wagons. You can rob parts from them to fix yours, if you were taking one. Hudson's Bay

Company did not want emigrants flooding into their territory, so they kept the broken wagons to show travelers, and told them that the earlier folks had to go ahead on foot, carrying what they could. They tried to paint a dismal picture that might send folks back to Independence.

"They have trade goods. Twists of tobacco, and leather bags of beads. Hudson's Bay Company blankets are a good quality choice. Good wool. If you need one, get the one with the most stripes. That's the quality code. They will have moccasins with good, thick buffalo hide soles. Some clothes. Maybe some rations, if they don't figure they need them all themselves."

Buddy reached across the table and picked up a small deerskin pouch and spilled its contents on the table. "Here's my small gold. How are their prices?"

Uncle Jack shook his head. "You never want to show what you have. Let them name their price. If you think it is too much, turn away. They will likely call you back, and offer a better price. If you want to buy, slip a little out, or maybe have your money out already. Be a little short, and then dig around for the rest. If they know you have plenty of money, you won't get a decent price if you need to buy anything else."

Wiggins reached for his other packet. "Here's the answer to your issue at the other end of the journey. Raise your right hand. Do you solemnly swear to uphold and defend the laws and constitution of the United States of America?"

Puzzled, Buddy edged his hand upward and said, "Um, yeah, why?"

Wiggins untied the bundle, and pulled out a belt with a thick pouch. Opening the pouch, he pulled out a small packet. "I told you I'm a U. S. Marshal. I can deputize those I need to do a job. Here is your badge. That will give you authority at the forts, and once you get to the Oregon Country. Joe Meek is a marshal there in the Willamette Valley. He is down at Jason Lee's mission station. Lee is dead now, but the mission station carries on. You may never see Meek, but if you do, you can show him this certificate with my name at the bottom. He'll back you if you need him to. Keep this with you. The belt goes around you, under your shirt. It also has your six hundred dollars in gold. You have thirty twenties. With what you have, you should be able to meet most any expense, along the way, or once you get there."

Buddy gulped. "I'm a lawman? What does that mean?"

Wiggins rose, putting on his coat and hat. "Means you can arrest the man who has Sarah, though what you'd do with him, I don't know. You can't try him and hang him. You likely won't find a jail anywhere to lock him up. But you will have the authority to take Sarah into protective custody.

He might object. You then would have the authority to protect her. Now, we both have things to do. I'll come by for you early Friday. Have your stuff ready to throw in the buggy. We will have a steamer to catch. Oh, put those tickets in that belt." Heading for the door, Uncle Jack slapped Buddy on the shoulder. "See you Friday, Deputy Wilson."

Chapter 10

Friday was another sunless day, with heavy clouds scarcely able to hold altitude above the soggy fields of Ohio. Half way through summer, creeks and rivers still ran brim full. Had it been visible, the sun would have stood two fingers above the eastern horizon as Jackson Wiggins and Buddy Wilson pulled away from the old Wilson farm. Potatoes in the lower forty flourished in orderly rows. Joe Simmons' cattle and horses grazed in the upper forty.

Half to himself, Buddy asked, "Wonder if I'll ever see this again? It's all the home I remember."

Uncle Jack sighed. "It'll be here. Likely it won't change. Cabin's solid, outbuildings are good. You'll change. You might get out to Oregon and like it there. Government wants it settled. They're giving away land, or selling it cheap. You just have to build a house of some kind, and live in it for a time. You can get a quarter section. If you have a wife, you can double that. Rufus says the east is good for ranching, and the Willamette Valley is good for farming. You can plow and plant, or you can run stock. You just have to get it there. With the money you have, you might buy a patch of ground from some geezer who has proved up on his, built his house and barns, and got old. Find someone who is tired, but not too tired to carry a bit of gold.

"If you find that is what you want to do, you might even buy the place, build your own house, and let the old folks live in theirs. They could help as they have strength, and advise as they have wisdom."

Buddy pulled out of his reverie as the buggy jostled toward West Union. "I'm not even started yet. Don't plant me there before I've set foot on the Emigrant Road."

Wiggins laughed. "Well, I'm not counting my chickens, but I might be cracking the eggs to let them out."

It was Buddy's turn to laugh. "A merry heart does good like a medicine, the Book says. Guess we might as well laugh as I leave everything behind that has been home to me, even if it was not mine."

Uncle Jack nodded. "The Book also says we are strangers here. We are not of this world. Our home is in heaven. We are looking for the Savior to come and conduct us to what He has prepared for us. But until then, we have a purpose here. Yours has been here, and now it may be a couple thousand miles away. He will let you know. Don't hold on too tightly to things of this world, or in this world. Don't be anchored when the Lord says move."

The two rode in a comfortable silence, each lost in his own thoughts. Uncle Jack waved at a couple of men he knew as the buggy rattled through West Union. The town behind them, they passed scattered farms, and an occasional cluster of houses that formed the germinating seed of a town.

Uncle Jack broke the silence. "I've got a couple moving to the farm next weekend. Jacob and Esther Jennings. Early twenties, but hard workers. They've leased the farm for a year. Jacob would like to buy it, but he does not have the money right now. I did not know if you want it sold or held, so I agreed to a lease. Part of your gold came from him."

Pulled from his own meditations, Buddy said, "I don't know, either. In a year, I might have a better idea. How are they going to make any money, with the upper forty taken by Joe Simmons, and the lower forty in potatoes?"

"He does not need an income from the farm. They just want a country place. Jacob has money from his father's business. His dad is in railroads. It seems Jacob invented some gizmo that makes the engine more efficient. They had a small acreage on the Kentucky side, but the Ohio took everything in the flood. They escaped with the clothes on their backs. They could have gone to

Chicago, but they wanted the quiet and uncrowded ways down here."

Buddy pondered the issue while the buggy rolled another mile toward Cincinnati. Finally, he said, "Do what you think best. You were the Wilsons' attorney and the executor of their...stuff. I don't know if they had a will. If you think it best to sell the farm, I'd say go ahead. I don't know what the post is like out in the Oregon Territory, but if I can get a letter to you, I'll let you know what I find out, and what I will be doing.

"If Tom gets there first, he might marry Sarah. That would mean the two of them would be staying in the Territory. If I get there first, and if she marries me, I don't know what we would do. I don't like the sound of this. As I told Tom, it sounds like we are fussing over the last slice of pie. Marriage is more sacred than that."

Whiskers hid Uncle Jack's smile. "It is. The Lord uses marriage to picture our relationship with Christ. He is the Bridegroom and the church is His bride. God holds marriage to be very sacred."

Another mile passed in silence. Buddy noticed Uncle Jack slip his hand up to brush away a tear, so he turned his gaze to the sky, and prayed silently for his friend.

Uncle Jack cleared his throat, and continued as if there had been no break in the conversation. "I had a wife. She was a precious part of me. She and my little one are waiting for me in the presence of our Lord. You are correct. It is sacred. Our Lord said back at creation, 'It is not good, the man, alone. I will make a helper to complete him.' Since my Susie died, I feel sorta incomplete, like part of me went on ahead. My little Todd went with her. Guess that's why I latched on to you." Wiggins noted the look of consternation that passed over Buddy's face. "But, don't change your mind about going. The Lord directs our steps, and He can meet all of our needs, whether they are physical or emotional. His grace is sufficient. I cling to that promise."

The morning was measured by the steady hoof beats of Uncle Jack's mare. Feeling the weight of silence, Wiggins drew a deep breath, and said, "There's something else I have to ask you, Son. Did you do anything with the stuff the Wilsons had? If Jacob and Esther are moving in, they might could use some of it, but what about personal stuff? Did you look through it, or store it or anything?"

Buddy shook his head. "No. I got Grandpa Wilson's guns, but I have not felt up to sorting stuff. It seems too, what shall I say, sacred? Personal? There wasn't a lot. Their clothes are still where they left them. Grandpa's stuff is probably still in the pockets of the pants he took off that night. Grandma Wilson had stuff she kept in a big chest at the foot of the bed. I stayed out of their room. I felt their private stuff was off limits."

Wiggins let another mile slip by, then said, "I'll take care of that for you. I understand how you've felt about it. I'll get Grandpa's britches and the chest before the Jennings couple moves in. The furniture and kitchen stuff isn't so personal that they shouldn't touch it or use it. They can even sleep in the bed. The Wilsons wouldn't mind. They used to let guests sleep there, and they shared the loft with Sarah. I might even find some answers in that chest." Uncle Jack shook his head. "Eight years, and you haven't looked in it. But, I understand why not."

Uncle Jack's mare measured another ten miles before either spoke. Uncle Jack broke into Buddy's thoughts. "When you get to Independence, see if you can find a livery stable. If the hostler does not sell mules, maybe he can direct you to some place you can buy one. If he can't sell you one, rent a rig, pick up your stuff from the steamer, and drive to where the hostler sends you. You know about mules. Find one that isn't spooky. Find one that has been broken gently, one that has not been mistreated. Mules take a lot of loving. Hurt them and they will kick, bite and balk. They will hate you forever. Some people are like that. Find a young mule, five or six years old. Get some oats, and some carrots for treats. Mules respond to kindness and bribery."

"Yeah." Buddy laughed silently. "I learned that from Grandpa Wilson and Benedict Arnold. Grandpa had nothing but contempt for mule whackers that used a bullwhip. He said they were creating no end of trouble for themselves."

Uncle Jack continued as if he had not heard. "Once you find your mule, pay the man to take the rig back to the livery. Saddle your mule and load the pack behind the saddle. Lead him out onto the trail and find a place to camp for a couple of days, so the two of you can get to know each other. You won't have much time for a real bond, so be sure you have hobbles for nights as you go."

Buddy nodded. "Grandpa hobbled old Ben now and again, when we were camping on the way somewhere. Ben understood, and stayed close. It was as if the hobbles anchored him. We didn't need to stake him out."

"You might need to stake a new mule, though. Stake him where he can feed, and he won't try to pull the stake." Uncle Jack pointed to a house with two large barns. "Ten more miles to Cincinnati. You'll see more houses, now."

Wiggins reined the mare to a sudden stop. "That farm had several mules in the corral. Let's see if they might have a young one they might sell."

He turned around, and headed up to the driveway. Seeing the farmer leaving one of the barns, Wiggins turned the buggy in that direction. The farmer stopped and waited while Wiggins pulled the mare to a standstill. He held his hand out for the mare to nuzzle, then reached into his pocket and pulled out a carrot. The mare's lips gently plucked the morsel from his open hand.

"Lose something?" He looked to Buddy and Uncle Jack.

Uncle Jack's eyes twinkled between crow's feet. "Yeah. A mule. Got an extra?"

Buddy turned and stared at Uncle Jack.

The farmer extended his hand in greeting. "Alton Rogers. An extra? I sure don't have one of yours."

Uncle Jack gripped the offered hand. "No. Buddy's mule was long in the tooth. He is headed out west, and needs to buy a younger model."

Alton Rogers dropped his hand, and turned his gaze to Buddy. "You want to buy one?"

Buddy nodded. "I need one that has a bit of gentling, and hasn't been abused. One that has potential to bond, and responds to kindness, with maybe a bit of bribery. Got anything like that paragon of virtue that you might part with?"

Rogers flashed Buddy a crooked smile. "You know mules, Son. I might could trust one of my kids with you. I don't know what fate sent you here, but I could sure use the money. My wife needs some medical attention, and I just don't have the loose change to cover the expense. Here, get down, and I'll let you into the corral."

Buddy lowered himself to the ground. "The Lord's leading brought us here."

Rogers scowled. "If you swallow that stuff. Guess it's all right for you. I trust what I can see and touch. Come on."

Uncle Jack looked at Buddy, but kept quiet. Alton Rogers walked with Buddy to the corral gate, opened it, and let Buddy in with the mules.

Rogers walked back to the buggy, and turned to watch. The mules had crowded to the opposite side of the corral. Buddy leaned quietly against the gate. The mules relaxed, but stayed against the far fence.

Rogers looked up and smiled at Uncle Jack. "I think he knows mules. He will wait to see who comes to him. There! That's the one I thought. That one has no bad habits. He's six and rides and drives and packs."

Buddy smiled and spoke quietly to the one that left the fence and walked slowly across the corral. Ears turned slightly back, and nostrils slightly flared, the mule walked confidently up to sniff Buddy's jacket. He did not flinch when Buddy took his hand from the top rail of the corral and reached to scratch the base of the mule's ear, then slid it down to scratch under his chin.

Uncle Jack cleared his throat. "Well, Rogers, what do you think of that one? Is he up to the trail? How would you rate him?"

In the same quiet tone, Rogers answered, "He's sound. Long legs will shorten the miles. I think he got more of the horse than the donkey. That's my mammoth jack over by the other barn. But back to the mule. Six years, and he's been the picture of health. I'd rather keep him. But, like my daddy used to say, he's only worth selling if he's worth keeping. If you want him, you've got me over a barrel. I've got an extra halter, and he's not opposed to being ponied behind the buggy."

Buddy had let himself out of the corral, and closed the gate. As he approached the buggy, he said, "That young roan thinks he wants to go west. Would you consider selling him?"

Rogers chuckled. "I've been watching the two of you. You know how to communicate with mules, and he knows it. If you had walked across the corral, you wouldn't have gotten any of them. You didn't say anything, but he heard you call him, and he came. I'll sell. His name's Tramp. Always begging."

Buddy looked up at Uncle Jack, who nodded slightly. Buddy reached in his pocket and pulled out some of his small money in gold. Holding out his palm, he said to Rogers, "Count out your price. You know what you need. I know what he is worth to me. Take what's fair. It can be a blessing to both of us. I thank both you and the Lord."

Rogers had started to reach for the gold. Pulling his hand back, he said, "You make that God stuff seem almost real. What if I took all of it? What if I cheated you?"

Buddy smiled. "Well, if I cheated you, I'd have to live with myself. When I closed my eyes at night, I'd still see the hopeless look in your eyes I saw when you greeted us. Your need has been troubling you for a while, hasn't it? Take what's right."

Alton Rogers shook his head, but said nothing. With an unsteady finger, he sorted through the handful of gold coins, and counted out a few of them. Tears filled his eyes when he looked up, first meeting Buddy's, and then shifting to catch the gaze of Uncle Jack. In an unsteady voice, he said, "Your religion is real. I wish..."

Buddy smiled. "You can. My Lord Jesus gave an open invitation. 'Come unto me, all you who labor and are heavy laden, and I will give you rest...' Sometimes He picks me up along with my burden and carries both me and it. You as much as said you don't believe what He has said, but I'll pray for both you and your wife. Your tears told me she is dear to you, and I read relief in your eyes now, not anxiety.

"You say you have a halter for him. I have a mule saddle I brought along. Do you have a bridle he's used? And maybe hobbles?"

Rogers nodded. "I have everything you will need. I'll throw it in."

Buddy picked another gold coin from his pocket. "No, you will have to replace it, since you breed mules and train them. Here. Take this. Folks in Cincinnati don't give their stuff away."

Taking the coin, Alton Rogers said, "I won't refuse it. Lord knows I can use it."

With a half smile, Buddy said, "You mention the Lord, but you say you don't believe."

"Just an expression." Rogers frowned, then headed to the barn.

Uncle Jack looked at Buddy. "Kind of plain spoken, aren't you? But he will think about that transaction. What you did spoke volumes to him. What made you hold out a whole handful of gold?"

"I don't know. It was like I was nudged in that direction, and then you nodded. Confirmation. Doesn't the Lord offer blessings in an open hand?"

"He does. That was flood money, wasn't it?"

Buddy nodded.

Uncle Jack said, "The Lord blessed you with it, so you could bless Rogers in turn, even though he isn't one of His. At least not yet. But what you did and said, the Spirit can use to turn his heart, and maybe draw him to the Savior."

Alton Rogers came out of the barn with the needed tack items. He handed the bridle to Buddy, then walked to the corral. He slipped the halter on Tramp and led him out of the corral. After closing the gate, Rogers led the mule to the back of the buggy and tethered him.

Coming around to where Buddy stood, Rogers started to extend his hand, then, changing his mind, he threw his arms around the younger man in a tight hug. Clinging to him, Rogers murmured, "Thank you. And I'll think about what you said. Hope you have a safe trip west. Keep your eyes open on the trail."

Rogers stood with his hands on his hips, watching as Uncle Jack turned the buggy into the road to Cincinnati, Tramp following without resistance. The man pulled the gold from his pocket, and walked slowly toward his front door, gazing at the provision that had fallen to him, as if from the clouds.

As the road took them through town, Uncle Jack said, "That was less than half what a mule would have cost you in Independence. You would have been cheated there, and the cheater would have felt no remorse. I'll pray the Lord uses that encounter to draw Rogers. Maybe I'll stop and check on him on one of my trips to town here. I think the Lord was leading in that whole encounter."

Uncle Jack drove the buggy onto the steamer dock, where the steamer was moored, waiting for the next day's departure. To Buddy, he said, "Wait here. I'll see if the captain is on board. I did not say anything to him about taking a mule on board. But, I'm sure they take the animals folks are riding. I'll find out, and ask what time he figures to head down river. Then, we will find a place for you to park for the night, and I'll head for my meeting." He pulled out a turnip-sized pocket watch, popped it open, and said, "We'll grab a bite to eat before my appointment. Then you'll be on your own."

Part Two

The Trail

Chapter 11

A small wagon train, fewer than thirty wagons, had headed out on the trail. Iron-rimmed wheels and iron-shod hooves had crushed the prairie grass, which lay like winter-blasted cornstalks across the trail where the oxen, horses and mules had drawn the burdened wagons through the mud left by unseasonable rains. On both sides of the trail, the prairie grass towered as high as Buddy's shoulders as he rode Tramp out of Independence, Missouri on a trail he could not miss. The Platte River had resumed its banks, and was again 'a mile wide and an inch deep, too thin to plow and too thick to drink.' Clouds still crowded thick and gloomy above them, and Buddy could see blue sky ahead, beyond the edge of the clouds.

To Tramp he said, "The folks who left these tracks camped along here, so we should find where they turned aside. But we should be able to hit every second or third camping spot. We will make better time than the wagon train. We might even catch them, depending when they headed out, and how fast they could go through this swamp."

Tramp plodded on, with little indication he had heard.

Buddy went on, his words ripped away by the wind that swept the prairie grass into apparent long ocean swells. "We'll walk here, but maybe you can trot as we get higher. Fort Laramie is our first stopover, but it is about six hundred miles. It'll be just the two of us, so I'll talk, and you listen. And when I don't talk, you listen anyway. I'll watch your ears, and you give me a signal if you hear any trouble ahead."

The way ahead opened into a wide trampled area with a black circle in the middle. Here the wagon train had circled, and the travelers had lit a large fire for light and cooking. Half-burned branches showed that the fire had sizzled out in the pouring rain. Buddy found that some, arching above the ground, were dry enough for a cooking fire. These he collected, and managed to light a small fire. He boiled water from his canteen and made a cup of tea. While he drank that, he simmered some shredded jerky, making a thin soup. His tin cup drained of tea, he poured out a cup of soup, and set it to cool.

While he waited, he surveyed the campground. The area to the south, between the camping area and the river, was littered with the animal droppings left by the livestock. To the east of the paddock area he saw the structure of the latrine. The travelers had not dug a pit. Water seeped through the mess, and made its way into the Platte.

As Buddy sipped his broth, he said to Tramp, "No wonder Tom said not to drink surface water. That's enough to sicken anybody. What did he say killed people? Cholera. That was it. Those headed west poisoned the folks who came after them. We'll find you a clean place to get a drink."

Buddy gathered the driest branches he could find, and tied them on behind his bedroll. "We'll be able to boil water for the canteen, and cook a bite of supper. You will have to carry whatever wood I can find until we get across this ocean of grass. We should eventually find some real trees. But for now, let's be moving." He scattered the remaining embers of his fire, and stomped them into the mud. Remounting, he headed the mule back to the trail.

Buddy smelled the next camping area before he reached it. The mule snorted. "I agree. Snort, yourself. Lets pass this place and look for a tributary. That crowd will continue west, but we will turn aside and go upstream a ways. Maybe we will find moving water. That should be clean."

Two miles later, Buddy spotted a line of willows that led to the north. Turning the mule, he followed the meandering thread of water to where it emerged from under the roots of two cottonwood trees. The spring divided, and the two branches formed two small pools, before reuniting and plunging into the willows.

Buddy gave the mule his head, and said, "Take your pick. Which ever one you drink from, I'll dip from the other."

Tramp slurped the impounded water, raised his head, and belched.

Buddy laughed. "I've heard that in some places, that is the way to say thank you. So, you are welcome. Now, lets get you unloaded."

Buddy found a hummock beyond the cottonwoods. With his knife he cut prairie grass. After stomping down the stubble, he piled the grass to form a mattress. Dense as it was, the grass retained the moisture of weeks of rain. There was no danger of a prairie fire, but then, there was no dry grass to use as kindling.

From the willows below the cottonwoods he broke dead twigs and branches. He shaved bark and fibers of dead wood into his tinder box, and, pulling his flint and steel from his possible bag, he struck sparks into the tinder.

Striking a fire in the cabin had been easy. Out on the prairie, the sparks fell into the box and went out. He turned, using his coat to shelter the tinder box from the incessant wind. After several minutes of futile efforts, one spark started a tiny orange glow in the charred part of the tinder.

Like a tiny orange worm, the glow crept under the fibers of willow.

Buddy gently blew on the tiny glow, and it expanded. At last, a tiny flicker of flame touched the fresh shavings and flared into a miniature campfire in the tin.

Poured into the pile of willow twigs, the flame faded, then ignited one, and then another. Ribbons of smoke were ripped away by the wind as Buddy broke willow branches and built them into a log cabin around and over the burning shavings. As the branches caught fire, he broke some of the charred branches he had tied behind his saddle and managed to build a fire that would sustain itself while he boiled water and prepared dinner.

To himself, Buddy said, "Might as well be prepared for morning." He set a pot of water on to boil, then shaved bark and willow fibers into his tinder box. Picking a glowing end from the fire, he lit the shavings on fire, then put the lid on the tinder box to suffocate the small flames. It would be ready for the next fire.

When the pot of water had boiled for several minutes, he crumbled jerky in his tin cup, and poured water over it to have it ready for breakfast. Then he set the pot aside to cool, and scattered the fire so it would go out. From the left pannier, he dug out his funnel and a canvas bag.

Once the water had cooled, he put a cloth in the funnel to act as a filter, and filled the canteen. When the burned ends of the scattered firewood were cool enough that he could pick them up by the charcoal end, he filled the canvas bag, pulled the drawstrings tight, then folded the mouth of the bag down and tied the strings. The ends would stay dry, and he would have first fuel for his next stop.

Hobbled and staked, Tramp was well supplied for his own dinner. The rasping of his tearing mouthfuls of prairie grass blended with the rustle of the wind that kept the grass in constant motion. Night noises lulled Buddy into a fitful sleep. His mind would not shut down. Just below the threshold of sleep, he kept calculating. He had come only about thirty-five miles, instead of the fifty he had planned. Mules did not move as fast as horses did, but they could go farther on poor rations.

At thirty-five miles a day, three weeks would put him a little over two hundred miles closer to Fort Laramie. August would be a week old by then. Unless he could make better time farther up the Platte, it would be a week into September when he reached the fort. Another month would put him at South Pass. That would be into October, and he would be less than half way.

Tramp, who had been grazing in the darkness, shook himself and heaved a rattling sigh. Buddy stirred, and thought, "I'll have to start earlier. I should have fourteen or fifteen hours of light. If I keep going, I can make fifty miles."

He settled back into half-sleep. His mind started recalculating. No. Thirty-five would get him to Fort Laramie in eighteen travel days, and fifty would get him there in twelve. Throw in a couple of rest days, and he could be a third of the way in two weeks.

At that point, he drifted into deep sleep. The light of dawn aroused him. Before the sun was above the horizon, he had downed his reconstituted jerky, saddled and loaded Tramp, and was on the trail. He crossed and recrossed the Platte, gaining altitude as he went. He sipped water from his canteen and ate jerky in the saddle, not stopping to build a fire or brew tea.

Through the afternoon, Buddy noticed that the prairie grass grew shorter and shorter. The prevailing wind still whipped it into waves, but he could now see beyond the walls that had closed him in as he left the Missouri River.

At length, Buddy reined Tramp to a stop, and, stiff and saddle-sore, he swung to the ground. To the mule he said, "I'll walk a bit, and you can follow without my weight on your back. That might be a bit of rest, but I'll tell you now, I'll be back up in a mile or so." Stiff at first, he eventually was able to stride out.

Another mile, and Buddy stopped. The prairie ahead was clipped short. The wind swept unimpeded over miles of shorn land. Ahead and to the south, the prairie looked black.

Buddy dug into the right pannier, and pulled out his spy glass. Focusing on the dark mass, Buddy said, "Buffalo! Thousands of them!" The undulating herd oozed southward, grazing. Swinging the glass to the north, Buddy saw another mass, even larger.

Buddy looked back and forth at the huge herds of buffalo. To Tramp he said, "Well, my friend, we won't have any place to hide now. It is all open country, and where the herd is, there may be hunters. We'll both have to be alert."

The way ahead led between the two herds. Buddy figured he had another five hours of light before he had to find a place to camp. With the spy glass he searched the area around and between the herds. Seeing nothing that was not buffalo, he mounted Tramp and started forward. "Step lively, Tramp. We need to get between those herds before they close ranks." He urged the mule into a trot, to cover more ground more quickly.

The air between the herds reeked of urine. The puddles on the ground were yellow. Buddy choked with each breath. He debated pulling Tramp down to a walk, to avoid the splatters thrown up by the mule's hooves. He kept up the trot to get beyond the putrid air as quickly as possible.

Knobs that might pass for hills rose on the right and left, and the trail passed between them into another long stretch of prairie. Here, too, the grass was clipped close by grazing beasts. Buddy reined in, and reached for the spy glass again. To the south, he spotted a knot of riders on horseback swinging to intercept the buffalo herd. He slipped off the mule in order to present a lower profile. The mule without a rider might pass unnoticed, while the mule with a man aboard would be much more likely to attract attention, even at that distance.

When the hunters were no longer in view, Buddy remounted and set Tramp into a trot. Another five miles passed behind them, when again Buddy pulled the mule to a stop. The breeze brought the transient smell of wood smoke.

"Well, Tramp, I think where there are hunters, there is bound to be a village. Guess this is where we walk circumspectly, as the Book says."

He pulled out the spy glass, and scanned the way ahead. The wind was out of the northwest, so that was the way he looked. With a pause in the wind, he spotted two threads of smoke rising toward the clouds. He could see no shape of dwellings, but noted that the encampment was beyond a ridge well off the trail, and he could cross the Platte and circle south around the smoke without encountering the hunters.

The thought led to action. Crossing the river, he angled south and west to skirt the camp. He kept an eye on the prairie behind him, watching for any sign of the herd or the hunters. He prayed, "Lord, could You shut their eyes until we get past all of this? The way ahead seems open, but I'm hedged in on the right and the left. You made blind eyes see, but I'd like You to make seeing eyes blind, at least where we are concerned. I'm trusting You for safe passage. And guard Sarah, for her good and for Your glory..."

Buddy swung Tramp back across the Platte. At a trot, the miles melted under the mule's hooves. Another two hours, and the light was growing dim. "We should have at least ten miles between us and the buffalo, and maybe that much between us and the camp." Buddy reached forward and patted the mule's neck. "Here's a tributary. We'll swing south and find some faster water so you can get a clean drink. I'm thinking we will have a cold camp tonight. A fire would be visible if they send out any scouts."

A mile south of the trail, Buddy found where the stream flowed instead of oozing. He kept going until he found where it tumbled over a buried log and fell into a pool, aerating the water. "Here's your fountain, and I can unroll my bedroll up there on that rise. No grass for a mattress, though. It's the hard ground for me. I don't sleep standing on my feet like you do. I'll stake you along the stream here. The buffalo have left you a bit more grass here than they did on the plains back there. You'll have to work harder than you did last night, but fill up, and get some rest."

The next days followed a similar pattern of monotony and watchfulness. The sameness of the prairie with the swaying of the mule lulled Buddy into drowsiness and his chin would drop toward his chest, jolting him awake, and he would hurriedly scan the area around him, only to doze again. He passed several points where the earlier wagon train had camped, and at two of those sites, he noted fresher hoof prints, some in the ash circle of the communal fire.

After six days on the trail, Buddy scanned the sides of the trail with his spy glass. He noted two rocky promontories to the south of the trail, with a gap between them and willows around the base of them. To Tramp he said, "That might be our resting place for tomorrow. You've moved right along, and it's time for a break. It looks like we can have a fire there without it being seen, and there should be plenty of feed for you. Maybe even some water, with those willows. Let's try it." He reined to the left, and approached with a degree of caution. As he neared the sheltered spot, he heard the sudden pounding of hooves. He had spooked some large animal that took an unseen departure. Tramp's ears pointed forward. Whatever it was, the mule was interested.

Riding into the gap, Buddy saw what appeared to

be a stone basin. Water trickled into it, then over the edge, to wander into the prairie grass. About twenty feet away, it formed another pool, larger than the goblet. The prairie grass beyond the second pool was only knee high. On a rock outcropping opposite the goblet Buddy saw the remains of a campfire, wet, cold and mostly washed away. Somebody knew this shelter. "Oh, well. It's ours now. But that tells me where to kindle a fire. It shouldn't be seen from there."

He pulled the panniers from Tramp's rump, then removed the saddle. The mule stood quietly as Buddy fastened the hobbles, then led him to the lower pool. Tramp balked.

"What's the problem?" Buddy asked. "See something you don't like?" He patted the mule's neck to calm him. Tramp shied, then reared, coming down with both front feet on a coiled snake at the edge of the grass. Writhing, the serpent tried to strike with the front third of its body. Tramp reared again, and came down on its head and slid, rolling and crushing the dangerous portion. The body continued to thrash, attempting to coil. After diminishing convulsions, the snake lay inert.

Buddy patted the mules neck. "You're more observant than I am. I would have blundered right into a snakebite. That was a close one. Not for you, though." Buddy cut a willow stick, scooped up the snake, and threw it out into the grass, as far from the camp as he could.

Tramp lay down in the prairie grass, rolled onto his back, and with a series of satisfied grunts and growls, twisted back and forth. For a moment he lay relaxed, legs to the sky. Rolling over, he scrambled to his feet, shook himself and turned to the next item on his agenda. He began tearing at the prairie grass, working out to the end of his picket. In the twilight, Buddy cut grass for a mattress, prepared his supper, and put water on to boil. As the pot began to sing over the coals, he prepared his tinder box for the morrow, and unrolled his bed. "I wonder why they call this a soogan. Maybe someone at the fort will know."

He scattered the coals, strained the water into his canteen, and fell asleep to the music of Tramp's grazing.

Chapter 12

Fort Laramie had been a disappointment. Supply wagons had been unable to reach the fort, and the tribal encampments arriving for the treaty negotiations had depleted the meager stores. Buddy did learn that there was an uneasy truce between the parties to the negotiations maintained by former mountain man Thomas Fitzpatrick, who now served as the government's Indian agent. His long-standing relationship with the chiefs kept underlying anger from boiling over into open hostilities. However, Fitzpatrick had warned Buddy that his mollifying influence was limited to the tribes of the prairies, and that the trail ahead became increasingly dangerous.

The Indian agent had been able to obtain a limited supply of jerky for Buddy, but it would not be enough to get him to Fort Bridger or Fort Hall. Fitzpatrick told him, "You are lucky to get anything from them. There was an idiot on that last wagon train that stopped here that nearly got us all killed. Rube Weston was his name. He tried to kidnap a Sioux teenage girl. There would have been no pow wow. That little incident will cost the government some concessions in the negotiations. We had a handful of men, and they had over a thousand warriors putting on the paint. I turned Weston over to the wagon train captain, and got the girl back to her father. The trail captain was as big an idiot as Weston. He had never been west, and had no guide. But he sure had authority! Figured he was king, and endowed with all powers. Sent Weston to his wagon, and headed everybody out on the trail. Between Weston and his dilapidated wagon, it's an even bet as to which one will perish first."

Fitzpatrick had repeated Tom Flannagan's warning. "Watch out for kids who want to be warriors. This is their time to prove their manhood. They are to come back to the village with tales of valor. Their first mission is to survive on their own. They go out on horseback, but with nothing but traditional weapons. They get a bow and arrows, a knife and a piece of flint. With that, they can fashion weapons, light fires, find food and build shelters. But then they have to do something worth telling around the campfire with their elders.

"They'll be skulking around the buffalo herds on this side of South Pass, and who knows where on the other side. The Arapahos aren't so bad, but watch out for the Pawnees and any Blackfeet who might wander down this way. Some of the tribes have been so offended by the whites that they can be downright cruel. And that includes the young ones. They have been stirred up by their elders."

Buddy was skirting the Black Hills that rose to the

south of the trail. Fitzpatrick had filled in some of the blank areas on Tom Flannagan's map. The Platte picked up the Laramie River at the fort, and the Black hills would rise just to the west of the river, but south of the trail. Within a hundred miles from the fort, he would cross six creeks that seeped out of those hills, and ran a short distance into the Platte. The trail held to the south side of the Platte, and the creeks were only twenty to twenty-five miles long. Some ran through gullies, but a man on a mule should have no trouble crossing, according to the former mountain man. He, like Jim Bridger, had a map of the West etched in his mind.

"After you pass those six creeks, there are three Platte River crossings, to the north bank, then to the south, and back to the north. Then you'll cross Poison Creek and angle away from the Platte, and pick up the Sweetwater, south of Devil's Gate. I suppose you can skip a couple of crossings, but don't miss Red Buttes crossing. If you do, you will follow the North Platte, headed south instead of west. You'll run into ravines and canyons following that stream. It'll be a struggle to get back to the trail. You will have to retrace your path. Don't just try to swing back north. Find your way back to the crossing." Fitzpatrick had thumped the map to emphasize the point.

In his reverie, Buddy had not been paying much attention to the trail. Tramp paused, and Buddy saw they had come to another creek. "Well, this makes number three. We followed Cottonwood

Creek upstream a little before we crossed it yesterday, and then Horseshoe Creek. I think it was halfway between that we came to the camping area where we saw those two fresh graves, but no wagon. It looked like they had camped there for two or three days. This would be LaBonte Creek."

They passed between the cottonwoods on the bank of the creek, and splashed across the gravel shallows. Ahead, Buddy could see a rocky prominence bathed in sunlight. The previous afternoon, the setting sun had peeked under the far edge of the cloud blanket that still covered the trail behind him. To the mule he said, "We're getting closer. Tomorrow we may even get warm. We have not had sunshine in weeks. Or in months."

Tramp's ears turned abruptly forward. Ahead, south of the trail, Buddy saw an abandoned wagon. It had been stripped of its canvas, and one wheel was missing. As he rode past the derelict, he noted that it had been emptied of everything. Near it, he saw three fresh graves. To the mule he said, "They were here for more than a night. Three graves. Mother, father and a child. The trail can be cruel." Looking to the clouds above, he prayed, "Father, these graves remind me of the need for Your grace as I go into an unknown situation. I do want to ask for Your protection of Sarah. You know her circumstances, and Your purpose for her. I need Your wisdom, and I need You to guide my footsteps on this trail. I thank You for Your sustaining grace that is ours in Your Son."

Buddy's was an ongoing prayer that he didn't close. Leaving the site of tragedy, he pushed on. Crossing Box Elder Creek, he rode out from under the clouds, into the warmth of the August sunshine. Deciding to camp and enjoy a couple of hours of warmth, he turned upstream and found a site away from the creek where a bluff rose straight up some thirty feet high. Unburdening the mule, he spread his bed roll, and opened the flaps of canvas so the sun would freshen the blanket inside. Then, taking his spy glass, he sought out an access to the top of the bluff.

Scanning the area to the south, he saw nothing moving. Being in the foothills of the mountains, it seemed that everything sloped upward. Rocky promontories marked the boundaries of dry gorges. Tawny grass-covered hills sloped down to the flood plain through which the Platte flowed. To the north, more rounded hills formed the fore drop of distant mountains. On one of those hilltops he saw perhaps a dozen buffalo grazing. They looked like ants crawling slowly over a pebble. Leaning against the wall of the ledge on which he sat, he closed his eyes, and dozed in the sunshine.

The declining sun stirred a breeze that carried more chill than warmth. "Supper time. Guess I'd better get down there before the sun sets." He had noticed that as he climbed higher toward the mountains, darkness came more suddenly. Twilight might linger on the western slopes, but here on the east side, night fell with a thud.

Buddy closed his bed roll to save what warmth it might have soaked up, then prepared his meal. His jerky bag told him he would have to ration his consumption, or find game to replenish it. As he crawled into his blanket, he prayed, "Lord, maybe tomorrow You will provide. Please show me the path You have chosen."

Morning dawned clear, with the promise of being a scorcher. Buddy finished his chores, saddled and loaded Tramp, and headed west. "Ten miles to Deer Creek, my friend. You'll be surprised this morning. They name things for a reason, and Deer Creek just might have what I'm looking for. A yearling doe would fill this jerky bag. I'll picket you, and wander upstream to see what I might find."

Near the Platte, it was shallow and rocky. Willows and cottonwoods lined its banks. Buddy rode a mile or so upstream, then unburdened and picketed Tramp. Pulling his rifle from its saddle boot, he checked the loads and put fresh percussion caps on the cylinder's nipples. He hid his packsaddle under some willows, and hung his money belt on the back side of a cottonwood. That done, he took his rifle and began a slow stalk up the creek.

An hour later, he was a mile upstream and had

seen nothing. Rounding a bend in the willows, he spotted a lone buffalo with its head hanging so its nose nearly rested on the ground. An arrow protruded from high on its side, behind the last rib. The arrow angled forward and downward, so Buddy guessed the arrowhead was buried in the animal's liver. It was a mortal wound, but the animal had escaped, but only to slowly die.

Kneeling, Buddy raised the rifle, sighted, and with a sigh, pressed the trigger. The black powder smoke drifted aside, and he saw the buffalo hunch its back and stumble forward two steps. Its head drooped, and blood dripped from its nostrils. With Buddy's second shot, the animal's legs buckled, and it sank to the ground. It raised its head, straining its nose upward, then collapsed limply.

Buddy looked skyward. "I'm sorry, Lord, but I do thank You. This is more meat than I can cure or carry. Maybe some of Your other mouths need feeding." He turned north and looked down the valley toward the Platte. Nothing was in sight. The hill across the Platte did not show any of the buffalo he had seen the previous afternoon.

Pulling his belt knife, he walked slowly to the beast he had killed. He circled it, then prodded its rump with his foot. It was dead. He walked to a cottonwood and leaned his rifle against it. The animal had been wounded, but the backstrap should be good. He would slice down each side of the backbone, peel the hide back, and filet out the long chunk of meat on each side. He had heard that the best part of the buffalo was the hump, but he wanted the lean meat on each side of the backbone for jerky. The lean meat would cure and keep well. The fat meat would not.

Buddy started at the shoulder, and slipped the blade of his knife under the hide, then pushed it along the ridge of the spine to the hip bone. Seizing the edge of the hide, he sliced between the hide and the meat, working his way forward. With the hide opened and folded back, he cut between the meat and the ridge of the backbone, then used his knife to free the meat from the ribs.

Hefting it, he figured he had about sixty pounds of meat. He carried it to the willows, and hung it over a sturdy branch.

From the direction of the Platte, he thought he heard the sound of Tramp's voice. He stopped to listen, but heard nothing more. Scanning the valley, he saw no movement. With a shrug, he turned to remove the other backstrap. As he was working the hide free from the other side of the backbone, he heard the thud of hooves. Had Tramp pulled his picket? Turning, he saw not Tramp, but half a dozen Indian horses ridden by youths. The one in the lead had fashioned a war club which he brandished over his head. Buddy dropped his knife, scrambled over the carcass of the buffalo, and ran for his rifle.

The teen with the war club uttered a whoop, and kicked his horse into a run. Jumping him over the carcass, he bore down on the fleeing man. As Buddy reached for the rifle, pain and flashes of light exploded in his head. And then, blackness.

Chapter 13

Buddy's first sensation was pain. His head throbbed with pain with each heartbeat. Next came the feeling of suffocation. Then came the stabbing of bright light, even though his eyelids were closed. A burning feeling seemed to cover his whole body. He could not move his limbs. His hands felt numb. Through the ringing in his ears came the sound of voices. Words he could not understand. Laughter.

He coughed. Pain shot through his head. The reflex act pushed a clot of coagulated blood from his throat into his mouth. With his tongue, he pushed the strangling blob out the side of his mouth. He could feel blood oozing into his throat. He tried to turn his head, but something pressed against his forehead, holding him down. The effort brought another stab of pain.

Another chorus of laughter, and Buddy managed to open one eye. The pain caused him to clamp it shut again. The sun must be overhead. His mind was foggy. How long he had been unconscious puzzled him. More laughter. More talk. Indians! Young ones...several of them. He remembered killing the wounded buffalo. When was that?

Morning. Maybe ten o'clock.

Buddy forced himself to open his eyes, and keep them open in spite of the pain in his head. He could not turn his head, but straining his eyes to look right, left and down, he saw that he was naked, and tied, wrists and ankles, with strips of raw buffalo hide which were shrinking in the heat of the noonday sun. The bands were growing tighter around his ankles and wrists, and the strips were growing shorter, putting a strain on his hips and shoulders.

Turning his eyes as far as he could toward the buffalo carcass, he could see the knot of youths. One wore his pants. Another wore his shirt. The leader had his rifle, and was examining the cylinder, hammer and trigger. The gun was pointed skyward, when it discharged. The noise hammered his aching head.

He managed to open his eyes again. Horses. He could see them beyond the would-be warriors. He coughed again, and the conversation and laughter ceased. Pants Boy walked slowly toward him, knocking an arrow in his bow. His shadow fell across Buddy's face. The pain of the glaring sunlight faded.

Tom had said he should show no fear. Fitzpatrick had said the same. With his face set, Buddy locked eyes with the youth, who drew the arrow back, ready to shoot. The glassy stone point shifted, first aimed at his left eye, then at his right. Either target would be fatal. The youth's eyes wavered. He looked back at his companions. The bow began to straighten as Pants Boy hesitated. Seeing his companions watching, he pulled the arrow again to full draw.

Buddy did not flinch. He did not allow his mouth to twitch. As he was looking into the eyes of the youth, there appeared to be two diverging arrows with one point wavering before his face. He prayed, "Lord, is this Your purpose? Am I to see You instead of Sarah? Your will be done. But could You make it quick?"

The arrow steadied. The youth's mouth firmed, and his eyes narrowed.

"Hah!"

Startled, Pants Boy jumped and released the arrow. Buddy felt the burn of the stone tip as it sliced his cheek, and plunged into the ground. Pants Boy turned, then looked in the direction Rifle Boy was pointing.

Straining his eyes to look north, Buddy could see a herd of buffalo draped over the crest of the hill beyond the Platte. Excited voices discussed a new plan. Gesticulations and a cacophony of overlapping words suggested a round-up and stampede of the herd. The youths abruptly mounted, and the group went careening downstream. Two of the horses leaped over Buddy. He saw one boy wearing his hat, and another wearing his boots and coat.

Buddy continued his prayer. "Your Word speaks of the trial of our faith. That was certainly a trial. But, I'm still alive. But, now what?"

In spite of the pain that wracked his brain and clouded his thoughts, he strained to turn his head. The drying hide was abrasive, but he felt it slip over his forehead in a sudden release. The sudden motion sent a new stab of pain through his head, and he clamped his eyes shut for a moment. Nodding his head toward his shoulder, he felt the band fall away from his head.

Free now to raise his head and look around, he discovered the extent of his bondage. The youths had driven ribs from the buffalo into the earth, anchoring the rawhide strips that held him fast, so the animal might have a bit of revenge, even in death. But now, the herd would be stampeded over him, and the living would avenge the death of one of their own. That should play well around the campfire.

When he turned to look toward the buffalo herd, his torn cheek bumped the arrow shaft. Buddy winced. In his pain-shrouded mind, he saw the stone point. If only he could reach the arrow, and pull it free, he might be able to cut his bonds. No amount of pulling would uproot one of the rib bones that held him.

In his struggle, he felt the arrow shaft under his

nose. Thought led to action, and he bit the shaft. Squinching his eyes against the pain, he struggled to turn his head. The resistance applied by the embedded arrow caused pinpoints of light to flicker in his brain.

Buddy turned his head farther in order to bite the shaft closer to the ground. He nodded his head, trying to wiggle the arrow free, then strained to turn his head again. The arrow came free. The suddenness of the release caused waves of pain and nausea.

He lay for a moment, trying to settle his systems. In the distance, he heard the yelps and whoops of the youths. They had skirted the herd and were starting the stampede down toward the Platte. With his tongue, Buddy pushed the arrow shaft from between his teeth. Gripping it with his lips, he twitched his mouth to the side. The arrow moved an inch toward his hand. An inch at a time, the point got closer to his numb fingers. When the feathers were in his mouth, he strained to see how far the arrow would reach.

At last, he gripped the knock in his teeth. It took some painful maneuvering to raise the stone point, twist it over his palm, and then with his tongue, push it between his fingers. Sheer will moved his fingers to pinch the shaft, inch it forward, and then move it to where his thumb and forefinger could grip it and turn it around. Then, working his way up the shaft, his puffy fingers brought the stone point's razor sharp edge into contact with the rawhide.

Numb fingers could not bring much pressure to bear on the shaft, but he worked the edge back and forth, getting only half an inch of movement each way. The stone began to slice into the skin. The tension on the cord helped, though time and effort seemed to creep by.

The tension of the shrinking rawhide snapped the remaining fibers, and Buddy's hand came free. Pain shot up his arm and through his shoulder. Free now to roll toward the other side, he cut the cord holding his other hand.

Sitting erect caused pain to slam into his head. He vomited a mixture of breakfast and blood. With his head bowed and his eyes closed, he waited for the pounding in his head to ease. Opening one eye, he reached down and cut one ankle free, and then the other.

He could hear the rumble of thousands of hooves as the massive herd thundered across the Platte. The ground under him shook. Buddy prayed "Lord, I need Your strength. Show me the way of escape."

He rolled to his stomach, and struggled to his hands and knees. With his head hanging, he crawled up past the remains of the buffalo. Reaching the cottonwood where had leaned his rifle, he worked his way up the trunk. Standing made him dizzier. Walking was difficult. His bare feet were numb, which was a blessing. The foot pain would come later. Looking west, he saw where a deer trail angled up a bluff to a ledge. It was a race against the running herd. He was not running.

His steps were short and stumbling. He reached the bottom of the deer track, and crawled up the steps their hooves had cut in the ascent. Some fifty feet above the foot of the bluff, he collapsed on the ledge, and rolled back from the edge.

He still clung to the arrow. With the edge of the arrowhead, he cut the loops of rawhide from his wrists and ankles, and began trying to rub life back into them. The first sensation was tingling as blood coursed back into his numb extremities. Pain followed.

Below him, the undulating mass of buffalo was chivied upstream along Deer Creek by the six youths. The animals smashed through the willows, churned the creek into a muddy soup, and left only the cottonwoods unscathed. The remains of the dead buffalo got ground into the earth and buried by the dirt thrown over it by thousands of hooves. Above the carcass, the herd veered away from the creek.

When the herd had passed, the six youths rode around where they had stretched Buddy on the ground. Apparently convinced he had been ground into the earth, they celebrated. They now had a story to carry back to their homes.

Buddy listened as their voices faded into the distance. His pain-addled mind tried to take inventory of his situation. Destitute. Naked. Helpless. "Where does my help come from? My help comes from the Lord." The words came unbidden in the midst of his miserable reflections.

"Lord, I need Your help. I need Your supply. I need Your strength." With those thoughts, Buddy relapsed into unconsciousness.

The warmth of the morning sun roused Buddy, and the reality of hunger, pain and nakedness raised him to his hands and knees. Looking around, he wondered where he was, and how he got there. Looking over the edge, he could see the plowed gash in the grass where the stampede had passed. "I wonder where Tramp is. Did they leave any of my stuff?" The drop to the grass below dizzied him afresh. The broken arrow slipped from his fingers, and plummeted to the foot of the bluff.

He stumbled to the top of the deer trail. He went down backwards, sometimes on hands and feet, and sometimes on hands and knees. He paused often, closing his eyes to ease the pain and nausea. Finally, he reached the bottom of the bluff, and rested, leaning back against the wall.

Crossing to the creek, he found two broken willows he could lean on as he walked back down the creek. His shoeless feet protested against the coarse way he had to tread. He had to rest often as he covered the mile down to where he had picketed Tramp. As he approached his intended camp area, he groaned. "Oh, no! They wouldn't!"

Tramp lay on his side, six arrows sticking out from his ribs. The sound Buddy had heard was Tramp's death cry. "They must really hate mules to do that." The stampede had swerved toward the creek to avoid the dead mule. He found where one of the would-be warriors had dropped an arrow in the game of killing Tramp. Picking it up, he snapped the shaft a hand-breadth above the stone point. "At least I have a knife. Of sorts."

Buddy walked haltingly to where he had stashed the packsaddle. It lay crushed and scattered. The spy glass was smashed. He found the revolver, with its frame broken and bent. The salt was scattered and trampled into the mud. His bedroll was shredded. Within the folds of his canvas food sack, he found a handful of unsoiled jerky. His money belt and canteen still hung in the cottonwood, but were now exposed to the morning sun. "I don't know how they missed seeing those! Thank You, Lord."

Buddy salvaged what was left of his bedroll. With the stone arrowhead, he cut chunks of canvas and blanket to wrap his feet. Those he bound in place with twisted strips of canvas. He managed to salvage a strip of canvas wide enough and long enough to fashion a loincloth, which he strapped in place with the money belt. A square of blanket held in place by a strip of canvas formed what would have to serve as a hat.

Buddy had just tied his improvised hat in place when he heard distant laughter, and juvenile voices. He grabbed his canteen, hung it over his shoulder, grabbed his willows, and hurried back up Deer Creek. As he passed the scene of his capture, he stopped to listen. The youths were following him up the creek. Farther upstream, the ground rose above the creek where it flowed through a willow choked ravine. Looking down, he saw that the side of the ravine dropped about twenty feet to a shelf above the creek. Excited voices carried up to where he stood listening. "They must have seen my footprints. They'll come at a gallop. Maybe I can hide in the willows. They will be following by sight, and not tracking. It's grassy here, and the herd sheered away to the right."

Stepping to the edge of the ravine, he slid down the steep bank to the shelf, then ducking down, he plunged into the willows. Deer trails ran like a rabbit warren through the tangle. He had to run bent low, and he jostled the willows as he stumbled forward. The waving withes traced his progress for anyone watching from above.

The path he was following turned left, and he dodged that way. His head crashed into an obstacle, and he collapsed into black unconsciousness.

Chapter 14

Voices roused Buddy to consciousness. Above him, horses clattered southward along Deer Creek, their riders calling back and forth as they searched for his trail. In case they looked into the ravine, Buddy lay still where he had fallen. The yelling above masked his groan. Renewed throbbing pounded the pain alarms in his head. He had clobbered himself this time, running blindly into something that did not yield.

Turning carefully onto his back, he opened his eyes and gazed upward through the willows. Below their canopy he saw the wheel and box of an upturned wagon, its tongue angled across his path. He surmised he had collided either with the iron-rimmed wheel or the wagon tongue. Broken fragments of harness were dark icicles hanging from the reach.

"What is that thing doing so far up from the trail?" he wondered. Somebody had come the wrong way, turned back, and lost control.

Sounds from above faded into the distance. Still Buddy did not move. He struggled to gather the simplest thoughts. He closed his eyes, trying to still the throbbing in his aching head. Surely two blows to the head were not helpful. His clouded mind groped for a thread of direction for the way ahead. Where he was, and where he was headed were muddled in the ocean of pain.

He sank into semi-consciousness, from which he was roused by the sounds of approaching voices and hoof beats. The mounted youths thundered by, galloping their mounts down toward the Platte.

Buddy rose to his hands and knees and looked around. In front of the overturned wagon, he saw the scattered bones of part of the team that had pulled it. Beside the wagon box he noticed a patch of gingham, then black canvas and flannel. Under the willow lay the remains of a man and a woman, if he read the clothing correctly. On what would have been the woman's lap was a man's skull. Disassociated neck bones disappeared into the collar of the flannel shirt. The woman's skull lay where it had rolled down from the collar of her gingham dress. Blonde hair beside the collar told Buddy the couple was young. What dreams had filled those heads? That question reminded Buddy that he had plans and dreams to try to recover.

Looking at his own attire brought memory of his situation. He stared blankly at the food bag and canteen. He ate. He drank. He slept.

The breeze rustling the willows above awakened

Buddy. His mind was a little clearer after a night's dreamless sleep. He stirred, rose to his hands and knees, and looked at his companions of the night. "I don't know who you were, but you may be God's way of providing for me. I'll tuck you in for your long night, and then I'll see if you have anything left that might be useful. You headed west. I may be able to finish your journey for you."

He chewed a mouthful of jerky, drank a little water, and shook the canteen. "Not much left. I hope you had a cooking pot. I'll have to boil some water."

Laboriously, he began to gather the bones of the couple into their clothes. In gathering, he found the remains of a leather pouch near the man's hand. The stitching had rotted, and gold coins lay scattered around it. To the bones, Buddy said, "Well, friend, if you knew the Savior, you've gone to where this is just used for streets and stuff. But, it has other uses here. You won't need it, but I might. I thank you and the Lord."

Buddy dropped the gold into his empty food bag, and continued gathering bones. The man had a torn possible bag. The tear had exposed a rusted steel and several pieces of flint, along with a tinder box.

"Fire makin's!" Buddy exclaimed. Those went into his food bag.

Near the woman's hand bones lay a silk bag. He picked it up and emptied it into his palm. He stared at wedding rings, both his and hers, and other jewelry. He hesitated, then dropped the jewelry back into the pouch, and added that to the gold coins. To the woman he said, "These were symbols of love. If you knew Jesus Christ, you are now in the presence of perfect love. Sarah might delight to wear them in your memory and honor."

Buddy shook his head. "I'm talking to dead bones!" Again he shook his head. The pain of that motion turned him again to the solemn task he had set for himself. Fastened to the side of the wagon box was a shovel. Freeing it, he tested the handle. It was sound. At the foot of the bank, he opened a trench. When it was a couple of feet deep, he was too tired to carry on. He crawled around the wagon, and, folding the clothes together with the bones, he dragged them to the hole he had dug, and lowered them gently into the earth.

Bowing, he prayed, "Father, Your Word says You know those that are Yours. I don't know anything about these two who died here, but You hold all of our days. I'll pray this, trusting You had drawn them to Christ Jesus. Maybe You could let them know that someone cared enough to lay their mortal bodies to rest in the anticipation of eternal life. Thank You for sparing my earthly life. I don't think taking what they don't need any more is stealing, so I will thank You for whatever has not been corrupted by the passage of time."

Buddy rested beside the open grave, then began shoveling dirt in to cover the bones. When he had mounded the dirt over the grave, he used his waning strength to move stones from the creek. Those he piled over the grave to protect it from flood waters that might rise to that level. He took the shovel and gouged away at the embankment that towered over it, concealing the mound.

Weary, he crawled back to the wagon. It rested on broken ribs, with some of its contents spilled onto the canvas. There was just enough clear space for him to curl up under the shelter of the canvas. Groping in the shadows, he felt a blanket, and pulled it to the front of the wagon. Reaching again, he found another, and used it for a pillow.

After another dreamless night, Buddy awoke to filtered sunlight dappling the canvas above him. Groping among the treasures he had stowed in his food bag, he found three sticks of jerky. He chewed those slowly savoring the flavor as saliva reconstituted the meat. Sipping a ration of water, he turned to the task of inventory. He had needs the wagon might meet.

The first thing he found was a cape gun toppled downward behind the seat of the wagon. Pulling it out, he examined it for soundness. It turned out to be a side-by-side shotgun with one rifled barrel and one smooth bore. It looked like fifty caliber. He pulled the hammers back. They worked smoothly. Looking through the nipples, he could see that it was not loaded. Somewhere in the wagon should be ammunition and percussion caps. His caps were somewhere underground down the creek.

Blanket, check. Gun, check. Canvas? The canvas that had covered the wagon seemed sound, but he would have to see. It had been torn when the wagon toppled into the willows. Buddy felt a twinge of guilt, pillaging through the belongings of the deceased.

Clothes? He pulled out an overturned trunk, and popped it open. In the tray on top he found the man's clothing. The pants were a little big. The shirt and coat were his size. He had guessed the man's stature was about the same as his. The man's waist had been a little bigger, but a belt would cinch up the extra girth.

Under the tray were women's clothes, but tucked in beside them the man had an extra pair of boots. Buddy unwrapped one foot, and tried the boot. It fit loosely. It was still loose when he tried it with a sock. When he put on a second sock, the boot fit well enough that it would not blister his foot. The woman had knitted her husband a hat for cold weather. Buddy thought of the mountains ahead, and added that to his supplies. From the trunk, he took the man's linens, shirt and trousers and dressed. The trunk yielded a belt that held up his pants. Socks and boots made him ready for further explorations. Digging beneath the woman's dresses and dainties, he found a set of bed sheets. He took one. He closed the trunk, and pulled out another smaller chest. He was amazed at its contents. Oilskin bags were marked 'Chicken Soup' and 'Vegetable Soup,' along with 'Porridge' and 'Beef Tea.' Another was labeled 'Coffee', and underneath were two bricks of tea.

Buddy took two bags of chicken soup and one brick of tea, and added those to his supply stack. From the chest marked 'Utensils' he took a tin cup and plate, and a knife, fork and spoon. There was a covered cooking pot that would nest all of his utensils, and hold the tea.

Looking at his growing stack, he contemplated carrying all of that when he had to walk, at least to Fort Hall. It was questionable whether he would find an animal available there, at any price. Walking to Dalles City gave him pause, since he would have to ford rivers, who knew how deep.

Digging deeper into the tumbled contents of the wagon, he found a coiled rope. A large canvas bag had arm straps and a tump line with a padded section to cushion where it crossed the forehead. A bucket that usually hung below the tailgate of the wagon was also lodged inside. The bottom was rusted, but the inside was clean. To his great joy and surprise, Buddy found a folded reserve canvas tarp, good for a ground cloth for camping, or a replacement cover for the wagon. Rodents had gnawed along the folded edge. Wedged beneath the upturned wagon seat, he found a powder horn. Shaking it, he found the powder was dry and loose. As he pulled it free, the thong holding the powder measure broke, but he could replace that.

There were still things he needed that he had not found. Remembering the torn possible bag, Buddy backed out from under the wagon, and went around to where the couple had died. He carefully picked up the bag. Its weight told him there was lead inside. Pulling it apart, he found bullets and a tin of percussion caps for the cape gun, and a rusty belt knife. He could polish it with a cloth and sand from the creek. The leather sheath had been well oiled, but the moisture had reached the blade. He unbuckled his belt, and slipped it through the loop on the sheath. From the condition of the possible bag, he decided his canvas food bag would have to fill that need.

Dividing the new canvas with the knife, he put together a new bedroll. With gaping holes in the canvas, there was enough sound fabric for a bedroll. He filled the tump line bag with supplies, and put the rope in the bucket. He used the drawstring on the bag to hold his bedroll in place. A long strip of canvas allowed him to hang the improvised possible bag cross-body with the canteen. Another allowed him to suspend the bucket from one of the tump line bag's shoulder straps. He cut a walking stick from one of the stout willows. Lifting everything into place, he stood with the walking stick in his left hand and the cape gun in his right. He felt balanced, and ready for the trail. His regret was that he did not find a spy glass. He would have to keep a sharp eye on things, and keep his ears open, since he could no longer rely on Tramp's long ones.

On a whim, he added one more bag of chicken soup to the bucket, and paused to pray before he looked for a way out of the ravine. "Lord, You do indeed supply our needs. Now, I need wisdom as I head out. You know where the danger lies. You guide me with Your directing hand. Show me the way, and Your purpose in all of this. I pray, too, for Sarah. I'm delayed, but it is by Your will. Your grace is sufficient for me, and for her. I would ask that You protect Tom as well, and bring him safely through."

As was his custom, he left the prayer unended.

Downstream through the willows he came to where the side of the ravine was only a few feet high, and sloping. A deer trail angled up to the top, and he crept up to where he could look all directions. Seeing no danger, he climbed out of the ravine.

He turned toward the Platte and the trail. Looking beyond the river to the slope the stampede had descended, he saw a line of horsemen angling across to the northeast. Looking skyward, Buddy asked, "Upstream, Lord? What lies upstream?

That's where the buffalo herd went. Show me what You have in that direction. I can't see it. But, I'll go."

Buddy recalled that if he looped westward from the head of Deer Creek, Tom's map had showed he would cut the upper reaches of the North Platte. Following it downstream, he would come to the confluence of the Sweetwater, and put him back on the trail. What lay between Deer Creek and the North Platte, he did not know. But, he accepted the prompt that he must go that way. He turned upstream. He would have to get out of sight somewhere so he could build a fire, boil water, and try some of that chicken soup. He had to do that before night fell.

An hour later, he reached a bend in Deer Creek that hid him from the Platte. Another hour, and he was moving upstream again. His canteen was full, as was his stomach. However long the wagon had been down that ravine, the soup had not spoiled. The couple had diced everything small, made the soup, and then dried it. Once all the moisture was removed, they had ground it into powder. He would have to experiment with how much to put in a cup of water. A little made a broth. A lot made a thick, creamy soup. He could detect carrots and potatoes. Something green gave it an odd color, but a good flavor. It was easy on the tongue, and easy on the stomach.

He reached the headwaters of Deer Creek.

Turning, he walked back toward the Platte as he crossed the stretch plowed up by the buffalo, so his tracks, should anybody see them, would appear he was headed downstream. Once he cleared the loose dirt and was again walking on grass, he turned and backtracked up the slope, gradually swinging westward.

About a mile ahead, he saw a crease in the broken hills that suggested a camping site. He counted the days in the ravine as his day of rest, having lost track of the days he had been on the trail. He would count this as day one, and rest a day after a week.

The slopes and ravines of the Black Hills shaped his travel. The fifty miles from Deer Creek to the North Platte stretched into nearly a hundred miles before he saw the upper North Platte. He had trended more southwest than west, and traveled through more broken country when he headed downstream. In places, the river ran through deep ravines. Seldom did he find himself beside the stream. Often, to get water, he had to swing his bucket down on the end of his rope.

On his third day traveling down the North Platte, Buddy saw wagon tracks. It appeared that several wagons had reached this point, and turned back. There was a confusion of wagon, animal and boot tracks that circled, and without camping, headed back downstream. At a point where the bank dipped to the river's edge, the wagons had crossed the Platte, then angled to the northwest. On the east bank stood a broken, abandoned wagon. A broken wheel lay beside the back corner where the axle rested on the ground. The wagon itself was empty, and its canvas had been removed. It gave the impression of a carcass picked clean by scavengers.

Buddy continued downstream, and two hours later found a spot where the toe of a bluff reached nearly to the edge of a ravine where the Platte looped to the northeast. The nook would be a good place to camp, sheltered from the wind and from view.

Buddy prepared his campsite, and with water from his canteen, prepared his cup of soup. Settled for sleep, he looked at the stars that filled the night sky. To himself he said, "The heavens declare the glory of God...and tonight, they certainly are declaring. Lord, I'm running late. Please show me Your purpose in this delay."

He drifted off into a restless sleep. He did not know what time it was when he was startled awake. From somewhere came an agonized voice: "Just let me die!" It was almost a scream. It was followed by another voice: "I don't want to die!" They seemed to come from the depths of the ravine.

Buddy crept from his bedroll, and felt his way to the rim of the drop-off. The voices were silent now. Was that a dream? No, he could hear someone crying below.

Not knowing what else to do, he began to sing:

How firm a foundation, O saints of the Lord,
Is laid for your faith in his excellent Word!
What more can he say than to you he has said
Who unto the Savior for refuge have fled?

The crying ceased. Buddy continued singing.

Fear not, I am with you. Oh, be not dismayed,
For I am your God and will still give you aid;
I'll strengthen you, help you, and cause you to stand,
Upheld by my righteous, omnipotent hand.

From the depths of the ravine Buddy heard a scream, "Help us!"

Buddy sang on.

The soul that on Jesus hath leaned for repose,
I will not, I will not desert to his foes;
That soul, though all hell should endeavor to shake,
I'll never, no, never, no, never forsake!

Again came the plea, "Please help us!"

Buddy shouted into the darkness, "Tomorrow! Help will come tomorrow!"

Journey Chapter 15

Buddy was restless before the cry for help. Afterward, sleep would not come at all. He kept hearing Sarah's voice calling, and he could not hurry. Tossing and turning on the hard ground was tiring rather than restful. He was up at first light, searching for a way into the chasm. Having found no way down as he walked downstream, he turned to retrace his steps. Movement ahead caused him to kneel and freeze in place. A coyote had materialized seemingly from nowhere. As he watched, two more came up over the edge of the ravine. There had to be access to the river at that point.

He stood up, and the coyotes fled. He hurried to where they had come up, and looking over the edge, saw what would pass as a stairway that zigzagged down the face of the cliff. It appeared as if deer and other animals used that access. Unsure of the stability of the steps, Buddy went for his rope. He threw the coils over the edge to be sure it would reach the bottom, then coiled it up again. Back from the ravine, a dead tree trunk rose some ten feet into the air.

Buddy kicked the trunk, then threw his weight

against it. It stood solid. He tied the rope to the trunk, and walked to the edge. Holding the rope, he stepped backward onto the first step, then the second. Letting himself back step by step, he reached the a ledge that was the first change of direction. Standing on the ledge, he looked down to the river's edge. Frowning, he saw a point downstream where a wrinkle in the cliff bulged out into the river. The call for help last night came from farther down the river. He could reach the bottom, but there was no way to move downstream.

He climbed back to the top, moved downstream, and lying on his stomach he peered over the edge. There was a gravel bar on the inside of the river bend, but looking upstream, he saw the bulge that blocked access. Pondering the issue, he decided the only access would be to swing on the rope out over the river and around the bulge and land on the gravel bar.

Scrambling to his feet, Buddy grabbed his blanket to cushion his rope where it went over the edge. Grabbing the rope, he descended to the upper ledge, then down the remaining steps to a large rock beside the water. Holding the rope, he pulled himself off the rock. It was plenty stout. He tied a slip knot in the rope so he could hold it without sliding. He took two running steps and leaped out over the river. His momentum took him around the bulge, and landed him on the gravel bar. For security, he put a rock on the end of the rope. Turning, he saw a figure kneeling by the water. It looked like a child, stark naked.

Buddy hesitated. Should he approach? He started down the gravel bar, singing, **"How firm a foundation, ye saints of the Lord, is laid for your faith in His excellent Word..."**

Hearing his voice, the child scrambled away from the water and crouched behind a boulder. Buddy stopped well back from the rock. He asked, "Did you call for help last night?"

Wide eyes stared back at him. The head nodded.

"Who are you?"

A trembling hand reached to brush back wet blonde hair from her face. The lips formed words, but no sound came.

Buddy asked, "Are you 'Just let me die,' or are you 'I don't want to die'?"

Sound came with the words this time. So did tears. "I don't want to die!"

Buddy smiled. "You can talk. What is your name?"

"Mary."

"Well, Mary, if you could have anything you want right now, what would that be?"

"Something to eat. I'm so hungry!"

Buddy took a step closer.

Mary wailed, "Don't come here! I'm all nakey." She crouched even lower behind the boulder.

"All right. I don't want to see you all nakey. Are you here all alone?"

"No. Jo's here."

"And where is Joe?"

Mary pointed toward the cliff. "In the bedroom."

Puzzled, Buddy asked, "And where is the bedroom?"

"It's behind that big rock."

Looking toward the cliff, Buddy saw where a big slab had broken free, and fallen to the foot of the cliff, where it leaned with a gap behind it. It provided the only shelter available on a crescent of flood-deposited rubble and gravel. He turned and strode to the opening behind the slab, saying, "Wait there. I'll check on Joe, and see what's wrong with him."

Three things happened at once. Rounding the slab and peering into the dim recess, Buddy saw a naked figure drawn into a fetal position. From the shelter came a scream, "Don't come in here!" From behind him, Mary called, "Jo's a girl!"

Buddy stumbled back, mumbling, "Sorry!"

Mary had started to run up behind him, but when he turned, she scampered back and crouched behind the boulder again. She called, "She don't got nothing to wear."

Buddy shook his head. "Lord, what have I stumbled into? No. Forgive me. What is the purpose of this? You have led me here. Please keep me looking unto Jesus."

To Mary he said, "So you are both nakey. Is that the bigger problem than you being hungry?"

Mary squinched her eyes shut, and a little voice said, "I can eat nakey."

Buddy laughed. "Well, you can't eat behind that rock, and I can't talk with you when you are nakey. You wait here, and I'll be back."

Mary began to cry. "Don't leave us here! Please help us."

"I won't leave you. I don't have anything for you to eat down here. I camped up there on top. I'll get stuff that will help you. You go and tell Jo... Who is she, anyway?"

"She's my sister. Her whole name is Johanna."

"Well, you tell Johanna that I'll be right back. I'll see what I can do to fix your problems. First, I've got to cover you up, then I'll have to get you something to eat."

As Buddy walked away, Mary called, "You will

come back? For real?"

He turned, and caught the flash of pale skin as Mary dodged back down behind her boulder. "For real!"

Buddy grabbed the rope and launched himself out over the river, swinging around the bulge that trapped the girls, landing awkwardly on the boulder at the bottom of the path to the top. More confident of the firmness of the steps, he clambered up the cliff, leaving the rope hanging. He pondered the possibilities of clothing the girls. He had no change of clothes that he could share. Remembering his own loincloth, he pulled the sheet out of his bed roll. Tearing strips from it, he checked against himself to see if they were long enough to cover the girls. He tore two more strips to serve as belts, and folded the strips inside the rest of the sheet. With the bed roll tied up on the tump line bag, he was ready to descend into the ravine. Feeling a little unbalanced, he clung to the rope and backed down, lowering himself hand over hand as his foot groped for the next step.

At the bottom, it took two tries to swing around the bulge. The first try, he swung out over the river, but collided with the bulge instead of landing on the gravel bar. On his second attempt, he landed awkwardly, thrown off balance by the pack on his back.

He made a second trip, coming back with the

canteen, possible bag and cape gun. This time, it only took one attempt to reach the gravel bar. He weighted the rope again, and walked to the boulder Mary had used as a screen.

He called, "All right, Mary. I'm back. Come on out here."

The girl peeked around the slab of stone."You'll see me! Don't look!"

Buddy chuckled. "I won't look. I'll look back the way I came. You come here and stand behind me with your back to me. You can tell me when you are ready for me to turn around."

He heard a stone turn behind him. "Are you ready?"

Mary squealed, "But you'll see me!"

Exasperated, Buddy said, "Everybody's back looks the same. I'll only see your back."

In a squeaky voice, Mary said, "Don't look at my bottom!"

"I won't look at your bottom, but if we don't get it covered up, I won't be able to help it. Now do as I tell you. Stand with your feet apart, and reach back between your knees. You will feel the end of this cloth. Pull it through and pull it up as far as you can. I'll close my eyes."

When he felt the tug on the cloth, Buddy said, "Now, hold that end with your teeth. Reach your hands back on each side, and grab these ends. Tie them around your tummy. If it is too long, tie it so one end is really long, and the other end is short."

Mary mumbled around the cloth in her mouth, and Buddy said, "Now drop the end of the cloth. I'm going to adjust the back, and you can adjust the front."

He grabbed the edges of the cloth, and pulled them around Mary's hips. It nearly met the width of the strip in front, forming a skirt that fell just below her knees. He tore a wider strip from the sheet, and tore it in half. With his knife, he cut along the seam to make a strap to go around Mary's neck. He slipped it over the girl's head, and let the cloth fall in front of her. Pulling the sides around her shoulders, he pulled the fabric farther around the left, and cut a slit for her arm, and did the same on the right.

"Now, slip your hands through these holes. Right. Just like that. Now, tear off that extra part around your waist."

With the remnant, Buddy laced the fabric together in back. "Now turn around and let me see you."

Mary squealed, "But I stick out! I can feel my legs all the way up to here!"

Buddy said, "Yes, you can. But I've already seen up to there, and more, when I first got here and you ran for the boulder. Turn around."

Mary turned, and held her hands over her eyes.

Buddy nodded. "All right, Kiddo, you have underpants, a skirt and blouse. That's the best we can do." He handed Mary the other strip of sheet, and the narrow band to use as a belt. "Now, you go and do the same for Jo. Do it just like I did for you. But wait." Buddy unbuttoned his shirt, and handed it to Mary. "Give her this. She has more to hide than you do."

Mary giggled. "She says I'll catch up!"

Buddy laughed. "You go dress her, while I light a fire and get you a bit of soup."

Mary stood still, her eyes opened wide. "Soup? What kind of soup can you fix here?"

Buddy winked at her. "Chicken. Now scoot!"

Buddy gathered driftwood from the foot of the bluff. With the help of the rusty steel, flint and tinder box, he kindled a fire. Rather than use water from his canteen, he went back to the rope, and dipped river water. When it came to a boil, he stood watching the rolling water in the cooking pot.

Beside him, he heard Mary ask, "Is that the soup? There's nothing in it but water!"

Buddy turned, and saw that the two girls had joined him. Wearing his shirt and the improvised loin cloth, Jo glared at him.

Buddy smiled at her. "I'm sorry I barged in on you like that. I didn't know you were a girl."

Jo said nothing. Mary asked, "When do we eat?"

Buddy said, "You don't. First, you drink some tea. How long have you been here?"

It was Jo who answered. "About six weeks." Her voice was flat, her words clipped.

Mary said, "Don't be mad, Jo. He didn't know you were all nakey."

Buddy asked, as if he had not heard, "How long since you had anything to eat?"

Mary said, "A week. We ran out of food a week ago."

Buddy shaved tea from the brick, and poured water into the tin cup, which he set to steep and cool. "And you have been here six weeks. How did you come to be trapped here?"

Mary looked at Jo, who said nothing. "They were going to make Jo get married, so we came around a bend in the river to take a bath while the wagons crossed. A flood came, and washed us down the river for miles and miles. We grabbed hold of a tree that was in the flood, and it washed us onto this bunch of rocks before it floated away. The next day we found somebody's food box on the rocks. It had flour and cracked wheat in it. We ate that, but then it ran out. I'm really hungry."

Buddy pinched the tin cup between his thumb and forefinger, then lifted it, handing it to Mary. "Each of you drink half of this. It may come back up. That happens when you haven't eaten for a long time."

Mary gulped half of the tea, and handed the cup to Jo. She sipped it slowly, closing her eyes as the warm liquid trickled down her throat. Mary suddenly turned and retched. With a drawn out "Oh!" Mary started to cry.

Buddy turned to Jo and said, "Give Mary another sip of that. I think it will stay down now."

Jo's lips were pressed into a straight line. She handed the cup to Mary. Buddy looked at Jo, and shook his head. "You can be angry with me, but it is going to get worse than me seeing your bare back. There are three of us, and I have only one blanket."

Jo gasped, and turned away. Mary asked, "We'll sleep with you?"

Buddy said, "That's up to you. Thanks to the rodents, there was only enough canvas for the one bedroll. You can sleep in your bedroom if you like. But we can't stay here forever. On the trail, we are headed into the mountains. We may get caught in early snow storms. The Bible says 'If two lie down together they will have warmth.' But there are three of us. Three might be even warmer."

Mary frowned. "The Bible? Are you a preacher?"

"No, Kiddo, but the Bible tells me God's way of things."

Mary said, "God doesn't like us. We asked Him to make our mama and daddy better, but He didn't listen. They both died."

Buddy hugged the girl. "I asked God to direct my steps for His purpose, and even though the way He chose to direct me took away everything I had, He gave me what I needed and brought me to where I could hear when you called for help. I think He not only likes you, but He loves you. He was not ready for you to die. How did your mama and daddy die?"

Jo answered. "Cholera. They both died the same day. They were fine when they got up, but by suppertime, they were gone. They were buried side by side where we camped beside the trail. We had to go on without them. That's how I got in trouble."

Buddy nodded. He took the tin cup, washed the tea dregs out, and poured boiling water into it. Then he spooned the soup powder into the water, and stirred it to reconstitute it.

Mary looked startled. "Isn't that just flour? I thought you said we got soup!"

Buddy took a spoonful, blew on it to cool it, and said, "Open wide, Kiddo, and tell me if it is flour or chicken soup."

Mary's lips closed, and Buddy pulled the spoon back. Mary's eyes closed slowly as she savored the bite, then swallowed."

"Chicken!"

Buddy laughed. "That's all for now. I don't want it back." Turning to Jo, he handed her the spoon. "You don't want me to spoon feed you. Help yourself. Take it from the edge. The two of you will have to dine slowly, since you've been without for so long. That's it. Now swallow. Your mouth likes it, but your stomach has to get used to it. I only have one cup and one spoon, but there is more soup when you are ready. Mary's turn."

Jo's face relaxed. She smiled as she handed the spoon to Mary. To Buddy she said, "I'm mad at you, but I might get over it. Thanks for the shirt. But God's on His own. He lost me when my parents died."

Buddy smiled, but shook his head sadly. Looking up, he said, "Father, thank You that You don't discard us when we rebel against what You do, or what You allow. Give us light and strength for this journey we are on."

Mary handed him the empty cup. "Is there really some more?"

Buddy smiled at her and said, "There is. But let your tummy get used to that little bit, while I have some. And then I'll make you another cup to share, and put more in it. I made that first cup a little thin on purpose. If that stays down, I'll fix more for you both. Then you will get more in the morning."

Chapter 16

Morning dawned clear and promising. Buddy had the fire going, the water boiled and soup ready when the girls came out of their bedroom. He had rolled up in his canvas tarp, giving them his blanket. They all slept in their clothes. After they had all eaten chicken soup, Buddy made tea to pass around.

Breakfast finished, he said, "Time for a talk. Pull up a rock and sit down." Mary sat hugging her knees. Jo sat carefully and spread the front flap of her improvised skirt so it covered her thigh. She pulled her bare feet back to one side, and sat trying to work the tangles out of her auburn hair. Buddy noticed the freckles that spread from her nose to both cheeks.

He said, "I'm leaving. I may be gone for a week. You two have to stay here. Here you are safe. Can either of you swim?"

Jo said, "I can, a little. Why?"

"If I'm not back in ten days, go down to where Mary first saw me, and swim around that bulge. There is a sort of stairway to the top. That is the way you can escape your prison here. I'll leave you the blanket, the food and the cooking stuff. I plan to travel light and fast, but I don't know what might delay me. I know where I can get more supplies for our way ahead. I can't take you with me, but I will be back. When I get back, I'm heading for the Oregon Territory. I don't know what your plans are, but I have to get to Dalles City as fast as I can. We can leave as soon as I get back. Ration your food. Don't eat it all at once."

Mary's face twisted into an anxious frown. "Can't we go with you? We'd hurry."

Buddy shook his head. "No. You have bare feet. The way is rough. Besides, one can hide more easily than three. Don't worry. I won't leave you here. I'm sure I can get back within a week."

Buddy caught up the cape gun and possible bag. "I'm leaving the flint and steel so you can start a fire. Keep it small. There's plenty of driftwood along the bottom of the cliff. If you feed this fire a little at a time, you won't have to start another one. That means you would have to gather enough wood that you could feed it during the night, but remember to keep it small."

He slung the canvas over his shoulder. "I'll take this opened bag of soup. Go ahead and open another one." Adjusting his pack, he headed upstream, seized the rope, and before he swung out of sight, he waved to the girls. Mary waved back. Jo stood with her arms folded.

At the top of the cliff, Buddy coiled and hid the rope. "No use leaving a sign for someone to follow!" He decided it would be easier and maybe safer to loop back along the Black Hills than to go downstream along the North Platte to pick up the trail back to Deer Creek. That decided, he loaded the cape gun and set out up the Platte. The second day found him descending the Black Hills toward Deer Creek. So far, he had seen nothing of danger. He came to the area the stampeded buffalo had plowed, and turned north. As he followed Deer Creek downstream, he searched for landmarks his aching head had failed to record. He looked down into several deep cuts before he came to the shallow bank he had climbed with his burden from the wagon.

He slid down to the willow-choked shelf, and threaded his way upstream until he came to the wreck. He pushed to the front, and ducked under the hoops. He got the tump line bag out of his possible bag. This would be a full load. He pulled out the other half of the reserve canvas. Too heavy and holey. Large portions had been shredded to make up some rodent's nest. He set it aside. Opening the trunk, he added the other blanket. He hesitated, then grabbed the woman's underwear, socks and two dresses, and tucked them under the blanket.

The trunk yielded two new pairs of the lady's shoes, but he could not recall the size of the girls' feet. He put them in the bag anyway. Two of the man's shirts and two pair of trousers followed. One of the shirts he put on. The other, along with the trousers, he put in the bag. He felt around, and came up with another knitted hat. A silk bag containing a brush, comb and hair ribbons he tucked down the side. There were four plain knitted sweaters. Thinking of the mountains they had to cross, he added three of those to the bag. At the bottom of the chest, he found a Bible. Closing his eyes, he hugged it. "Thank You, Father. I need this, and I need it for the girls. Give me the words that You can use to draw them. Soften Jo's heart. She does not understand what You are doing."

The utensil chest was next. He put two more tin cups in the bag, then the rest of the knives, forks and spoons he wrapped in a cloth, and added them with two more tin plates and three tin bowls. From the food chest, he added all of the oilskin bags of soup and the cracked wheat. In the jumble behind the chest, he saw a misshapen man's hat, which he clapped on his head. Under the hat, he found another canteen. He mumbled, "You can never have too much water!"

He noticed an oiled canvas bag jammed between the wagon seat and the side of the box. He worked it free and opened it. It yielded an equally well oiled leather belt and holster, holding a Colt's revolver identical to the one the buffalo had destroyed. In the bottom of the bag were a box of patches, a bag of bullets, a tin of grease, and a tin of percussion caps. A flask of powder with its own measure was wrapped in the belt.

Backing out from under the wagon, Buddy stood and buckled the gun belt around his waist. The other items he transferred to his possible bag. He pulled the tump line bag out, and found it only partially filled.

Ducking back under the overturned wagon, he looked to see what else might be useful. He found two more large canvas bags with drawstrings, and a length of rope. A bareback pad he discarded. From the utensil box he pulled another cooking pot.

By the time he clambered back out of the ravine, it was only an hour to sunset. He hoisted the bag into place, leaned his forehead into the tump line, and headed up Deer Creek. "I'll camp at the head of the creek. There should be some clean water where it rises."

Buddy did not have to eat dry soup powder. With his belt knife and a chip of flint, he managed to start a fire. He filled the canteen with clean water he boiled, made up a bedroll, and fell asleep.

Before dawn, Buddy was pulled to the surface by something tickling his face. He turned his head slightly to the side, but the tickle followed. He shook his head slightly, then pulled his hand up to brush his face. A blast of hot air startled him awake. Something roared in his ear, and a clatter of hooves told him he had animal company. The roar sent him rolling away, bedroll and all.

From up the slope came a long drawn out "Haaaaaaw" followed by a rasping indrawn breath "Heeeee."

Laughing, Buddy crawled out of his blanket. "What a rude way to wake me up! But, don't you have that backwards? I always heard it was 'hee-haw.'"

The donkey brayed again, repeating the same pattern.

"All right, you win. I'll bet it was your hooves we heard thundering away from the fountain the other day. Like people, do you?"

The donkey stayed. His ears showed interest, and a desire for company. On a whim, Buddy dug in his bag, and pulled out his cooking pot and the cracked wheat. He pulled out the rope, and tucked the end in his back pocket. He poured some wheat in the cooking pot, and walked slowly toward the donkey, rattling the kernels.

The donkey stretched his nose toward the pan, then took a hesitant step forward. Buddy kept up a gentle conversation with the beast, and the two continued their slow approach. Within reach, the donkey sniffed the shirt sleeve and made a soft noise in his throat. He began licking the wheat from the pan. Buddy reached up and scratched the base of one long ear as the donkey turned his attention to the wheat in the pan. Buddy reached back, drew the rope forward, and looped it over the neck. The donkey stood quietly as Buddy deftly tied the rope into a makeshift halter.

"I'd say you belonged to that wrecked wagon back there. You knew this shirt I borrowed. I'll wear it until you get used to my scent, and get used to me." Looking at his load of supplies for the way west, Buddy asked, "Do you carry stuff? Come over here."

Buddy led the donkey to the willows, and tied the rope to a stout trunk. He returned to the wagon for the bareback pad. He laid his hand on the donkey's back, stroking him. Sliding the pad over his back, he reached under and caught the cinch. Fastening it, he got out an empty canvas bag and divided the load in the tump line bag into the new one. When they were balanced, he tied the drawstrings together, and eased the bags over the donkey's back. The animal did not flinch. Buddy said, "You were used to this. You'll be a big help. Do you also take passengers?"

He placed his hands on the pad, and pressed down. The donkey stamped one hoof, but stayed where he was. Talking gently to him, Buddy put both hands on the pad, and lunged up to where his weight was draped over the pad. The donkey danced, then steadied. Buddy swung to where he straddled the animal.

"You seem well trained. And you are certainly

big. I'm going to guess that you are a mammoth jack. You might even have some mule kiddos somewhere. Well, I don't have any mares for you, but I think the Lord has given you to me to help in a difficult situation. I've inherited a couple of girls who need to get to a safe place. There will be more for you to carry. You might even carry one of them now and then."

Buddy slid to the ground, and unburdened the donkey. "I'm going to leave you here for a bit. I have to go back, and you would not like the things you would see." He headed back down Deer Creek. When he reached the dead mule, he removed the halter, hobbles and picket rope. He found the broken mule saddle, and dug the bridle from under it. Turning, he said, "Good-bye, Tramp. Guess you'll have to beg somewhere else. But, we were a good team. I've got a donkey, now."

He kicked broken willows aside, and washed the bridle. As he hiked back up the creek, he rubbed the bridle against his shirt to get the smell of the donkey's previous owner on it.

Back at camp, he exchanged the makeshift halter for the one Tramp had worn, and adjusted the straps. The Donkey rolled his eyes and snorted at the smell of the leather. "Sorry, my friend. The one who used to wear this is dead, as you can smell, but that will wear off. We will do the bridle later, when I ride. For now, I'll lead, and you will follow."

Buddy loaded all his gear on the donkey, and, picking up his gun, he untied the rope and strode up the hill. At the first pressure on the rope, the donkey followed.

The way around the Black Hills was rugged, but familiar. With a blanket, Buddy did not have to sleep leaning against a rock.

The next day, Buddy bridled the donkey, loaded him, and, holding the reins, he mounted. Urging the donkey into a walk he rode down toward the North Platte, holding his gun across his lap.

It was late afternoon when he reached the dead tree trunk above the stairway to the river. He tied the donkey, then retrieved the rope he had hidden, and tied it around the trunk. He threw the coils over the cliff, and returned to the donkey. He opened the tump line bag, and pulled out the extra canvas bag. Pulling out the trousers, underwear and shirt, he stuffed them in the empty bag. Shoes and socks came next, along with the knitted hats. The dresses he left in the tump line bag. "I can hide the fact that they are girls, or I can let everybody know. For now, it is safer if nobody can tell."

Leaving the donkey tied, he descended the stairway, and with the gun stuck in the bag, he swung around the bulge, landing on the gravel bar. A thin ribbon of smoke showed the girls had been diligent fire tenders. Nobody was in sight.

When he reached Mary's boulder, he called, "Hello, the bedroom. Anybody here?"

Mary came running out, calling "He's back! Jo, he came back!"

Buddy laughed. "And two days early!"

Jo came out slowly. "You will probably say God brought you back early. Don't bother."

Buddy sighed. "I won't. I don't know who brought me back early. He does not have a name. But, he got me here. Sometimes I walked, and sometimes I rode. He carried all the stuff."

He looked critically at the four bare feet. Even though Mary was younger, her feet were about the same size as Jo's. The lady's shoes just might fit. He held out the bag and said, "Here. Go change your clothes. We are leaving this place."

Mary took the bag, and peeked inside. "Shoes! Jo, there are shoes in here!
And...and...well...things!"

In the bedroom, the girls shook out the contents of the bag. They traded loincloths for bloomers, then pulled on the trousers. Jo took off her shirt, and slipped into a camisole before she buttoned it on again. Mary took off her makeshift blouse, and donned the other shirt. Her clothes were big and baggy on her slender body. With socks on, the shoes fit each girl. Dressed, they walked out into the sunshine.

Mary was holding her pants up with her hands.

Buddy laughed. "Go back and get your loincloth belt. You can't walk all the way west like that! You might need your hands for something else. Then what would you do?"

When Mary returned, she had her pants tied up, and cuffed so she did not trip over them. Buddy looked at them critically. "You both look fine, except for one thing. There were knitted hats in there. You will have to put them on, and tuck your hair out of sight." Mary came running back with the hats. Both were a dull grayish brown.

Buddy said, "Now put them on, and hide your hair. Fellers on the trail don't have purdy hair."

Jo snorted. "We are not 'fellers', in case you haven't noticed."

"No, you certainly are not. But for the purpose of the trail, you have to look like you are. So, for your own safety, veil your beauty, Joseph!"

Jo glared at him. "I'm not Joseph!"

"For the trail, you are. And, like it or not, for your own safety, you will have to do what I tell you, and do it straight away. Some young would-be warrior would be right proud to parade you around the village campfire in front of his elders before he took you to his lodge. Do I need to be plainer?"

It was a subdued Jo who shook her head. "No. I understand. I'll do what you say." She put the hat on, and hid her hair up under it. "Does that look all right?"

Buddy looked at Jo's attire, and then at her face. "Looks fine. I know what's under it, if nobody else does. You'll do. I just need to keep you both safe. It's a point of honor."

With all of the supplies packed, Buddy said, "Let's go. There is someone I want you to meet." At the rope, Buddy made three trips with the baggage and gun. Climbing carefully, he carried everything to the top of the cliff. He checked the rope where it went over the edge. It did not show any fraying or wear.

He climbed back down to the river, then swung back around the bulge.

"All right, Kiddo, you are next. Wrap your arms around my neck, and your legs around my waist. Now hold on tight, and don't let go, even when we land. I'll tell you when. Ready? Say good-bye to your prison."

With quick steps, Buddy swung out over the river, around the bulge, and landed on the rock. When he stood steadily, he said, "All right. Down with you. I'll go back for Jo. You stand over there as far as you can go."

When he landed on the gravel bar again, he said, "Your turn. Do what Mary did."

"I won't. I'm not going to hug you!"

"Do you want to stay here?"

"NO!"

"Then climb aboard. I'm leaving. I have to get to Dalles City. Let's go!"

Jo reached for Buddy's neck, then drew back. "This does not mean anything. I don't even like you, so don't get any ideas."

Jo threw her arms around Buddy's neck, jumped up and locked her legs around his waist. She shuddered at the nearness and strength of him. He launched out over the river and felt the rope stretch with the weight of the two of them. He prayed, "Lord, please don't let it break!" The rope creaked as he stretched his feet to the rock, and lurched forward with their momentum. He caught himself against the cliff, and said,"All right. You can let go now. We are here."

Jo let her breath out, and laughed nervously. "That's what you have been doing each trip?"

Buddy nodded. "Right. Now, you climb up those stairs, but be careful. Hold on to the rope, and if you slip, squeeze the rope tight. Those steps have been gouged out by deer hooves, and used by coyotes. That's how I found you. You go first, Kiddo. There's a ledge up there where you have to move to the left to get to the last of the steps. Ready? Up you go!"

Mary grabbed the rope, and scampered up the cliff. When she reached the ledge, Buddy said, "Now you, Jo. I'll be right behind you."

Jo's climb was more uncertain than Mary's, and she dropped to one knee when she reached the top of the cliff. Buddy scrambled up beside her, and turned to coil the rope.

Jo said, "I didn't think I could do it. But, I'm here. Thank you. Who are you, anyway? I don't even know your name."

Buddy pursed his lips, then said, "I'm sorry, Jo. I don't know who I am, really. I go by Buddy Wilson. Buddy for short. I hope someday to find out my real name. It's a long story, and I guess we can hash it out on the trail. I think we both have stories to tell. So, you are Jo, or Johanna. Johanna what?"

"Feeney. It's Irish. I'm Johanna, and my sister is Mary Feeney. Mary is ten, and I am seventeen."

Buddy mused, "Sarah was ten when she disappeared. She looked a lot like Mary. She would be seventeen now, so I guess she would look a lot like you. I finally found out she is in Dalles City. That's why I have to get there."

Jo frowned. "And who is Sarah?"

"I'm not sure. That's what I have to find out."

Buddy shook his head, coming back to the

moment at hand. He pointed to the donkey. "I headed west on a mule. This fellow is his replacement. Tramp died with half a dozen arrows in him. This fellow woke me up a couple of days ago. I don't know his name. The strange part is that he liked me because I'm wearing a shirt that smells like his former owner. We all are. He didn't need the shirts any more."

Mary asked, "Why not?"

"He died. Both he and his wife died when their wagon toppled into a ravine. God led me to that wagon, and through someone else's tragedy, He provided for all three of us. We are all wearing their clothes, and we will sleep in their blankets. Their donkey will carry our stuff, and maybe even carry us sometimes. God is good, and gracious. He has a purpose for everything He allows, even if we cannot see it immediately."

Jo's look showed her contempt for his words. "And what was His purpose in mama and daddy's death leaving us out here alone? What was His purpose in allowing Rube Weston to lie about me, and make the wagon master try to force me to get married?" She tempered her hot words by saying, "I'm glad the flash flood washed us away so I did not have to be in his wagon."

Chapter 17

Three pilgrims followed the tracks of a wayward wagon train as they descended the upper North Platte River. A burdened donkey followed, patient between canvas bags that dangled over his ribs. The pilgrims presented a motley appearance, large, medium and small, two in ill-fitting attire.

As the westering sun tumbled toward the horizon, Buddy started looking for a campsite. In one of the wrinkles of the Black Hills, he spotted a splodge of green, indicating water.

He said, "We'll see what this looks like. It appears to have what we need. There's food for this donkey, at least. Maybe clean water, too."

They turned into the side canyon that opened slightly as they approached the green vegetation. A spring bubbled to the surface, and a trickle of water ran several feet before it vanished into a crevice to find its way, unseen, to the river. Willows and a scrub cedar drew life from the damp earth. Buddy tethered the donkey, and freed him from his load.

"Why don't you ladies clear the stones from an

area big enough for sleeping? Smooth ground will be more comfortable. Not much more, but if you try sleeping on a pebble, by morning it will feel like a boulder." Buddy indicated a flat area likely to be easily cleared. He took one large stone, and tossed it down toward the Platte. He watched it roll to a stop, then turned to the tasks of the evening. His first chore was the donkey. With his knife he cut a handful of bunch grass, and began rubbing down the sweaty back where the bareback pad had been. The animal stood with eyes half closed, enjoying what had to pass for currying.

"No rolling for you. We'll get our water, and then you can get a drink. Poor critter. You don't even have a name. What shall we call you?"

Jo did not hesitate. "Buddy. That is a name that will suit him."

Buddy scowled, then laughed. "Thanks, Jo. Is that to honor him, or me?"

Jo did not answer directly. Glaring at him, she said, "The name seems appropriate."

The girls were kicking or tossing rocks out of the way. Mary whispered to Jo, "That was mean. He's been kind to us, and is taking care of us."

Jo whispered back, "So's the donkey!"

Mary called to Buddy, "I think we should call him Grumpy. He has a long face. Or Trudge. That's all he does, is trudge along behind us."

Buddy laughed as he built a fire. "That's good. Trudge it is. He only plods along because that's all we do. But we will have to step lively, or we will run into snow before we get out to Oregon."

With the sleeping area cleared, Buddy laid out the canvas and spread the blankets while they waited for the water to boil. He folded the canvas over the blankets, and said, "That should do us."

Jo stared. "There's only one bed. Where are you going to sleep?"

Buddy pointed. "Here."

"With US?"

Buddy's voice was matter of fact. "Get used to it. We'll sleep in our clothes. We'll sleep on one blanket, and under the other. Once we get to South Pass, or before, if it's really cold at night, we will sleep under both blankets. You and I will sleep on the outside, with Mary between us. She's kinda small, and will need the extra warmth."

Jo looked skeptical. "You have it all figured out, don't you? Not even married, and you plan to join us in bed."

Buddy's face hardened. "Jo, listen. I have no desire to take advantage. If we had more blankets, I would sleep on a different hill from you, just to avoid wrong appearances. Some people would misunderstand, or make degrading comments. I understand your concerns, but necessity says to do it this way. If I get sick and die, where would that leave you two? Women are scarce out here, and there are those who would take what they want by force. My goal is Dalles City. Our next stopping place is Fort Hall. I might just leave the two of you there with the soldiers."

Startled at Buddy's vehemence, Jo settled into silence. She knew he was right, but did not like the sound of being left. She finally said, "Our parents were going to Oregon. That was their dream. They lie in graves back down the trail."

Buddy interrupted, "I saw those graves."

Jo went on, "We have to finish their dream."

Supper finished, they made preparations for an early departure. Buddy tied Trudge where he could graze, filled the canteens, packed the supper stuff, and crawled between the blankets. He said, "You're next, Mary, when you get ready. Then Jo. Good night."

The girls stayed up, whispering, until Buddy was asleep, then crawled in beside him. Mary snuggled up next to him. Buddy's arm came up, and she pillowed her head on his shoulder. Content to be held, she fell asleep. In the darkness, Jo wept silently.

In the half light of morning, Trudge began to crop

the spring-side vegetation. Buddy slipped his arm from under Mary's head. She turned, but slept on. He crept out from the bed, struck a fire, and began breakfast preparations. When the tea was cool enough to drink, he took two cups to where the girls still dozed, and said, "Day's busted. Rise up, you weary travelers. Here's your morning potion."

Both girls sat up and stretched. Jo said, "I must have missed a little rock. Ouch!" They took their tea, and sipped it.

Jo pulled off her hat, and began trying to pick the tangles out of her hair with her fingers. "I'm a woolly mess. You and your idea of hiding my hair. I'll be a tousle-headed sight the whole way to Oregon." Her fingers got stuck in a knot of hair. "Ouch!"

Without speaking, Buddy sipped his tea as he walked to the packs. Opening one of the bags, he groped until he felt silk. He pulled out the bag, walked to the bed, and laid it on the blankets on Jo's lap. She stared after him as he walked to the fire. Then, opening the drawstring she dumped the contents onto the blanket. Out poured the hairbrush, comb and ribbons. Looking down at them, Jo closed her eyes. Tears trickled silently down her cheeks. She angrily dashed them away.

By the time breakfast was ready, both girls stood by the fire, their hair neatly braided and tucked up under their hats. The blankets were folded, along with the canvas, and were stacked beside the packs. The cracked wheat was bland without salt, but nourishing.

Buddy washed the dishes and stashed them in their bag. He packed the blankets in the mouth of one bag, and pulled its drawstring tight, then packed the canvas in the other bag. He stashed the halter, and bridled Trudge. When the bareback pad was in place, and the bags tied on, he said, "Today, you ride. But you have to take turns. Who's first?"

Mary said, "Let Jo ride first. She's sore."

Jo whispered, "In more ways than one!"

Buddy knelt, and patted his knee. "Your mounting stone, m'lady. Put your foot here, and step aboard."

Jo threw her forearm across her forehead, and turned away. Then, lifting her imaginary skirt, she stepped onto Buddy's knee, and settled herself aboard the donkey, saying, "Gauche! I always ride sidesaddle, you oaf! Ladies don't ride astride!"

Buddy smiled as he took the lead rope and headed toward the Platte.

It was midday when they reached Red Buttes Crossing on the river. The afternoon took them across Poison Creek with its alkali flats and poison pools. They passed through an increasing mixture of stunted grass and sagebrush, up beyond Willow Springs to the Sweetwater River. Here, the trail was well marked by the wheels of earlier travelers. The tracks circled, then vanished into the river in the direction of Devil's Gate.

Since the afternoon was chilly and the sun was nearing the mountains ahead, Buddy turned off the trail, seeking a fold that would hide them from anybody headed either direction. Mary rode, and Jo walked on the off side of the donkey.

Buddy found a dry niche deep enough for a hidden camp. When they had eaten, they sat listening to the night sounds.

Jo said, "Here we sit. What deeds of darkness shall we contemplate?"

Buddy said, "Story time. Tell me about that Weston marriage."

Jo groaned. "Darkness is the appropriate setting for such a tale." She lapsed into prolonged silence.

Mary said, "Even before Mama and Daddy died, he would not leave Jo alone. He kept talking to Daddy, and he wouldn't stop touching Jo. He would even follow her when she had to go aside..."

"Mary!"

"Well, he did, and Daddy had to punch him to make him stop!"

"But you don't have to tell that part. We don't talk about some things."

"I know, but still, we do have to go..."

"Mary!"

"Sorry. You tell it."

Jo took up the tale. "After Mama and Daddy were buried, we took the wagon on up the trail. Daddy had painted the box a pretty green. He said it was for Ireland. There was a man, Mr. Anderson, whose wife was sick. He helped us harness up for the trail. He saw me crying after our parents died, and he hugged me. Weston saw him holding me, and told Mr. Thomas, the wagon master, that I was a hussy, trying to seduce Mr. Anderson even before his wife was dead and buried. He said I would be nothing but trouble for the outfit unless I was married, and that Daddy had promised that when we got to Oregon, he would give me to Weston. He told Mr. Thomas that since he was the wagon master, he could marry us, like a ship's captain, since he was king of his domain. Mr. Thomas told me I was to marry Weston as soon as we crossed the river.

"Mary and I went around the bend to take a bath while the wagon train crossed. That's when the flash flood washed us down the river. The tree we grabbed tumbled us, and then got caught crosswise in the river. We let go, and the river spun it away, and left us where you found us. Mr. Anderson warned me about Weston. He said he heard him say he was going to get me, and sell Mary to the Indians. Men!"

Buddy shook his head. "We aren't all bad."

"I know that. Daddy was not bad. Mr. Anderson was not bad. But they were special. They cared about people."

Buddy caught her eye. "I'm not Weston."

Noon two days later found them above Ice Slough on the Sweetwater. The river wound like a serpent through a narrow valley. Leading Trudge, Buddy turned up a narrow canyon away from the river, such as it was.

"If I have to cross that thing once more today, my feet are going to dissolve. I'm done with wet shoes and socks. This sunshine is a bit weak, but it might dry things out. If not, I'll have that fire going too long. If anybody comes snooping after our smoke, they'll smell burned gunpowder!"

Jo said, "I can't even feel my feet. I'll put on dry socks, and sit with my feet beside the fire. You can gather sticks and move rocks."

Mary looked up at the hills, and said, "I don't know what you're complaining about. My feet are dry and warm."

Jo whacked her on the thigh. "That's because you are riding that donkey through the crossings. We have been wading, and that water is not warm!"

Two doglegs and a quarter mile up the canyon, it widened into a bowl. A spring seeped out of the base of the wall, formed a small pool, but did not flow anywhere. The water was clear and cold.

Buddy swung Mary to the ground. She staggered and sat down abruptly. "My legs are asleep!"

Buddy laughed. "Well, when they wake up, you can help set up camp. Tomorrow we rest. I think we're safe here. We only have to watch the front door."

At some time in the past, a dead tree had fallen down the canyon wall, and its corpse lay ready to supply their fire. Buddy looked up and said, "Thank You, Lord. Now we won't have to hunt for sticks."

When the fire was burning well, he got out a blanket. "Give me your socks, Jo, and wrap your feet in this. I'll get you some dry ones as fast as the fire can handle this."

He stuck sticks in the ground around the fire, and hung the socks to dry, and upended wet boots on their own sticks to drain and dry. He checked the loads on his revolver, and changed out the percussion caps, repeated the chore for the cape gun, and walked over to where Jo sat. "Is there room in that blanket for a couple more feet?"

Jo shook her head. "Get your own."

Buddy looked quizzically at the back of her head, shrugged, and fetched the other blanket. "Suit yourself."

Jo muttered, "It's enough that I have to share blankets with you at night."

Buddy turned, and sat with his back to the fire. "I wonder if it's warm in Oregon. I guess it is a matter of where you are. They have mountains there, and Tom said they have a desert. I guess I'll find out." He dozed in the warmth of the fire.

"Who's Sarah?"

Without opening his eyes, Buddy mumbled, "Hmmm?"

Jo asked again, "Who's Sarah?"

"I don't know."

"Then why are you going to Dalles City?"

Buddy opened his eyes, and saw Jo looking at him with narrowed eyes. "She needs me. Tom Flannagan came all the way to the Wilsons' farm to bring me a message. It ended with Sarah's words of command, 'Point of honor'."

Jo frowned. "She sent for you, and you don't know who she is?"

Buddy sighed. "Story time. My turn. I guess

that's only fair. You shared yours, Jo."

He began with wading in No Name Creek, and recited the account up to the fire. "And that's the story of Sarah. Sarah Wilson? Maybe. Or perhaps the name Sarah Wilson is like Buddy Wilson, borrowed. Given to us by Grandma Wilson."

Mary looked at him wide eyed. "You waded nakey with a girl?"

"Yeah, Kiddo. She was four years old. I was eight."

Jo said, "You were old enough to know better."

Buddy smiled. "But I didn't. We were just a couple of kids with the same goal, to get cool in the hot sun."

Mary said, "And you sat nakey on the same rock?"

"To get dry, Kiddo. We didn't have a towel."

It was Jo's turn now. "You didn't realize you were...um...different?"

"No."

Mary asked, "How 'bout when you pulled her burning dress off, and rubbed eggs on her?"

Buddy sighed, and answered, "Yes, Honey, I knew then. But I pretended not to see. She was already badly hurt in her body, and I did not want her to suffer embarrassment in her mind."

Mary asked in a small voice, "Did you pretend not to see me?"

"I did. But it did not take much pretending for you. You were far away. Sarah was right there in front of me. I saw you did not have any clothes, but that's all. Relax, Kiddo."

Mary mused, "We used to swim nakey in the pond before we came west. We would run from the house to the pond, and jump in. Then we would run nakey back to the house, and dry off and get dressed. But we were both girls."

"Mary!"

"Well, we did."

"But you don't have to tell it!"

Concern clouded Mary's face. "Were we naughty?"

Buddy laughed. "No, Kiddo, you were not naughty. You were probably nakey a lot when you were smaller. Little children often are."

"Was Jo?"

"Mary! That's enough!"

Looking at Mary and winking, Buddy said, "No. Jo was born wearing a dress and bonnet, and socks and boots. She has never been nakey. Well, except by the river. Or in the pond back home."

Jo muttered, "I hate you!"

Buddy stirred up the fire, and put water on to boil. He took Jo's boots and socks in one hand and his own in the other. He dropped Jo's boots beside her, and handed her the dry socks.

"Here. Put these on and warm your toes."

Returning to the fire, he brewed tea, and took cups to the girls. Setting his own cup on a rock, he sat down and reached for one of his boots. Grasping the leather, he began bending and twisting it. To Jo he said, "Grab a boot and do this, or it will be too stiff to be comfortable when you put it on again. It'll wear blisters on your feet."

He drank some of his tea, and reached for the other boot. Once he got it softened, he put on his socks, tied his boots, and finished his tea. He took the cooking pot of boiled water to the spring, and added enough cold water to make it tolerable. Digging in the pack bag, he pulled out two wash cloths and a towel. He laid those by the pot of water.

"Here. You may want to wash. I'm going down to check things out. I'll be gone half an hour or so."

Out of the canyon, he climbed to a ledge that gave a good view of the trail ahead, and the ground they had covered. He sat watching, looking each way. Below him, the Sweetwater meandered through its loops and switchbacks, as if it had no intention of reaching a goal. "Lord, that looks like my path. Is that what You have chosen for me? Loops and wandering that gets nowhere? Here I am, where I should have been more than two weeks ago, and now You have put two helpless orphans in my care. Is that for Your glory? They don't even know You."

Immediate conviction hit him. "You are right, Father. I have not shown them the light of Your Word. Forgive me. I will. Prepare their hearts, Lord. Mary is tender, but Jo seems so hard. But nothing is impossible for You."

Seeing no threat, he climbed back down to the tracks they had been following, and turned back up the canyon. As he approached the camp, he began whistling, then started singing, **"When I survey the wondrous cross, on which the Prince of Glory died..."**

The girls sat before the fire, each wrapped in a blanket.

"Keeping those warm for night?"

Mary turned. "See anything?"

"No. We are all clear. Not even a sparrow. But there might be a trout in the river. Too bad the buffalo stampede took all of my fishing stuff. We could have a trout dinner."

Mary gasped. "Buffalo stampede? When was that?"

Buddy recounted his adventures on Deer Creek that led him to the wrecked wagon and to the two girls. He made the telling as dramatic as he could, and wove God's gracious hand all through it.

Jo said, "Lucky you!"

Mary said, "God did all that for you? And you think it was for us, too? I wish I could know God."

Buddy smiled at her. "I think you will. Your wishing is His working. Maybe I can help you."

Mary asked, "Would you? For real?"

Buddy nodded. "For real."

Chapter 18

The next day was a rest day. The sun was two fingers above the horizon outside the canyon when Buddy awoke, but the camp was still in shadows. He kindled a fire and boiled water for tea, and roused the girls.

"Here's your tea. I'm going to take Trudge to the river for his drink. I don't want him drooling in our water supply. I'll whistle a tune to let you know I'm coming. When you hear me whistling, I'll be close."

When he headed back up the canyon, he launched into "How Firm a Foundation." When he rounded the last bend in the canyon, he saw Mary coming to meet him.

She reached for the donkey's lead rope, and said, "Jo wants to know do you have a hanky she can borrow."

He noticed Jo still lay in bed. "I do. I grabbed three bandannas from the wagon. One for each of us."

While Mary tethered the donkey, he reached into the pack, and pulled out all three. He handed two to Mary. "Does she have a cold? After all she has been through, I wouldn't be surprised."

Mary's look was solemn. She whispered, "She said her tummy hurts."

Buddy nodded. Reaching back into the pack, he pulled out a cloth, tore it in half, and folded the pieces. "Here. Take her these."

Mary frowned. "You mean, you know?"

"Yes, Honey, I know. Grandma Wilson was reading in the Bible to Sarah. I was listening. Grandma read about when Rachel's daddy was searching for his idols that Rachel had stolen. When he got to her tent, she told him she couldn't go out, because the way of women was upon her. Sarah asked Grandma what that meant. So, yes, I know, but don't tell Jo. Pretend I don't. I'll fix breakfast, and you can take some to Jo. Then I'll go back down the canyon. Jo can get up when she is ready."

Breakfast finished, Buddy left the girls in camp. He returned to his lookout on the ledge, and scanned the trail ahead and behind. Nothing moved. A stone clattered down from above him, bounced off the ledge, and rolled to a stop on the trail below. Looking up, Buddy saw the disappearing hind quarters of a deer.

Checking the trail again, Buddy headed back to camp. He whistled his way around the last bend, and saw that Jo was still wrapped in blankets. He went to the pack, and dug out the Bible. "Come here, Kiddo. Lesson time."

Mary sat in front of Buddy. He turned to the first chapter of John's Gospel. Buddy read aloud: "In the beginning was the Word, and the Word was with God, and the Word was God."

Mary asked, "Who was the Word?"

"Jesus." Buddy kept reading through the chapter.

Mary asked, "God's name is Jesus? The Christmas Jesus?"

Buddy thought a minute, then said, "The Bible gives us many names for God. Each one shows us a little bit of His character. He's called Jehovah-Jireh. That means God my provider, or God will provide. Like He provided for us in our need. We don't understand what we can't see.

"God exists in three Persons, but He is one God. There's God the Father, God the Son, and God the Spirit, but only one God. The part I read says that the Word was made flesh.

"That's when God the Son was born as a human baby. We only understand what we can see or feel. He came as one of us so He could grow up and live a life that demonstrated what God is like. That was the Christmas Jesus."

Mary looked puzzled. "I don't understand. How did He become Jesus?"

"That was the name He was given when He was born. His parents were told, 'You shall call His name Jesus, for He shall save His people from their sins.' That's why he was born.

"It's like this. You know a fire is hot. You feel the warmth as you get closer, and you get burned if you touch it. If I tell you a rock is lava, you can hold it in your hand. If I tell you it came out of a mountain, it would not make sense, because you have never seen lava come out of a mountain. If I told you the lava coming out of a mountain was hot, and you had cold lava in your hand, you might think I was fooling you. But if I told you the lava coming out of the mountain was rock that was melted and like fire, you would start to understand because you have felt the heat of fire.

"Our chapter told us that nobody has seen God at any time, but that Jesus made Him known, or understandable, demonstrating what God is like. You said you wish you could know God. We will keep on with the lessons, and the more you learn about Jesus, the more you will know God. God the Spirit will teach you."

Mary sat quietly thinking about what she had heard. She asked, "How come they did not receive Him?"

Buddy prayed silently, "Thank you, Father. You are working. Please open her understanding. And Jo's, too."

To Mary, he said, "He came to the people related to His parents with a message they did not like to hear. They thought they were good people, and that those not related to them were the bad people. His people pretended to know God, but they lived wicked lives. He said they were sinners, and they did not like that. They rejected His message, and rejected Him, and when they rejected Him, they rejected God."

Mary nodded, then asked, "What are sons of God?"

Buddy smiled, thinking, "Thank you, Father!"

He said, "People who believe the message of salvation God sent are brought into God's family. They are called His children. Jesus is His message. The Bible says we must believe in God's Son. Believe, in the Bible, means to trust in, to rely on, to cling to, to submit to and to obey. All of them, not just one or two. We can only do that in the ability God the Spirit gives us, not by ourselves. I'm praying God will give you that ability."

Mary smiled. Then she asked, "What is sin? Am I a sinner?"

Buddy smiled, but said, "Yes, Honey, you are. Sin has two parts. It is deep inside us as a nature we inherited. Our first parents, Adam and Eve, were tempted to disobey what God had told them, to rebel against God's way. They chose to do just that. They became the first sinners, and that heart of rebellion has been passed on to each person ever since. The Bible calls us children of disobedience. There were consequences of disobedience.

"With that heart of rebellion, we decide to disobey. That is the other part of sin. It is what we do. God says, 'Don't lie.' We rebel, and say things that are not true. We rebel against the circumstances God allows to surround us. We grumble and complain. We want our own way, not God's way. That is what sin is, and we are all sinners."

"I'm not!" Jo had been listening, but now she turned her face away.

Buddy said, "The Bible says that we all are. It says 'All have sinned, and fall short of the glory of God.' It says nobody seeks after God. It says we suppress the Truth in unrighteousness. We push it away. But, if God wants you as one of His own, He will make that happen."

Mary asked, "How did you start believing? How did it happen? What did you do?"

Buddy said, "I didn't do anything. I couldn't. Grandma Wilson kept telling me more and more about Jesus, and reading the Bible to me. God's Spirit worked in my heart, and gave me a hunger to know more, a hunger for Himself. He opened my understanding, showing me His truth, and the love He had for me. His Spirit gave me God's gift of faith, so I could believe what I could not see. One day, I realized I believed. He did it all. Since then, I've wanted more and more of His Word. It's nourishment for the new person I am in Christ Jesus."

Mary asked, "Will you keep telling me more and more?"

"You precious girl, I will. As long as you are willing to listen, I'll keep telling you."

Buddy glanced toward Jo. He caught a glimpse of the hunger in her eyes, and tears on her cheeks. Catching his glance, she turned away again.

Mary was quiet for several minutes. Then she asked, "What's the glory of God?"

Buddy pursed his lips, then said, "God is good and perfect and right in everything He is and does. He is pure light, and there is no darkness in Him. Darkness represents sin. There is no sin in Him, and He can't allow sin in His presence. His glory represents all that He is in His nature and His character. We don't measure up. We are not like God."

Mary frowned. "How can God be good when He allowed Mama and Daddy to die?"

Buddy said, "Honey, we can't see all of God's purpose for what He allows, or what He does. How much of this world can you see right now?"

Mary looked around. "Just this canyon."

"Can you see the Sweetwater?"

"No."

"But you know it's there. It winds and twists down its valley, and runs into the Platte, which runs into the Missouri, which runs into the Mississippi, which reaches the ocean. That's God's purpose for the Sweetwater. It gets carried along, and gets to where God planned for it to go. God's purpose for us is like that. We don't understand the reasons for the twists and turns in our lives. But, God knows what He is doing. That's why we have to trust Him, and let Him do what He has planned."

"Do you trust Him? Do you rely on Him?"

Buddy said, "I'm like the Sweetwater in its twists and turns. I had to trust God when that Indian almost broke my head. When I woke up tied with rawhide, and that Indian pointed that arrow at my eye, I had to trust Him that if they killed me, I would see my blessed Savior face to face."

He ran his finger along the scar healing on his face. "When they went for the buffalo herd to trample me, I had to trust Him to deliver me. He had already provided for my escape. This scar will always remind of His greater deliverance from sin.

"I wanted to get back to the trail, and head up

the Sweetwater toward South Pass, and on to Oregon. He had other plans. He used the Indian kids to chase me around the Black Hills to the upper Platte, and you. I knew nothing about you and your situation. God did. He used circumstances to direct me to you, and rescue you, just like He used circumstances to direct Jesus to the cross, to rescue me. Yes, I trust Him. I submit to Him, although sometimes I don't like it. Sometimes I protest. I want my way. But, I have found it is best to listen when He speaks."

"He speaks to you?"

"Yes. He speaks through His Word. He speaks through circumstances. He even speaks through wise people who know more than I do. It's smart to listen. The Bible says He speaks to us through His Son, Jesus. The more we know of Jesus, the better we can hear Him. His Spirit uses all of these ways to guide us."

Mary looked Buddy in the eyes. "Was it a lie to pretend not to know?"

Buddy bowed his head. "Honey, you got me with that one. I pretended not to know that Sarah was naked after the fire. We did not say anything. She knew that I knew, but we did not acknowledge it. Jo knew that I knew the minute you gave her the stuff. But I led you wrong when I said to pretend I did not know. I led the way in that lie. That shows how easily the sin nature inside us can take over. It can make us say the wrong things, feel the wrong way, and do the wrong things. I'm sorry. Please forgive me."

Mary nodded.

Buddy took the Bible to the pack, and brewed some tea, which he took to the girls. Going back to the fire, he boiled more water from the spring, and filled the canteens. As he was refilling the pots, Mary came up to the fire.

"Jo wants you to heat some water, and then go away. She wants to wash some clothes and dry them. Can you put the sticks back around the fire, so she can dry them?"

Buddy nodded. "I'll go, and be back in an hour and a half or two hours. Do you think that will be enough?

"Maybe. I'll help with the washing."

"When you are finished, rinse the pots, fill them at the spring, and put them on to boil again."

Chapter 19

The next morning, Buddy announced, "We will rest here another day. I'm going to try to get us some meat, and we can put that with the vegetable soup. That should stretch our supplies. It will be a long way from Fort Hall to Dalles City. I don't know if the Army will have fishing supplies, or if the fish will be safe from us. I'll be ready for breakfast when I return."

He brewed tea, and took it to the girls, who still snuggled under the blankets. Taking an empty canvas bag from the pack, he picked up the cape gun. As he passed the girls, he asked, "Jo, can you shoot? Have you ever used a gun?"

"Yes. Daddy taught me before we headed west."

Buddy took the revolver, belt and holster, and laid them beside the bed. "This is in case you need it. The smoke and noise could be enough, but don't shoot to miss. If you need to fire, aim to hit. I know you are mad at me, but when I come whistling up the trail, I don't want to be dodging bullets."

With that, he strode down toward the

Sweetwater. Two hours later, whistling his way into camp, he returned with one cottontail he had managed to snare. With fresh tracks of unshod horses on the trail, he didn't use the gun.

Mary held his bowl of soup out to him. "The mighty hunter returns." She went back for his cup of tea. Jo sat beside the fire, wrapped in a blanket.

Buddy pulled the rabbit, skinned and cleaned, from the bag. He cut it in pieces, discarding the ribs in the fire. Half filling one of the cooking pots at the spring, he set the meaty pieces to simmer.

Buddy cleaned a spoon for stirring the pot. "It's a good thing they mixed salt in the soup mix. I wonder if Fort Hall will have any salt to spare..."

Mary asked, "Shall I get the Bible?"

Buddy looked at her in surprise. "Hungry, Kiddo?"

"My heart is. Can you tell me more about Jesus?"

Buddy said, "I'll get it." He went to the pack, praying and praising God. "Thank you, Father. Your Spirit is at work. I pray He might soften Jo's heart, too, and prepare it to receive Your truth." Returning to the fire with the Bible, he sat beside Mary, deliberately sitting between the two girls.

When he had read the second chapter of John, Mary asked, "How could He change the water?"

Buddy said, "Remember yesterday? It said all

things were created by Him. The whole world, and everything in it. He created it. He did not need anything to make it. When we make soup, we start with water, and add the powder. We can't just take an empty cup, and say, "Here is some soup." He did not need to start with stuff. He created everything, so He could make it over, because He was God. He can make us over. When He was made flesh, or born, He did not stop being God."

"Oh." Mary pondered the rest of what she had heard. "Why did he chase people out of the temple? Was he mad? Wouldn't that be sin?"

Buddy took a deep breath, and said, "They were cheating the people who came to worship God. They sold them animals for sacrifices, and charged much more than they were worth. The money changers told the people that they could only give God gifts of special temple coins, and charged them silver and gold for cheap coins. They made the people sin. How could they worship God in the right way with angry hearts?"

Buddy heard Jo gasp.

Mary asked, "What did it mean when it said 'when He was raised from the dead'? Did somebody kill Him? I thought He was God."

Buddy prayed silently, "Father, help me say the right things. Help her understand."

To Mary, he said, "Yes, Honey, they killed Him,

but it was God's plan. Remember yesterday when it said 'His own did not receive Him'? They crucified Him. That means they nailed Him to a wooden cross, and left Him there to die. He died. He was born to die.

"Yesterday, we read about when that man pointed to Jesus, and said 'Look! The Lamb of God that takes away the sin of the world.' The Bible says we are like sheep who have gone astray, and God piled on Him, Jesus, the iniquities of us all. Iniquities are all the wicked things we say or think or do. Remember how Jesus showed how mad God was at the men in the temple? He demonstrated the wrath of God against sin. God has to judge sin. He put all of our sins on His Son, and poured out His wrath on Him on that cross.

"They buried Jesus in a tomb. On the third day, Jesus came out of the grave, alive again, alive forever. That is eternal life. He promises eternal life to all who believe that He has satisfied God's wrath against sin. Our physical body will some day die, but we will live forever with Jesus if we believe."

Buddy got up, went to the fire and stirred the soup. Going to the spring, he brought more water and poured it into the pot. Both girls sat thinking.

"I'm going to take Trudge down to the Sweetwater for a drink, and then over to where I got that rabbit. There's plenty of grass there, so

I'll let him graze. I'll be back in an hour or two."

When he was gone with the donkey, Mary said, "I told him that I wished I could know God. I think I'm starting to. How come we did not know about Jesus?"

Jo mumbled, "I don't know."

Mary went on, "Mama and Daddy took us to church sometimes, and they had a Bible, but we never heard about Jesus at church, and Mama and Daddy never talked about Him at home, except at Christmas. They told us when we were naughty, but did not tell us why it was naughty. They did not tell us about sin."

Jo was silent.

"Do you miss Mama and Daddy?" Mary moved to another thought. "I miss them. Sometimes at night it hurts so much I cry. Buddy holds me until I can go to sleep."

Jo threw her arms up, and the blanket fell from around her to the ground. "I need somebody to hold me!"

Mary thought, then said, "We could trade places. But it would have to be after he goes to sleep. I could climb over you so you would be in the middle. But you hate him. How could he hold you when you are mad at him?"

Jo pulled the blanket back up around her

shoulders. "I wouldn't have to look at him. And before morning, we could trade back."

Mary savored the conspiracy. "We could."

"How do you get him to hold you?"

"I snuggle next to him, and he puts his arm up. I put my head on his shoulder, and he hugs me. Then I go to sleep. Sometimes I stay there, and sometimes I turn over."

It was Jo's turn to stop and think. Then, "Let's try it tonight. When you are sure he is asleep, we'll trade places. But I hope he doesn't catch us. He might get mad."

When Buddy returned, whistling up the last stretch of the trail, the meat was falling off the bones in the soup pot. He carefully spooned the bones out of the water, and tossed them in the fire. With two forks, he shredded the meat that remained.

Later, he added the vegetable soup powder, enough to make a thick, meaty stew, which he reheated, and served out into three bowls. There was enough left for breakfast. He put the lid on the pot, and set it in the spring. If cold water from a spring kept milk, butter and eggs cold in the springhouse, it should keep the soup overnight.

Planning to head on up the trail in the morning, Buddy prepared their gear for an early departure.

Then, rearranging the tarp and blankets, he crawled between the blankets, calling to the girls, "Come on when you are ready. I'm tired." He was already asleep before they stepped softly to where he lay.

Mary steered Jo to the middle part beside Buddy. "We won't have to trade until morning!" She giggled silently.

Jo trembled slightly as she slipped in beside Buddy.

Morning came. Buddy awoke abruptly. He was not holding Mary's bony frame. His hand rested on soft flesh. He quivered, then stiffened. Slowly raising his arm, he nudged the warm body next to him. Jo sighed, and turned over. Buddy slipped out of the bed, and hurried to stir up the coals into a cook fire. He set the soup to heat, and filled the other cook pot with spring water, and took it to the fire to boil for tea. He checked the canteens. Both were full. He put the bareback pad on Trudge, and readied the bags for the rest of the gear. It would be quick to load them so they could be off. He calculated the distance ahead. He planned to be over South Pass by evening.

"Day's busted! Roll out!" Buddy awakened the girls as he dished up the stew and poured tea. "Breakfast!"

Awakened, Mary looked at Jo, wide eyed. She

whispered, "We didn't switch back!"

Jo groaned. "He knows!"

Buddy called, "Come on, you sleepyheads. Let's get started!"

Breakfast over, Buddy packed the bedding, washed the dishes and packed them in the bags. He left the pot of warm water and the cloths. "I'm going down to check the trail, if you two want to wash. Then pack up the bags. I'll load Trudge when I get back."

Jo and Mary were both troubled by his stern expression. As he strode down the canyon, Mary asked, "Did we do something bad? I don't think he liked it. I don't think I did wrong."

Jo said, "I don't know if I did, either. But I sure slept. Until morning, anyway. It was...assuring...I guess. I felt safe for the first night in a long time, just feeling him there."

Mary agreed. "That's how I felt. Safe. I wondered if that was what it would feel like if God was holding me."

They heard Buddy whistling up the trail, and hurried to finish their chores. When he reached camp, they had their hair braided and tucked out of sight. The camp gear was packed, and the wash cloths were in the cooking pot, packed away. They had drowned the fire, and scattered the remains of the wood. They had even collected some of the charred ends for first fuel for the evening.

Buddy found them ready, standing beside the bags. He loaded the donkey, then turned to Jo. "You ride today. Mary and I will walk."

Jo was puzzled by his consideration, and her face showed it. He knelt, and she stepped on his knee and mounted the donkey.

They had covered about ten miles of the last thirty miles to South Pass. Trudge had hobbled a couple of steps, so Buddy stopped, leaned against him, and picked up his front hoof. He flicked a jammed pebble out of the frog of the hoof. "That better?" he asked.

Mary stood with her knees rubbing together. "I have to..."

Buddy pointed. "Over there. Behind those bushes."

While Mary was gone, Buddy turned to Jo. "For your own good, and mine, please don't do that again. I woke up with my hand on your...body. I don't have that right."

Anger flared in Jo's face. "Fine. I won't. I just needed someone to hold me. It won't be you! You can just hold Mary!"

"Jo, listen. Mary is like a tiny rose bud. All green. She does not show any of the color God has planned for her. You are a woman. You are a rose in full bloom, with all of the fragrance and attractiveness God purposed for that flower. Please don't do that again."

Slipping off Trudge's back, she said, "I'm going over with Mary. You stay with the donkey. You are fit company for each other."

The girls came back, whispering to each other. Jo started to walk up the trail. "Mary's turn."

Buddy said, "No. You ride today, Jo. Come back here, and mount up."

Jo stood on the trail, defiant. "I'll walk!"

Buddy knelt, holding the lead rope. "Mount up!" At the snapped words of command, Jo yielded.

"If you so demand, Master. I'll ride." Sarcasm and disdain flavored Jo's words.

They forded the headwaters of the Sweetwater where it turned east, and in another ten miles found themselves on South Pass. Buddy checked the height of the sun, and said, "Let's push on a bit farther."

Four more hours brought them to the sandstone marker at the 'Parting of the ways.' On the stone, someone had etched an arrow pointing left, with the words 'Fort Bridger'. The arrow pointing right said 'S. Cutoff'.

Buddy stopped at the stone. Tracks wandered

both directions. Most of the wagons had gone left. Buddy turned to the girls. "Wet or dry?" If we go right, it is about eighty miles shorter, but it goes across a little desert between a creek and the Green River. If we go left, we cross several rivers, and loop around by Fort Bridger. Tom Fitzpatrick at Fort Laramie said go right. Do you want to cross the desert, which is dry, or the wet rivers?"

Both girls said, "Dry."

"All right, dry it shall be. Drier than you think. We have only two creeks to cross on the way to the river instead of eleven crossings, and this way, there's a ferry across the Green River, and we only have to cross it once. Not sure what it will cost, though."

They turned right. Less than five miles later, they crossed the first creek. Buddy turned off the trail and found a place to camp. When everything was set, and dinner eaten, they crawled between the blankets. Buddy had cut and scattered sage under the canvas. The aromatic mattress was a welcome change from the hard ground.

Jo crawled under the far edge of the blanket. Buddy said, "Cuddle up, you two. At this altitude, it is going to be cold. If it gets too cold, crawl under both blankets. G'night..."

Mary murmured, "Night."

Jo snorted.

The next morning, Buddy gathered dead sage, and branches from a fallen balsam. He cleared an area down to the dirt, and kindled a fire. He topped off the canteens with boiled water, and brewed tea for their breakfast. Chicken soup warmed them for the journey ahead.

When the donkey was loaded, he said, "We will all walk to start the day. That should warm us up. Fitzpatrick said we are over a mile above the level of the ocean. He said it is not uncommon to have first snow in late August up here. I have lost track of the date, but we will have to move. We are almost half way.

"We cross that fifty-mile desert today. If I forget to stop for a drink every so often, remind me. Ready? Let's go. We want to make the Green River Crossing before nightfall."

A little over five miles brought them to the Big Sandy. Buddy had Jo mount the donkey, and led Trudge across the river. He left Jo on the sage covered shore, and went back for Mary.

When they were across, he said, "All right, Mary. Slide down and walk some more. Whoever gets too tired to walk first gets to ride for a bit. We are going to move right along. Ready?"

The girls nodded, and they strode out. The tracks were plain. The wagons had straddled the sage, but the axles had trimmed the brush that grew between the ruts. To avoid the dust of the desert, the wagons had traveled side by side, spread across the arid ground. Bleaching bones showed where livestock had perished. They passed several derelict wagons, mute testimony of the difficulty of the way they had chosen.

Buddy watched the ascending sun. Two fists above the eastern horizon, he called a water stop. The girls held their cups, and he filled them from the canteen. He filled his own, and let the water slide down his throat. Hanging the canteens over the donkey's back, he said, "Forward, march!"

He called three more water stops as they went, figuring they were about ten miles apart. On the third stop, he took off his hat, and poured water into it for the donkey, who drank it all, and licked the last drops out of the felt. "That's all for now, Trudge. Now, trudge along. You are doing fine. How about you girls? Anybody need to ride yet? No? All right, I think this will be the last segment. If you look west, you can just catch the sunlight reflecting off of water, unless that is a desert mirage."

The sun sank slowly toward the western rim of the desert. At last, Buddy saw buildings in the distance. At their approach, a chorus of barking dogs announced the arrival of strangers. A man's voice yelled, "Shaddap, all of you."

Buddy approached the man who stood with his hands on his hips. "Can we get across yet tonight? We got slowed down a bit crossing that dry stretch."

"For a fee. Five dollars a head, including the donkey. You help pole the barge across. Pay in advance."

Buddy held out a twenty dollar gold coin. "Tom Flannagan said to tell you not to skin me."

"Know Tom, do you? Good man, Tom. Ten dollars, then." He fished in his pocket, and tossed Buddy a ten dollar coin in change.

On the other side, as they went ashore, the ferryman pointed at Buddy's pistol. "That thing work? You'll need it, with those two girls in tow."

Buddy flipped the ten dollar coin back to the ferryman. "Here's ten dollars to forget that you know they are girls. I found them on the North Platte. Got swept away by a flash flood, and abandoned. Their folks died of cholera."

The ferryman caught the coin. "You found them, you say? Rescued them? Say, there was a wagon train through here a while back. Had one purty green wagon. It was pulled by a team of mules. The off lead mule was missing half of his right ear. Cut off, flat across."

Mary cried, "Smokey!"

The ferryman scowled. "You know that mule?"

"That was our wagon. Somebody took it when we

got washed away."

"And who was the yay-hoo driving it? Looked like gallows bait to me. Said he inherited the outfit, sorta. Said the parents died and the daughters drowned. Said he searched for them for days and days."

Buddy said, "If he had searched for them, he would have found them. I'd say he just abandoned his broken-down wagon and took theirs. He headed west to escape being charged with armed robbery. Stealing the girls' outfit fits him like a glove." To Jo, he asked, "Did your parents have any money in the wagon?"

Jo nodded. "They had six hundred dollars in gold. It was in the tray in their steamer trunk. It wasn't even hidden."

Buddy turned to the ferryman. "How did he pay for his crossing?"

"In gold. A twenty."

"I may have to track him down. Did he say where he was headed?"

"The Willamette."

"Thanks. Remember, if anybody asks, you took three fellers and a donkey across. I tried to make them look like fellers, anyway."

"I can't be too careful out here. I look close. Those are girl faces. You take good care of them.

There's trouble afoot with the tribes. Be extra careful. Some of the trouble has white skin."

Buddy raised one eyebrow. The ferryman tapped his hip, as if he carried a revolver. He winked, and nodded. "Go upstream 'bout a mile, and you'll find a stream flowing into the Green. There's a clearing in the sage there where you can camp, and be out of the way. But be on your guard."

With camp set up, Buddy opened his money belt, pulled out his badge, and pinned it inside his coat.

Chapter 20

Morning dawned chilly, and a breeze swept down from the hills as Buddy loaded the packs on Trudge. The sound of hooves splashing in the stream changed to the crashing of branches. Buddy hissed to the girls, "Company coming. Get in those bushes and hide. Don't make a sound." Two thin, ill-kept horses walked into the clearing, ridden by two equally ill-kept men. Seeing Buddy, they reined in the horses, and sat watching him with narrowed eyes. One, sporting a scraggly beard, held a rusty muzzle loader across his saddle.

Apparently the leader, the man with the rifle said, "Well, looky here, Bill, a pilgrim. That's why we seen the ferry come acrost." To Buddy, he said, "Travelin' alone, are you?"

His hand hidden by the pack hanging from the donkey's back, Buddy slipped his revolver from the holster, and hooked his thumb over the hammer. "See anybody else?"

The bearded man said, "Bill, why don't you climb down and see what he has in them bags?"

Buddy stepped away from the donkey, and raised the revolver covering the bearded leader. He said, "Bill, if you get off that horse, you'll never get back on. Fuzz-face goes first, then you'll be dead before your second foot hits the ground. Stay put."

Bill, who had started to swing his leg over the horse's rump, settled back into the saddle. His partner started to swing his rifle toward Buddy. He froze at the click of the revolver's hammer.

"No, you don't." Buddy raised the pistol slightly. "Drop it on the ground, and be quick and careful. My finger gets twitchy. I said, drop it!"

The end of the rifle barrel hit the earth, then the weapon toppled and rolled under the horse.

"Now, unbuckle your belt and throw it down."

"My pants'll fall off!"

"They won't as long as you are on that nag of yours. Drop it!"

Buddy raised the revolver. "Now, unless you want to sprout a third eye in the middle of your forehead."

The leader stared at the muzzle of the revolver that seemed to grow larger before his eyes. When Buddy raised it, his coat fell open.

Bill yelled, "The law! Jake, you've held up a lawman!"

Jake growled, "There ain't no lawman out here."

"I seen his star! Jake, I tell you, it's the law!"

Jake still stared at the unwavering gun covering him.

Buddy said, "Unless you want to be buzzard bait, drop those belts. Now!"

Both men unbuckled and ripped off their belts and threw them on the ground. Belt knives clattered on the rocks beside their horses.

"You can circle around and come back here tomorrow to look for your weapons. I'll give you a hint. They will be wet. My advice is that you clear out of this part of the country. It won't be safe for two men wandering around unarmed. I'd arrest you, but there is no jail where I could lock you up. I'd either have to shoot you or hang you. If I see you again, you'll catch hot lead. Now, get!"

The two would-be robbers turned their horses, and clattered back the way they came. Buddy heard the rapid splashing up the stream.

"All right, Mary, Jo, you can come out now."

Two very frightened girls came out of the brush.

"They were going to rob us!" Mary's voice bordered on hysteria.

Buddy lowered the hammer on his revolver, and

slipped it back into its holster.

Jo's face showed her consternation. "Are you really a lawman?"

Buddy turned back his coat, showing the star. "I show this only when it is necessary. The ferryman hinted to me that we might have trouble, so I got this out. Yes, Jackson Wiggins back in Ohio is a U. S. Marshal. He deputized me before I left. He says this is good in all states and U. S. territories, including the Oregon Territory. He said I should take it for Elmer Gilson in Dalles City. I guess we can add Rube Weston to the list. Let's see. A wagon, four mules and six hundred dollars in gold. That's just from you two."

Mary gaped at the badge, then asked, "Would you really have shot them? I was so scared."

Buddy's face was grim. "To protect you, I would. His hand trembled as he unpinned the badge. He dropped it, picked it up from the ground, and slipped it into his possible bag. "I've never come so close to taking a life. You were scared then. I'm scared now."

Buddy stooped to gather the weapons. Going to the stream, he picked out pebbles that would almost fit in the rusty barrel of the rifle, and with a stone, he pounded them down the bore. He picked the percussion cap off of the nipple, and threw it to the middle of the creek. Tossing the rifle and belt knives into a deep pool, he hung the two belts on a willow as a clue as to where the weapons lay. Turning to the girls, he said, "They won't use that rifle again. Let's head back to the trail."

As they reached the ferry landing and turned to follow the wagon tracks that now angled southwest, Jo noticed Buddy's knotted jaw and labored breathing.

"That was hard for you." She made it a statement, not a question. "You were brave."

"I didn't feel brave." Buddy's teeth were chattering when he spoke. "My innards felt like jelly."

Mary asked, "Does that gun really shoot?"

Buddy said, "I don't know. I've never shot it. I pray I never have to find out."

They walked in silence, each processing troubled thoughts. An hour after they hit the trail, Buddy said, "I heard there were bandits along the way. I knew the tribes were stirred up. Keep your eyes open. If you see anything move, let me know."

Mary nodded.

Jo gasped and pointed toward the north. "Horses!"

Buddy looked. "Wild ones. No riders. But watch to see if anybody is trying to catch them."

At Emigrant Springs, they stopped. Buddy built a small fire and boiled water from the spring for tea, and mixed a light soup. A cottontail pushed out through the grass by the pool.

"Close your eyes, girls. You might not like this."

Buddy groped in his possible bag, and pulled out his slingshot. He reached into the bullet pouch for a round lead ball. Fitting it into the pocket, he drew it back, raised the weapon to where the upper arm aligned with the top of the rabbit's shoulder, and released the missile. Struck in the ribs, the rabbit was knocked kicking.

Buddy dropped the slingshot back into the possible bag as he ran around the pool. He grabbed the rabbit by the hind legs, and with his other hand, he broke it's neck. He carried it to the rock outcropping above the spring, and dressed it.

He took the carcass to the fire. Dipping a fresh pot of cold water from the spring, he washed it, and leaving it curled in the cooking pot, he put the lid on it and stored it in the pack.

"Meat for our supper. We'll stop early so we can cook it, and make a stew."

Mary said, "That was a good shot!"

Buddy smiled. "Quiet, too. It took me two weeks

of practice before I could hit the side of the barn."

In a reproachful tone, Jo said, "You hurt the poor thing."

Buddy nodded. "I'm not very good at it yet. If I had hit it in the head, It would not have felt anything. But then, a lot of things I say or do miss the mark."

Jo mumbled, "Me, too."

With the cooking pot in the pack, Buddy said, "Let's go. I want to leave those two knotheads as far behind us as I can. We will probably have a dry camp tonight, unless we can reach the Bear River. But that's another thirty or thirty-five miles. So, no. Let's go another five hours and find a spot to stop."

Her fear allayed, Mary fairly bubbled with the thrill of excitement. "We almost got robbed! But we're traveling with a real deputy! Jo, he's a real lawman!"

Jo's disdainful snort did not diminish Mary's enthusiasm. "There were two of them, and only one of him. But he made them throw down their weapons, and run away!"

Jo said, "Will you be quiet? Stop trying to make a hero of him."

"I can't. I have to talk. My tummy is still all

jumpy." Mary's nervous laugh made Jo scowl.

"Well, mine isn't. It's had tea and soup, and I don't care to chatter. Especially about this morning."

An hour later, Mary could no longer hold her tongue. "This is all the same. Nothing but rocks and sage brush. It must have been boring riding in a wagon. Do we always have to follow their tracks? They wander all over the place."

"It's better to follow where somebody has already marked the way," Buddy said. "Back at Fort Laramie, Tom Fitzpatrick told me the mountain men and trappers came first, and found all of the wrong ways to go, and the right ways. Then the wagons followed the right way, but had to wander a bit, because wagons need a smoother road than a man on horseback or on foot. We could travel in a straighter line, but we don't know just where we are going."

"Oh." Mary thought about that a moment, then asked, "How did the people with the wagons know where to go?"

Buddy smiled at her, and said, "They had mountain men to guide them. The mountain man would say, 'Head for that pointy hill,' and the wagon driver would keep that pointy hill in sight, even if he had to go around something like these high rocks. You'll see. Once we get around them, we will straighten out again. It makes the trail longer, but it will get us there.

"If you look ahead, you will see that it is not all the same. The hills are all different shapes, even if they are all covered with sage brush. You look and pick out a landmark, and keep moving toward it. Once you reach it, you pick out another one, and move toward the new one. Try it. Pick out some feature of the land up ahead, and watch to see if the trail keeps moving toward it, even if the trail wobbles."

Jo said, "Maybe that's why we went the wrong way. We did not have a guide. Mr. Fitzpatrick said he would go, but he was stuck at Fort Laramie. He said he was too old to wander around the mountains anymore. He was working for the government."

Another hour passed. All three were panting from the exertion at high altitude.

"It works!" Mary pointed to a jagged ridge ahead. "I've been watching that toothy hill, and even though we turn and turn, we keep getting closer to it."

"We'll make a guide of you yet," Buddy said. "I've been watching that same landmark. It looks like there is a gap on the north side of it. Watch and see if the wagon tracks don't sneak through there."

They did. Buddy found a box canyon off the trail between the hills.

"This looks like our inn for the night. There might even be water and grass back in there."

They turned into the mouth of the canyon. Trudge, who had patiently followed, sensed a stop, and brayed. The sound echoed off the walls of the canyon. Mary laughed at the chorus of donkeys the canyon threw back at them.

Buddy said, "Well, if there is anyone in here, we can't sneak up on him. But with all of those donkeys yelling at him, he's probably halfway up the wall by now."

The canyon doglegged to the left, and opened into a small basin surrounded by sheer walls of stone. Buddy looked around, and nodded.

"We'll camp here. I don't know what lies ahead, but it's about twenty miles to the Bear River. After that, it'll be a little over a hundred miles to Fort Hall. At the rate we are going, that's about three days travel. We might as well rest here tomorrow. That was a hard push today. Donkey's tired."

Jo sank to sit on a rock. "It's not just the donkey. We have to take two steps to your one. You just about wore my feet up to my knees."

"Sit tight. I'll set up camp, and get the soup going. It looks like there is a seep of water over there in that green patch. Trudge can start on his dinner, and then I'll start on ours."

Buddy unburdened the donkey, and set the bags near where the girls rested. Four stunted trees grew near the seep, and a dead one had fallen across the patch of grass. He tethered the donkey to a boulder where he could not reach the water that gathered at the foot of the wall. Where the water trickled away from its source, he scooped out a small basin, which began to fill with water for the donkey.

Gathering dead sticks, he carried them to a bare patch of ground and kindled a fire. He dismembered the rabbit, and dropped the meat into the simmering water, and then turned his efforts to clearing a place to sleep. The floor of the canyon was uneven, and after clearing the stones away, he kicked and scraped with his boots to make a flat place for their bedding.

He called to the girls, "It'll be hard ground, but I don't think I've left anything to bruise you." On the far side of the grotto he saw the opening of a small cave.

Mary watched him disappear into the rock wall. When he reappeared, she called, "What's in there?"

"Lions and elephants and crocodiles, all ready to eat you!" Buddy laughed.

Mary said, "No, there aren't. They don't live here!"

Buddy said, "Oh. You're right. No monsters in

there. We got an en suite place at the inn."

Mary turned to Jo. "What's that?"

Jo frowned. "He's naughty. That means a bedroom with a bathroom."

Mary giggled. "Oh."

Buddy brought them tea. "Have some of this while dinner is cooking." He sat on a rock near the fire, and took off his boots. "Free at last. Poor feet!"

Mary went to the pack, and took the Bible to Buddy. "More?"

Wiggling his toes, Buddy said, "Pull up a rock. Plenty of seats in the house." He opened to the third chapter of John. When he finished reading the chapter, he said, "All right, Kiddo, you have an inquisitive mind in that head of yours. Let's hear your questions. I'll do my best."

Mary poked her left pinkie with her finger. "Why does it say condemned?"

Buddy was startled that her first question went there. "Condemned means judged and sentenced. When God created Adam and Eve, He put them in a big orchard. They could eat all the fruit they wanted."

"Yummy!"

"Yes. But God told them not to eat from one tree.

The Bible calls it the tree of the knowledge of good and evil. God is good. He wanted them to know Him, and to know nothing of evil. He wants the same thing for us. He wants us to know Him. They ate what they were not supposed to eat, and to them it was the fruit of disobedience. They rejected the good, and now they knew the evil of rebellion. Once you know something, you can't unknow it. Once you experience something, it stays with you.

"God had told them that the day they ate of it, dying, they would die. That would be the consequence of knowing evil. They would be separated from God by their sin, not only in this life, but forever. God had to punish sin, and that would be the condemnation. If there was a jail here in this country, Jake and Bill would be judged guilty, and condemned to years and years in jail. They would be separated from everybody else for what they have done."

Mary nodded, then poked her next finger. "It said God loved the world. Doesn't that mean He won't have to judge?"

Buddy shook his head. "No. It means He wanted to offer a way back. He sent them away from the place they had called home, where they had enjoyed God's presence. But first, He showed them how to demonstrate they were sorry they had sinned. He showed them how to offer a sacrifice of a lamb as a substitute, so it died instead of them dying. But the animal that died only pointed to when Jesus, the Lamb of God, would die for our sins."

"Did you sacrifice that rabbit?"

"No, Honey, we don't do sacrifices now, since Jesus is our sacrifice. We read that God loved us so much that He gave His Son, so that we could have everlasting life. Jesus is the way back to the presence of God. Jesus offered Himself, His own life, His own blood, to open the way to God forgiving our sins. That's why it says that whoever believes is not condemned.

"Because Adam was the father of all people living today, what he decided to do, and the consequences of what he decided, he decided for his whole family. That includes us. So, because Adam was condemned, everybody is as if they were born in jail, and are prisoners with Adam. Those who do not believe stay condemned, because they do not accept the way back."

Mary poked the next finger. "What's born again mean?"

Buddy smiled. "Remember we read that those who received Him were given the right to be children of God? That means we have been born spiritually. The Bible says without Jesus, we are dead in our disobedience, our trespasses and sins. But God makes us alive in Jesus. When Adam was created, he was made from the dust of the ground. Then it says God breathed into his nostrils the breath of life. That word breath is the same word as spirit. That's when Adam became a living soul. When we are born again, God's Holy Spirit comes into us. That's how He makes us alive in Jesus. That's how we are born again. When you were born, you took your first breath. When you are born again, spiritually, God's Spirit is your first breath. Then, God is your loving Father, and you are His dear child."

Jo asked her first meaningful question. "So, if you choose your own way again, are you condemned again?"

Buddy looked at Jo, surprise showing in his face. "No, Jo, once God takes you into His family, that's permanent. Jesus said that all the Father gives Him, He will never cast out. He did not give any exceptions. Remember I talked about the three persons who are one God? Well, all three work to keep you. The Bible says God's purpose for His own is that they do not sin. But, we do. But then He says that when we do sin, we have an advocate with the Father. That's Jesus. So when I sin, God the Son defends me in the presence of God the Father, while God the Spirit takes me to the place of confession. And the Bible says if we confess our sins, God is faithful and just to forgive us our sins, and to cleanse us from all unrighteousness. It says there is no condemnation for them that are in Christ Jesus.

Jo said softly, "That seems too easy."

Buddy answered, "It cost Jesus everything. Before He was crucified, He prayed, 'Not my will, but Yours be done.' The work of our forgiveness, our salvation was not easy. God did it all. We can't help Him. His call to us is to believe. But we are skeptics. We can only believe by His grace, when He opens our hearts to His truth, and opens our understanding to our need. That's my prayer for you, Jo."

Mary asked quietly, "And me, too?"

A tear trickled down Buddy's cheek. "Yes, Mary, and you, too."

After supper, Mary walked slowly over to Buddy. Looking up into his eyes, she said simply, "I believe."

Buddy's eyes opened wide, and he asked, "What do you believe, Honey?"

With shining eyes, Mary said, "I believe that Jesus died for my sins. I believe that He has brought me into God's family. I want to know more, and I want to do what He wants."

Buddy knelt and embraced the girl before him. He prayed, "Oh, Father, thank You. All the hardship has been worth this moment. I praise You, and I'm rejoicing with the angels."

Chapter 21

Two days later, they camped on Thomas Fork of the Bear River. Climbing the Bear River Divide had been gradual, and they had been able to keep up their three-and-a-half mile an hour pace. They had stood panting at the top of the ridge. Surveying their surroundings, they could see the Uinta Mountains and the Wind River Mountains. Below them stretched the green canyon of the Bear River.

The wagon tracks fell steeply away ahead of them. The descent into the valley of the Bear was not as easy as the climb to the top of the ridge, and the tracks were gouged deeper into the earth, because the wagon wheels had to be locked for the downward journey into the valley. The skidding wheels ground the earth into a fine powder that mounded the edges and middle of the Trail.

In camp, Buddy cut a willow withe, and after dark, he searched the sky and located the north star. He aimed the willow stick straight at the star at the end of the handle of the little dipper. Stabbing it into the dirt, he crept back under the blankets without awakening the girls. Next morning, he told the girls, "Tom Fitzpatrick said when we got here, I should go around Pegleg Smith's trading post. Said it would be swarming with tribes and bandits. We'll go ten miles north, and then head west. Then we'll catch the trail to Fort Hall."

Mary asked, "Why do they call him Pegleg Smith?"

"Well, he was a mountain man and a trapper. At some point it seems he hurt himself. Since he was alone, he ended up cutting off his own leg so it would not kill him. Now he hobbles around on a wooden leg."

Mary looked around the camp. "How will you know which way is north?"

Buddy pointed at the willow stick. "I set our compass while you were sleeping. That stick is pointed at the north star, so it is leaning north. We go that way. See that peak way over there? That's our landmark. Keep that in sight. Tom Fitzpatrick said there will be a treat for you down the trail when we get back to it."

Mary could not repress a squeal. "A treat? What treat?"

Buddy picked up the lead rope, and led the way away from the trail. "You have to wait. But I think you will like it."

"Will you get some?"

"No. Just the two of you. You would definitely not want me to share. It'll be all for you."

The girls exchanged puzzled looks, but said nothing as they followed Trudge through the sage brush.

Three hours later, Buddy figured it was time to head west. "We should hit the trail about five miles beyond Smith' trading post. Fitzpatrick said it was not much. Not even a fort. Just a bunch of log cabins. It'll be good to miss it."

He stood facing their landmark to the north, and stuck his left arm straight out. "That way. What do you think, Mary? Do you see a landmark?"

"There's a mountain way over there with a flat top."

Buddy reached over to pat her on the back. "That's the one I picked out. Let's head for it."

It took four hours to reach the trail beyond Pegleg Smith's post. Far behind them, they heard the lowing of cattle.

"Fitzpatrick said Smith had quite a herd of cattle. I'd like to have picked up some jerky from him, but it's better we missed. We'll go another three hours and stop."

"For a treat?" Mary could not hide her curiosity.

"For a treat."

The Bear River Valley was crossed by a series of rocky inclines and valleys. The river itself, therefore, flowed sometimes through rock-walled gorges, and sometimes through gently sloping banks. The trail meandered down the valley, where the wagons had followed the easiest path available. The hills were covered by sagebrush, with dry bunch grass between the bushes. Throughout the valley they saw scattered tufts of trees. With abundant water, balsam trees swayed softly, while the leaves of white-trunked aspen trees shivered in the breeze.

At the top of one of the ridges, Buddy stopped. Looking ahead, the three saw they would drop into a long valley, flat and marshy in places. "We're getting there," Buddy said. "Fitzpatrick said I should look for a game trail that takes off toward a knot of trees. But we have a couple more miles to go. I think you can see it from here, but there are a lot of groves down in the valley. But if you look down there, you can see the sunlight reflecting off of a bunch of scattered pools. It should be somewhere there."

They headed into the valley, and after about a mile, Buddy spotted a narrow trace leading off the trail and disappearing into the towering sage, some of it rising over ten feet. "We'll turn here and head for those trees. I think that's the place. If not, we'll check out other groves

Under the shelter of the grove, they saw a rock-rimmed pool about twenty feet across. Buddy tethered the donkey, and reached into the pack for their tin cups. He filled two cups from the pool, and handed them to the girls. "Here. Drink this." He filled and drained his own twice.

Jo and Mary sipped the water.

Jo gasped, "It's hot!"

"And fizzy!" Mary took a big gulp. "It tickles my mouth! Is this the treat?"

Buddy nodded. "It's part of it. The best is yet to come. You had to drink some first."

Mary lowered her empty cup. "There's more?"

"Yeah. There's more. See those big rocks under the water?"

Mary nodded.

Buddy said, "You sit on those. The water should come up to your chin. You lean back against the rocks on the side of the pool. Trudge and I will go back and guard the trail. You two slip off your clothes and enjoy a hot bath. Here, I'll leave you the towel. You'll have to share, since I only found one. Or...wait. Mary, you can dry off with these two wash cloths. You're smaller. Let Jo have the towel."

Mary scowled. "You won't look?"

Jo caught Buddy's glance, and said, "No, Mary. He won't look."

Buddy said, "Give me five minutes before you undress. I should be back on the trail by then. I'll look for a dry grove off the trail on the other side where we can camp. I'll stay away for an hour. That should give you plenty of time. You haven't had a hot bath in months.

"When I come back, I'll sing a song. If I'm singing, take your time getting dressed. When I stop singing, you'll have a couple of minutes before I come out of the sage.

"But if you hear me whistling, get out and get dressed fast. That will mean there is trouble afoot. If I'm whistling, don't take the time to dry. Get dressed and hide in the sage."

Mary said, "Singing means safe. Whistling means danger, right?"

"You got it. Now, give me a few minutes to get away from here, and then enjoy your treat."

Later, as Buddy prepared soup and tea, the girls sat by the fire drying their hair. Then they took turns brushing and braiding each other's shining tresses. Buddy set out the bowls of soup and cups of tea. "Supper!"

"What makes the water so warm and bubbly?" Mary sipped her tea. "My tea isn't bubbly."

"It's a hot spring from under the ground, Fitzpatrick said. 'Sodee Springs', he called it. He said the water seeps down to where the earth is hot, and then bubbles back up in this valley as hot springs. He said he has seen a place out here where there are hot springs that will cook you, and where water and steam come shooting out of the ground. He said those fountains shoot about a hundred feet into the air, or more."

Buddy finished his soup, and gulped his cooling tea. "Fitzpatrick said the people on the wagon trains stop here to bathe and do laundry. Some have even baked bread with the soda water. He said they get really tender bread, and don't even have to use leavening. They use the other pools for washing and stuff. He told me to get a drink from the pool back there under the trees. Said I could soak there as long as I wanted, and nobody would know, because it was hidden from the trail."

Jo said, "That bath was wonderful. My hair is the cleanest it has been in ages. Thanks."

Mary whispered to Jo, "We were nakey in the pond again. But this time it was warmer."

"Mary! Hush!"

Buddy walked into the grove. They could hear him working, but did not see what he was doing. When he came out of the grove, he scattered the remains of the fire, and said, "Time to turn in. We'll sleep under the trees tonight. Feels like it might get a little cold."

The girls disappeared into the grove while Buddy

tethered the donkey where he could graze. When he found his way through the shadows to their bed, the girls were already snuggled in.

Mary's sleepy voice came from under the blanket, "This is so soft! And it smells so good!"

Buddy slipped in, and said, "Good night, you two. This should make up for hard ground."

Two voices mumbled, "Mmmmm...."

Ice covered the water in the cooking pot the next morning. When Buddy awakened, he discovered the two girls had crowded to the middle of the bed, and the three of them were huddled together for warmth. He slipped out, and tucked the blankets next to Mary, then walked out to where he could survey the trail and the area around the springs. Nothing moved. A light fog arose from the hot springs, and spread like a blanket over the valley floor. He had heard hooves on the trail during the night, but nothing stirred in the half light of morning.

Buddy kindled a fire and prepared breakfast. Sunbeams cascaded over the Bear River Divide and swept the valley floor, and still the girls slept. He walked to the edge of the grove and called, "Hey, you sleepyheads. Breakfast is ready, and the day is half used up. Roll out, and roll up that bedding!"

He heard yawning, followed by sleepy grumbles.

He called, "Let's go. Tea's getting cold, and we have a ways to go today."

As the girls stumbled out, stretching and yawning, he poured some of their tea into his own cup, and added hot water to all three, and handed the cups to Jo and Mary. Both girls shivered in the morning chill.

Buddy dug in the pack, and pulled out the sweaters. Handing one to each girl, he said, "Here. Put these on over your shirts. It'll warm up later, but for now, these should help." He put one on himself, and reached for his tea, cupping it in his hands to warm his fingers.

Mary straightened her clothes, and said, "That was the most comfortablest bed I ever slept in. What was that mattress?"

"Balsam tips. I cut the tips off the low branches I could reach, and piled them a foot deep before I laid out the canvas and blankets. If the softness didn't help you sleep, the aroma would."

Jo sipped her tea. "Between the softness and the aroma and the hot bath, I'm ready for...a nap!"

Buddy laughed. "You'll have to sleep on your feet, then. I plan to reach Fort Hall today. Have you had enough of this trail? I can leave the two of you there. I don't know whether you would be safer on the trail with the tribes on the prod, or in a fort full of love-starved soldiers. I'm going to leave it up to you, Jo. I know I'm a rock in your shoe. But you have today to decide." Turning to face Jo, Buddy saw brimming eyes, and watched a tear trickle down her cheek.

"Buddy, I have to talk to you. Sit down. I'm going to sit behind you, so you can't see me."

Puzzled, Buddy sat.

Jo began, "I've been hateful to you. You are not a rock in my shoe. I've been piling the rocks in my own shoes. You have been kind and caring, and I have been pushing you away, trying to make you hate me. I made everything your fault. I'm sorry."

Without turning, Buddy said, "I used each of those pushes as a prompt to pray for you, Jo. I forgave you immediately."

Jo drew a shuddering breath, and went on. "I tried to make you Weston. I took out all of my anger at him on you. You bore it. I resented it more than you knew when you came and found me, well, without any clothes to wear. You gave me a c-covering, and d-didn't make me feel ashamed." Sniffles broke her words. "I was so lonely. I needed someone to comfort me. That's why I traded places with Mary that night. Then you were so stern when you told me not to do that again. Why were you?"

Buddy's silence stirred concern in Jo's mind. "I should not have asked that. I'm sorry."

"No," Buddy said. "But what I say may offend you."

"It won't. Go ahead and say it."

"You asked for it. When I woke up that morning, I felt the warmth and softness and nearness of you. That awakened a hunger within me, within my flesh. I wanted you. I suppose I could have taken you."

After a moment's silence, Jo spoke. Her voice was barely above a whisper. "You could have had me. I was only half asleep. I...I wanted you."

"Jo, understand this. My flesh said yes, but God's Spirit within me said no. That embrace is only for the deepest, godliest kind of love. It is for marriage. Taking you would have been seeking to satisfy my own wants. God's love seeks the best interest of the object of that love. I would have dishonored you, dishonored myself, but worst of all, dishonored my Lord Jesus Christ. That was why I said it was for your sake and mine. And, though I didn't say it, for the sake of my Lord Jesus Christ."

After a moment, Jo said, "Mine, too."

"Your sake?"

"No. My Lord. You thought you were talking to Mary, but your words went right to the center of me. I...I believe."

Buddy's prayer of rejoicing quieted Jo's heart and mind.

She hesitated, then asked, "It wasn't Sarah, then?"

It was Buddy's turn to hesitate. He said, "That is a sacred subject for me. I... How shall I say this? My body wanted you. My heart and mind were not looking your way. My focus is to find Sarah, and maybe find myself. I know who and what I am in Christ. But here, in this life, I don't know who I am. I have to find out. It may be connected to who Sarah is. I just don't know.

"Please understand when I say this. You and Mary are a burden and a blessing to me. That does not mean that you are a burden and Mary is a blessing. The two of you are a burden only in the fact that you have slowed me down in trying to get to Sarah as quickly as I can. But, you are a blessing in that it was and is God's purpose for me to find and rescue you. He planned my steps. I cannot rebel against what He has done. What Sarah will be to me is unknown. But I have to say that, yes, she was a protective wall between us that morning.

"I tell you all this for our protection. You are a new child of God, since you told me you believe. I have believed for more years, and have learned more of God and of Jesus. But we are both still subject to our passions. The Bible calls them the desires of the flesh.

"As a new believer, you have God's Spirit living in you. He will guide you, using God's Word. He will cause you to come to the Bible like Mary did, saying, 'More, please?' The Bible says we are to walk, or order our lives, being responsive to the Spirit's leading, so we won't satisfy the desires of the flesh. That we are to desire the pure milk of God's Word, so that we can grow.

"I told Tom Flannagan that I don't have God's sacrificial love for Sarah that would be the foundation of a godly marriage. Nor do I have that love for you. That is something I would have to grow into, like those clothes Mary is wearing. It would take time. But first, I have to find Sarah."

Jo sat for several minutes in silence. Then she said, "Thank you for sharing your heart, Buddy. I think I am starting to understand. I'll be careful. I'm sitting here behind you, but in my mind I'm hugging you. But it is a hug I would give to my brother, if I had one."

Buddy turned, and saw the tears on Jo's face. "You do have one. You are a child of God. So am I. You are my sister in the Lord."

Mary stood and asked, "Me, too? Are you my big brother?"

Jo and Buddy had been deep in their own conversation, and did not see Mary sitting and listening, with her eyes and mouth wide open.

Jo frowned at her sister. "You were not supposed to hear all that!"

Consternation spread over the face of the younger girl.

Buddy said, "It's all right, Jo. Mary has to know what lies deep within each of us, even though some of it will come to her later. Now, we'd better load up and hit the trail. Let me know if you want to stay at Fort Hall."

Jo gathered what was left to be packed, while Buddy prepared the donkey.

As they left the grove, Jo said, "I don't have to think about it. I've prayed about it. I want to go on. I don't know if any of the soldiers will have a Bible. I'm hungry."

Chapter 22

Buddy's talk with Jo set them on the trail too late to reach Fort Hall by sundown. The sun climbed higher in the sky, but the temperature hovered just below freezing. The Bear River ran through a gash in the earth, and as the land sank to meet the river, the trail clung to its banks, only occasionally crossing the river for easier paths. Along the river, it was willows, always willows. But a short distance from the water, it was lava, always broken lava. The lush Bear River Valley, beyond Soda Springs, was nearly barren, sparse vegetation clinging to a landscape of broken volcanic debris.

As the sun rose higher, Buddy peeled off his sweater. He said, "Why don't you give me those, and I'll stuff them back in the pack. We may need them another morning, but not now."

Buddy muttered, "I wonder if this is the cut-rock Tom mentioned." To the girls he said, "We'd better walk in the wagon tracks. The wagon wheel rims have crushed the lava to dust. If we walk any place else, it will wear holes in our shoes."

By midday, the sun had broken through the morning chill. The girls carried their hats, ready to cover their hair at a moment's notice, but hoping for a cool breeze that did not come. The trail through the lower Bear Valley wound through broken rock that had fallen from the sheer rock outcroppings. Scrub cedars and sage clothed the high ridges, but the wagons had struggled over and between naked rock that wasn't really rock. The valley was baked clay studded with pebbles. Sheets of fossilized snails cooked under the blazing sun.

Buddy saw Mary stagger, then start to wander away from the wagon tracks. She did not respond when he called her. "Hold the donkey, Jo. Mary's in trouble." He caught Mary by the shoulders and steered her back to where Jo stood, concern lining her forehead.

"Too hot," Buddy told her. He poured a cup of water, and poured it over Mary's head. Then he poured another, and forced sips between her dry lips. Pouring another, he handed it to Jo. "Drink this. I should have called a water stop."

Buddy caught Mary as she collapsed, and laid her in the shadow cast by the donkey. Lifting her head, he trickled another cup of water down her throat. She swallowed reflexively. He gave Jo another cup, then drank two himself. To Jo he said, "She did not have as much reserve as we did. We can't stay here. I'm going to load her on Trudge. You walk alongside, and steady her so she does not roll off."

He lifted Mary and draped her astraddle on the donkey, leaning her forward over the packs. He arranged her so her arms hung down over Trudge's sides. "Hold her arm, and let's go. When she soaks up that water, she should perk up. We'll look for some shade. I should have known better than to travel this wasteland in the heat of the day."

A mile later, they came to a cut in the rocks that cast a short shadow over the trail. A cool breeze came up from the river, and moaned through the broken cliff. Buddy lifted Mary from the donkey and propped her against a boulder. Jo held her upright, and Buddy poured another cup of water. He began to pour sips into the girl's mouth. Mary's eyes fluttered open, and she began to gulp the water. She stared blankly ahead, then blinked and focused on Jo's anxious face. "Did I fall?"

Buddy gave her a relieved smile. "No, you didn't fall, but you came close. Did you know you were thirsty?"

Still dazed, Mary shook her head. "No. I felt hot. I think I felt dizzy. Then it got dark. I called and called, but you didn't come."

Buddy and Jo exchanged glances. He said, "I'm sure you did. In your mind, anyway. You started to wander away. Do you remember me bringing you back to Trudge? You didn't fall until then, but I caught you."

Mary shook her head. "It was dark. Nobody came. I couldn't find you."

Buddy said, "Well, we found you. You sit here and let that breeze cool you. Then you are going to ride, and we will look for a place to camp. The fort can wait. When you want more water, you tell me, will you?"

Mary nodded, and closed her eyes. "I'm better. We can go, now. You wanted to reach the fort today."

Buddy felt her forehead. Her skin was hot and dry. "We'll rest, Mary. Jo, hand me her hat, please."

Buddy soaked the hat, and pulled it down over Mary's head. The dry air began to draw the water out, evaporation cooling the girl's head.

Mary sighed. Without opening her eyes, she said, "That feels cool. But the water you gave me tasted warm. Can I have some more?"

An hour later, the shadow of the cliff had stretched clear across the trail. Buddy felt the side of Mary's neck, and found it cool to the touch. Reaching under her hat, he felt her forehead.

"I think we can go, now. Let's stand you up, Kid,

and see how steady you are."

Mary stood without swaying.

Buddy lifted her onto the donkey. "Hold onto those packs if you need to. Jo, you stay beside her, just in case. I'll look for a place to stop for the night."

Their pace slowed to only about two miles an hour, as Buddy calculated it. As the sun fell toward the horizon, the temperature began to drop. Buddy found a valley with willows and a few stunted cedars. They apparently reached deep into rocky crevices. There was no spring.

"Well, girls, it'll be a dry and cold camp on hard ground tonight. But we'll make the fort tomorrow."

Jo said, "We are still slowing you down. Sorry."

Buddy shook his head. "No. It's the Lord's doing. He orders our steps, and He knows what He's doing. Let's rest Mary a bit, and we'll travel early tomorrow morning. We should be there by midday, before the sun gets too hot. It'll likely get really cold again tonight, but we'll cuddle close."

Jo cleared her throat. "I'll stay on my own side."

"Right. I'll take care of one side of Mary. You take care of the other."

Morning saw them up and on the trail before the

sun peeked over the ridge behind them. The land lay in somber shadows. The cedars on the ridges showed black against the cliffs that would awaken to daylight colors of red, buff and gray. Had there been any moisture in the air, frost would have covered the rocks.

Buddy had loaded the donkey. He whisked Mary off the ground, and put her on the bareback pad. "You ride, Kiddo. When you need a drink, I want to hear about it. How are you this morning?"

"I'm feeling better. I don't feel so weak. But my head aches."

"Well, I'm not taking chances. Let Trudge do the walking today."

Through the morning hours, they descended from the high altitudes of South Pass and Bear River Ridge. As the trail reached the lower elevations, the cedars closed in around them on the lower slopes. Knots of aspens and balsam dotted the hillsides and bottom lands.

A little after noon, Mary asked, "What's that white thing down there?"

They were approaching a long flat plain, and, looking ahead, they could see the adobe walls of Fort Hall shining in the sun about five miles ahead.

"That must be Fort Hall," Buddy answered. "One thing I've noticed out here. It seems like you can see forever. I'd say we are about five miles out, but it almost looks like we could reach out and touch it."

An hour later, Fort Hall did not appear any closer, or any farther away. It looked like it just hung there, a desert mirage, gliding away as they approached. Another hour, and they descended into a valley, where they lost sight of the fort. Climbing out of the gully, they were surprised to see it looming large before them, about one hundred yards away.

"We're here!" Mary murmured. "We really made it. A real building. I was so tired of nothing but rocks. Can we go in?"

The gate stood open. As they approached, a man in uniform came to the gate and watched them. Surprise showed on his face.

"Stragglers? Where on earth did you come from? Is there a train coming?"

Buddy shook his head. "No train. Just us. Can you take us in?"

"I'm sorry. Lieutenant Crawford. Edward Crawford. Yes, by all means, come in. All my men are out on patrol. Don't you know there's trouble afoot? I sent one patrol east to the pass, and another to Fort Boise. You might have seen the one I sent east."

"No," Buddy answered. "I did see their tracks.

Shod horses rode over the tracks of unshod horses."

Lieutenant Crawford nodded. "Yeah, there was a troublesome-looking bunch rode by here a few days ago. They didn't see you?"

"No. We hid pretty well."

Mary whispered, "Can we take off our hats? It's hot."

Buddy looked speculatively at the lieutenant, then said, "Yes. Take them off. Both of you."

Lieutenant Crawford gasped, squeezed his eyes shut, then looked again. "Girls! You dragged girls out here? Wait here, mister."

He walked to what looked like the best quarters in the fort, opened the door, and called, "Jenny! Company. Come on out here."

A tidy-looking woman of about forty came out, wiping her hands on her apron. She stopped on the porch. Seeing the braids, she said, "Where did girls come from?"

The lieutenant said, "Take them inside, Jenny. Tend to them."

His face was stern as he looked at Buddy. "I see only one bed roll. Where did you sleep?"

"With them." Buddy's gaze did not waver.

Lieutenant Crawford's eyes narrowed. "You fool! You drag them out over the hazardous trail, expose them to danger, and dare to tell me with a straight face that you shared blankets with them? If they were my girls or my sisters, I'd horse-whip you. They'll sleep in the house. You will sleep in the barracks. Pick any bunk. They're all hard. And rustle your own supper."

With a shrug, Buddy led the donkey in the direction the lieutenant had indicated. He opened the door, then tethered Trudge, and unloaded their packs, carrying them onto the porch of the bunk room. When everything was set aside, he led Trudge to the trough for water, then turned him into the corral. In the shed beside the corral, he found hay, and fed the donkey.

When he woke up next morning, he dressed, and stepped out into the early-morning chill. Lieutenant Crawford was waiting for him.

"Young man, why didn't you defend yourself yesterday?"

Buddy faced the officer squarely and said, "Because, Sir, it was indefensible. You were right. The Book tells us to avoid even the appearance of evil. What we had to do had a bad look to it."

Lieutenant Crawford approached, holding out his hand. "I spoke harshly to you yesterday. I ask your forgiveness. The girls shared their story with Jenny and me last night. If you can forgive my rash words, I'm proud to shake hands with a better man than I am."

Buddy took the offered hand in a grip of strong friendship. "No offense taken. You didn't call me half the things I've been calling myself. But now, if I may ask for some advice, what do I do with them? Can they stay here?"

Doubt crossed Lieutenant Crawford's face. "We stay here for another month, then we head back to Fort William on the Willamette. We are only stationed here during the emigrant season. We do not expect any more wagons this year. We'll fasten all the doors inside, and bar the gate.

"In the mean time, having Jo here would be nothing but chaos. I have a squad of single men here, young men. They would be like wasps at a picnic. All over her, and at each other. Jo does not look like that kind of girl to me. Besides, she is adamant that she is going on to Oregon. With you."

"I left Ohio July twentieth, I think it was. My route has not been direct. I've faced some obstacles, and I've lost track of the days. What is today?"

"September tenth. You are past the highest points with only some frost. But snow could fly at any point. You have the Blue Mountains ahead, then the high desert, then the Cascades. Don't go down the Columbia. If you leave Dalles City, go over the Barlow Trail to Oregon City. The Willamette Valley runs south from there."

Buddy saw Jo and Mary come out of the lieutenant's quarters. They looked more trim.

Crawford said, "I went to the sutler, and found small britches that fit Mary, and some that fit Jo better, without showing her to be a girl. Got a couple of shirts, too. Jenny gave Jo some of her spare flimsies. Couldn't do much in that line for Mary.

"You have a bag of jerky, and about a pound of salt. Oh, and I fixed you another soogan. I got Hudson's Bay blankets for them, and for you. How are you fixed for powder? I see you have a couple of guns."

Buddy looked his surprise. "How much do I owe for all of that?"

"Nothing. After what you've done for those girls, I think the government owes you. Powder?"

Buddy showed his amazement. "Nothing? But I have not done anything for the government. Oh, I have plenty of powder. I have not dared burn any. Those hills have too many ears."

Lieutenant Crawford said, "I'm not sure who stands higher, a deputy marshal or an army lieutenant. Who knows, you might out rank me."

Smiling, Buddy asked, "Do you trust in Christ?

Are you a believer?"

Crawford smiled. "I am."

"Then we are equal in God's eyes. Sinners saved by grace, and trying to follow as He leads."

The lieutenant turned, and started toward where the girls stood beside the loaded donkey. "I fixed your critter. Now, I have two things for you. This envelope is an official complaint against one Rube Weston. If you go to the Willamette Valley, go far enough south to find Joseph Meek. He's a U. S. Marshal. Give this to him. I want Weston found and arrested. He is responsible for some of the unrest among the tribes. He outraged a young girl from the tribe, and when a young man came looking for him, he knifed him. Add that to what the girls told you, Deputy Wilson."

He gave Buddy another envelope. "This is new orders for the patrol that went to Fort Boise. Sergeant Carroll is leading that one. He is due back here tomorrow, so you will meet him somewhere soon. Give him this. I'm ordering him to send three men back here on foot, and you and the girls are to take their horses. The patrol is to see you across Three Island Crossing, across at Fort Boise, and up to the Burnt River. The three men who walk back here will take fresh supplies and meet the patrol on their way back. As a government man, all of that is covered for you."

The two men reached the donkey. Jo and Mary stood smiling at Buddy, looking comfortable in their new clothes.

Lieutenant Crawford extended his hand again. His eyes caught Jo's as he said, "I'm proud to know someone who exhibits real manhood. Those knights of old were rascals next to you, Wilson. Guard these two...and I hope to meet you again. Now, push off. Keep your eyes open."

Crawford hugged both girls. "Jo, Mary, I wish Jenny and I could keep you. You are dear girls. Now, go be fellers on the trail."

Reaching into his possible bag, Buddy found his badge, and pinned it inside his jacket. He checked the loads in his revolver, and checked the caps. He untied the lead rope, and the three walked to the gate. Turning, the girls waved a farewell to Jenny, then to Lieutenant Crawford. Buddy gave a crisp salute, and they were off down the trail.

It was mid morning the next day when they spotted the dust of the approaching patrol. Buddy stopped the donkey, and waited. The sergeant leading the men held up his hand, and the patrol stopped ten yards in front of the three.

Handing the lead rope to Jo, Buddy stepped forward. "Sergeant Carroll?"

"I'm Sergeant Carroll."

Buddy handed him the envelope. The sergeant read the orders, a look of respect on his face as he glanced at Buddy. Then he said, "I have orders, and I am to take yours if the need arises, Sir." Without turning, he called, "Adams, Davis, Henrys. Front and center."

Three men rode to the front of the line as the sergeant turned his horse. "You three are to give these three your mounts. Take the empty pack horse, and report to Lieutenant Crawford. He will give you instructions.

"The rest of you are to follow new orders from the lieutenant. We are to see these three to the Burnt River across from Fort Boise. They are to be treated with utmost respect, at all times, no matter what. Deputy Marshal Wilson will have authority to issue necessary orders. Is that clear?"

"Yes, Sir!" A chorus of disappointed voices showed little enthusiasm for the change in orders.

The sergeant reread the orders, then said, "Jo, Mary, please remove your hats."

At the sight of their braids, an excited murmur ran through the line of soldiers. The sergeant bellowed, "Utmost respect! I want you to know from the get-go that you are escorting two young ladies. They are especially dear to Lieutenant Crawford. It would be most unwise to offend them in any way. Is that clear?"

The men sagged back in their saddles. "Yes, Sir."

To Buddy, Carroll said, "I suppose that donkey will pony. Leave your packs on him, and give him a fair lead. Ride up here with me. You don't have to eat dust all the way to Burnt River. We've camped along here, and as we take you there, we will use our existing campsites. We will put up a tent for the girls' latrine, and one for their sleeping quarters. They will have no cause for concern." His eyes swept the patrol.

Trudge had to trot to keep up with the horses, but he did not protest. Eight days later, Fort Boise was behind them. Sergeant Carroll bid them a reluctant farewell, and the men of the patrol appeared to Mary to be riding backwards as they headed back to Fort Hall, waving until they were swallowed by the vegetation across the river.

Afoot again, Buddy said, "All right, girls, hats on. You have to hide your beauty again. Unless we can shrink the miles, we still have about five hundred miles to go and who knows what knotheads lurk along the trail. Blue mountains, here we come."

Part Three

Oregon

Chapter 23

The Snake River had been sluggish in its quest for the ocean. Leaving the valley of the Snake had been a challenge for the wagon trains, but horses and the donkey easily climbed the portions that had been a challenge for the teams pulling wagons.

Sergeant Carroll had said, "This country is steeper than a cow's face." Buddy agreed.

High, steep-sided ridges towered above narrow ravines that passed as valleys. In contrast to the lazy Snake, the streams that fed it rushed and raged down the side canyons into the valley. The ridges were mottled with silvery sage, cedars that were so dark green they appeared black, and tawny bunch grass.

Carroll had pointed upstream where the wagons had followed the course of the Burnt River. "Take the right fork up there. You'll leave the river after about five miles, and climb a long hill. Then you'll drop down to a huge grassy meadow between here and the Blue mountains. You'll have rivers that you follow or cross all the way to the Columbia. Keep your canteens full, but you should not have any dry camps the rest of the way. Wish I could take you all the way, but we have another month at Fort Hall before we leave this wild country."

Ten miles up the canyon, after a particularly steep climb, Buddy stopped. The three stood panting, then sat on a rock ledge. "Steeper than a cow's face was right. I don't know about you girls, but my legs are really shaky." Buddy got up and got a canteen and their cups. "Time for a drink. We don't want Mary falling over the edge!" He winked at Mary, who stuck her tongue out at him.

"I'm keeping Trudge between me and the edge," she muttered.

Finally breathing more normally, Jo said, "That last few days were rather interesting. I think I had a veiled proposal from every soldier except Sergeant Carroll. Each one wanted me to know when he got out of the Army, and wondered where I was headed. Oh, they were very respectful. Maybe they just wanted to get a close look at auburn hair or hazel eyes. Some kept looking at my freckles."

Buddy grinned. "Wasps at a picnic."

Jo murmured, "I had fun with them. They didn't dare sting. When Weston looked at me, I felt...well, dirty."

Buddy tapped the money belt under his shirt. "I

have some unpleasant news for Mr. Weston, and a badge to back it up. Here's my plan. First, I have to find Sarah. I have to deal with Gilson. Before I can do that, I have to find a place to stash the two of you. Maybe there's an inn at Dalles City. Or a fort full of soldiers." He winked at Jo. It was her turn to stick out her tongue.

Buddy looked at Mary. "More water?"

Mary shook her head. "No, that was plenty. Those soldiers were funny. Some of them wanted to know how old I was. One even told me he would wait for me to get older."

Buddy laughed. "Desperate, aren't they?"

Jo asked, "How will you find Weston? Do you have to?"

Buddy looked her way. His gaze was direct, his face stern. "I have to. Point of honor. His trail of misery is too long already. He owes you. A wagon and team, six hundred dollars, not to mention the anxiety of mind and physical danger on the Platte. Besides, I have a warrant for his arrest. I'm supposed to take it to a U. S. Marshal in the valley. Joseph Meek. I heard that was where he was headed. So, yes, I have to. And I can't take you with me. When we get to Dalles City, I think you will have had enough of the trail.

"Where will you go?"

"Tom Fitzpatrick said they've cut a road over by

Mount Hood. The road drops down into Oregon City, and from there you ride south along the Willamette. Before they cut that road, you had to get somebody to raft your wagon down the river through the Columbia River Gorge. But you had to portage all of your stuff around the Columbia Cascades. A lot of people died trying to raft the river. I'll go over the mountain."

"Will you be gone long?" Mary asked.

"I don't know. Weston leaves a stink along his trail, the rotten odor of his wicked deeds. Plus, he can't hide that green wagon. Or the lop-eared mule. People see those details, and they stick in their minds. I'll find him. When is the question. I suppose it depends on how far south in the valley he went.

"We're already into September. It might be the end of October or even into November before I get finished in the valley. If I find your wagon and team, I may have to wait until spring to come back over the mountain, or even into summer. But, I will come back, and let you know what I've discovered. I might even bring you your six hundred dollars. Even if I have to take it out of Weston's hide." Standing, he held out his hands, and helped both girls to their feet. "Off we go. Let's get to the top of these stairs."

The wagon tracks led upward over a series of benches, then along a ridge before it dropped steeply into the canyon of the right branch of the

Burnt River. In the shadowy canyon they came to a wide cleared area where wagon trains had camped.

"We'll camp here, too." Buddy located an area where he could lay out their bed rolls, and set up camp. He paused in his work, listening, then said, "Hide in those cedars, girls! I hear hooves on the trail. They are coming this way."

He reached for the cape gun. The clatter of hooves got louder. A herd of over a hundred elk walked into the clearing. Seeing the camp, and Buddy walking toward them, the herd stopped. Buddy thumbed the hammer on the smooth side of the cape gun, and pressed the trigger. The walls of the canyon both amplified and contained the sound of the shot. Heads raised, and ears pointed forward, the elk stared, then whirled and thundered back up the trail. As their racket faded into the distance, Buddy called, "False alarm, girls. Come on out."

Pushing their way through the cedar branches, Jo and Mary stood looking wide eyed after the elk. Mary squeaked, "Those were really big! And their horns had lots of points. Would they hurt us?"

Buddy said, "I don't think they would attack us. But they certainly could. I guess it would not be wise to sleep on the trail. They might not watch where they are going. I would not want them to step on me!"

As they ate their supper of jerky soup, Buddy said, "I don't have a map of what the trail does now. Carroll said we would follow and cross a series of rivers. I'm guessing there will be steep ridges and canyons in between rivers, and there is supposed to be a large meadow with one lonely pine tree in the middle of it. Somewhere ahead are the Blue Mountains. And there is a really marshy valley. He said the trail goes around that, clinging to the slope around the edge. I don't know what comes first, or how far we'll get tomorrow. But we had better get some rest tonight. See you two in the morning."

As they started along the trail the next morning, they found they had camped almost at the edge of the large meadow, a high plateau laced by streams, and walled in by lowering mountains. In the middle, they passed a lone pine tree.

Twenty-five miles north of their morning start, they began to climb again through broken ridges, a giant stairway to a short timbered hogback. Then the trail dived into a steep-walled canyon. The many tree stumps and scattered branches testified to the terror of the pioneers as they hewed large pine logs to act as dragging anchors behind the wagons as they descended the steep chute to the creek below. At the mouth of the canyon, the total of the wagons could be counted by numbering the discarded logs.

The narrow gorge through which the creek flowed opened into another valley, flat and lush, some twenty-five miles long and fifteen miles wide.

Buddy announced, "We'll camp here. There's water and wood, and lots of grass I can cut for mattresses. Let's get a good night's sleep, and see if we can break through the mountains tomorrow. We have to be getting close to the Columbia, I think."

As he was preparing the campsite, Buddy tried to add up the rivers and creeks they had followed or crossed since leaving the Snake. Somehow, those waterways did not add up to enough miles. However he figured it, he still had at least two hundred miles to go.

Next morning, they followed the wagon tracks as they skirted the south rim of the valley, along the foot of the Blue Mountains. About noon, the trail veered abruptly west along what barely qualified as a river that oozed out of the valley, and entered a canyon that slashed through the Blues. The way was rough, the steep-sided Blues towering on both sides of the trail. Emerging from the canyon, the timbered slopes of the mountains gave way to a flat, sage-covered plain that stretched to the horizon. In the distance, the peak of Mount Hood stabbed the sky.

Buddy said, "There! That's where we are headed. Dalles City is just this side of that mountain. It looks close, but we still have days to go. Over a hundred miles, yet."

Mary asked, "Do we have to cross that tall mountain?"

"No. I will, but you will stay on this side. At least for now. We'll see what we find when we get there."

Jo asked, "Do people really live around there? Are there buildings?"

Buddy looked around. "There aren't any here. But Dalles City is the bottleneck on the trail. Folks have stopped there, waiting their turn to float down the Columbia. While they waited, some found places where they decided to live. Supposedly, there are farms and ranches, and they are building a town. There was a mission there, but not now."

They came to a point where the trail forked. One branch headed north, while the fresher tracks headed west. A boarded-up building stood at the fork. The weathered sign read, "Indian Agency."

"Come on, Trudge." Buddy tugged the rope to get the donkey moving. "It looks like nobody lives here, either. Maybe it's abandoned because of the trouble."

With the miles and hills already covered, the girls were tired. The miles were slower underfoot. It was four days later that they approached the Deschutes Crossing. Hearing Tom Flannagan's message, the ferryman charged ten dollars to take them across the river. From there, the ferryman told him, the trail was more a road, and more settled.

Buddy led the donkey along a road that was more than ruts. He was scarcely three miles from the Deschutes when he saw a two-story house set back to the south. Two barns stood back from the house. A split-rail fence ran along the road they traveled. Buddy stopped and looked over the field between the road and the house. It was cross-fenced, and in one portion, he saw a dozen horses. In the next section he saw the long ears of mules.

Nodding approval, he started toward Dalles City. He had only covered about a hundred yards, when he heard rapid hoof beats. A horse was coming across the field at a gallop.

"Hey! Hold on! You with the donkey! Wait!"

Buddy stopped, and walked over to lean against the fence.

The rider reined in, and sat leaning on his saddle horn, surveying Trudge. Then he shifted his gaze to Buddy.

"A mammoth jack. And a big one. Young. You just in off the trail?"

Buddy nodded. "We are."

"Have any trouble? Where's your train?"

"No train. I started on a mule, and ended up with

a donkey. No trouble that can be shared without a cup of tea."

"Tea! Out here? I haven't had a cup of tea since Noah was a sprout. Got any?"

Buddy laughed. "Yeah, I've got most of a brick left."

"Well, bring it in. Alice will be tickled. I'll add some venison stew, if you are hungry. Alice made a berry pie. Oh, I'm Ben Hollister. I breed mules. There's a gate about another hundred yards ahead. Meet you there."

Hollister stood waiting at the gate, holding it open. He had ground tied the mare, tossing the reins over her head to lie loose on the ground in front of her feet. Buddy led Trudge into the field, and when the gate was fastened, he held out his hand. "I'm Buddy Wilson." His proffered hand was taken in a grip that equaled his own. "Glad to meet you. Alice is your wife?" Ben looked to be in his early forties.

"Yes. We came here back in forty-two, and stayed. We wanted no part of that river. Some pulled the wheels off their wagons, built rafts, and floated downstream. The Columbia Cascades is a twisting, churning, boulder-strewn meat grinder. Once you're in, there's no getting out, until it spits you out at the bottom. We stayed here, and started this ranch."

As they approached the house, Buddy asked,

"Any kids?"

Hollister was silent for several steps. "We did. Three girls. They died on the trail."

"I'm sorry." Buddy looked around for a place to tie Trudge.

Hollister said, "Go ahead and unload your donkey here. We can put you up for the night.

"Besides, I want to talk business with you. Unload, and put the donkey over in that small corral by the barn. That's where I kept my jack. He got old, and died three months back."

Buddy winked at Hollister. "Makes it hard to breed mules, then."

"Very hard."

Buddy turned, took off the packs, and set them by the steps to the porch. Turning to Jo and Mary, he said, "Go ahead and take off your hats."

The girls did, and shook out their braids.

Hollister looked puzzled, and turning to Buddy, he said, "Girls?"

"Yes. I found them on the trail. North Platte. The older is Johanna, or Jo, for short. The younger one is Mary. Feeney. The trail took their folks."

"And you brought them all this way? Alone?"

"Yes. I'll let them tell you. It's their tale."

Hollister opened the door, and called, "Honey, set three more places for supper. And get out your tea pot!"

A kind-faced woman came toward them, then stopped. "Girls! Ben, where did you find them?"

"Out by the fence. They just appeared. I just picked them off the girly bush."

Alice laughed at his jest. "Can we keep them?" Her question was tinged with tears.

Sorrow lurked behind Ben's answer. "We might have to do some horsetrading. This is Buddy Wilson. He doesn't look like an easy mark. See if you can pry them loose with a piece of that pie."

Buddy smiled at her. "Deal!" He turned to Ben. "I'll tell you straight out, I shared blankets with them from the North Platte to Fort Hall. Jo and I kept Mary between us to keep her warm. I only had one soogan when I found them. I did not dishonor them, or my Lord, by taking advantage of them. If you have a bed for them, I'll sleep in the barn. I'd enjoy the clean smell of hay instead of dust."

Alice's face showed her concern and compassion for the girls. She drew an unsteady breath, then asked, "Where's that tea I heard about? The water's boiling."

Buddy went out to the packs, and returned with the tea brick and a bundle. He handed the tea to Alice, who stood inhaling the aroma.

"Oh! Good stuff!" She handed it back to Buddy. "You do the honors. The Book says 'he brews,' not she brews!" Alice's laugh was low and musical.

When the laughter died down, Buddy handed the brick back to Alice. "You go ahead. Make it the way you like it. Don't stint."

He opened the other bundle, and pulled out the dresses that had resided in the bottom of the pack. He handed one to Jo, saying, "You can be a girl now. You don't have to be a feller."

Jo shook out the folds of fabric, and held the dress in front of her. Tears ran down her cheeks, as she stood shaking her head. Her voice would not work. She mouthed, "Thank you." Then squeaked, "Oh, thank you."

Buddy turned to Mary. "Yours will be too big, I think, but maybe Mrs. Hollister can take it up and in for you."

Alice looked to Ben, who nodded. She went upstairs, and returned with her own bundle.

"Mary, we left our own dear girls buried on the trail. We only have their trunk of memories. We'd like to share with you. Here. Try these on. If you don't mind sharing with our little one, I brought you some of her underthings. They are clean."

Ben's voice was broken and husky. "Show them where they can change, Ma. I'll warm the stew."

Jo came down the stairs in frilled calico. She had brushed out her hair, and gathered it in ponytails on each side of her head. She wore beaded moccasins on her feet. She twirled around, ending in a pose with her arms outflung. "I ain't no feller!"

Buddy smiled. "Stay off the trail, looking like that!"

Mary came bounding down the stairs, ahead of Alice, who was smiling through tears. Ben saw a sprite in his girl's clothes, and slowly bowed his head. He groped blindly for his wife, and held her in a fierce embrace. "It's all right, Honey. And it is right."

When Alice could speak, she gasped, "Marty...doesn't need...them any more."

Chapter 24

Ben Hollister went to the barn after sunrise next morning. Buddy was already up and caring for the donkey. Hollister brought out a bucket with a measure of oats. "Here. Bet he hasn't had these for quite a while."

Buddy took the oats, and held the bucket out for the donkey to smell. Setting it on the ground, he said, "Not while I've had him. I caught him with cracked wheat in a cooking pot."

"How did you find him?"

"I didn't. He found me."

"How was that?"

Buddy recounted the killing of the buffalo, his capture and escape, and finding the wrecked wagon. He went on to describe how he planned to return to the trail, but his captors were coming back, and that steered his course around the Black Hills to the North Platte. When he got to the point of finding the girls naked and marooned on a gravel bar, Hollister cut in. "They told us that part last night. And I don't mind telling you, it was an emotional evening for all of us. I sure wish this world was full of men of your character. Like old Boaz, you covered them with your skirt. You shielded and sheltered them. You even fed them from the Word.

"Alice and I have been really mad at God since our little ones died. Last night tore all that down. My wife wanted me to thank you first off for what you have done for us. It was through what you did for Jo and Mary. We can pray again. We can go on."

Impulsively, Buddy reached and embraced the weeping man. "God's grace is sufficient for the deepest need. He may not do like He did for Job, and give you back more than you lost. But, He gave you Himself."

When he recovered from his emotional collapse, Hollister said, "Back to the donkey, though. How did you really get him?"

"I think he belonged to the folks I buried. He sniffed me awake when I was wearing a shirt from the wagon. He let me get a rope on him and tie it into a makeshift halter. I talked to him all through the process. I put my hands on his back to see if he might pack, and he did not object. Then I hopped up and lay over his back to see if he could be ridden. He danced a bit, but steadied. That told me that he was well trained."

Hollister leaned back against the corral fence. "Can we talk business?"

Buddy nodded. "What do you want?"

Hollister smiled. "Everything. I want the donkey. My wife and I want the girls."

Buddy said, "Let's go inside. If I'm going to bargain the girls away, they should be part of the discussion. But before we go, tell me if you know of a man named Gilson in these parts."

"Gilson? Elmer Gilson? I know he's here. Why do you ask?"

"I have a bone to pick with him."

"You and forty-'leven others, if they were alive to do any picking." Thinking back to the last evening's story, he asked, "Sarah?"

"Yeah. Sarah."

"Gilson has an inn and hash house down above the Cascades. There's a girl working there who's about Jo's age. Folks wonder about her. And him."

Buddy asked, "Where's his place? I'll tell you right now, I'm here to find her. She goes by Sarah. That may be her name. I have not seen her in the last several years. She was taken by Gilson, who told her he was her Uncle George. If I find her, I will take her from Gilson."

Hollister stopped, one foot on the bottom step. "The trail runs along the edge of the river, down beyond Dalles City. As you go, you will hear the roar of the Cascades. A couple of miles above the Cascades, the trail runs along the top of a bluff over the water. Folks have fallen into the churning water there, and were never seen again. His place is there in a clearing above the bluff. The girl cooks a good meal. I would not stay there, though. Gilson has a way of finding out what you are carrying, and getting it. It's rumored that once he gets what you have, you vanish. Let's go in."

Inside, Alice said, "Breakfast is on the table. Good morning, Buddy." Her glance conveyed honor.

At the table, Buddy asked, "Mind if I pray?"

Ben said, "Please do. We're just getting back on speaking terms with the Lord. We've been blaming Him for all our troubles. Guess we always look for somebody to blame, and hold the wrong one guilty."

Jo cringed.

Buddy prayed, "Father, You know our hopes and dreams, and our disappointments and sorrows. You direct our steps, and give light to our paths. We thank You for your grace, and ask that You give us understanding in the things that lie before us. We need Your wisdom, and the grace to accept all that we receive from Your loving hand. Thank You for all that is ours in Your Son."

With a chorus of 'Amens', they attacked a platter

of pancakes and a sizzling skillet of sausage patties.

After breakfast, Hollister said, "Now for negotiations. Buddy, I want your donkey. What do you want?"

"Fair enough." Buddy thought a moment, then added, "Straight to the point. I want the use of your best riding mule. Trained, and ready to head out over the Barlow Road. I'll trade you the use of the donkey for the use of the mule. If I don't get back here, the donkey is yours. Fair enough?"

Ben said, "I'll take it. I'm getting the best of the deal, though. If that donkey cooperates, I'll have a dozen young mules next year, and you will have the use of one. Done.

"Next, we want these girls of yours."

Buddy waved the words aside. "They are not mine. They are their own persons. But I know what you mean. I'm moving on. I have errands that will take me away from here. I can't take them with me. I need a place that is safe for them to live...to stay. I know this is not an inn." He put ten twenty-dollar gold coins on the table. "It costs money to keep them. This is to help with those expenses. They had six hundred dollars stolen from them, along with their wagon and team. That is part of my mission. The girls are destitute. All they have is what was salvaged along the trail, or given to them by the

Lieutenant at Fort Hall. I'll trade you the girls for keeping the girls. If you are agreeable, I may throw in Sarah for safe keeping as well."

Jo and Mary gaped at each other, then at Buddy.

Mary asked, "Do you mean we can stay here?"

Buddy smiled at her. "That is up to the Hollisters. If they want you, I think you can get all the hugs you need. You, too, Jo. I'm sorry if it looks like I'm bargaining you away without asking you about it, but I wanted you to be in on the discussion of what is going on."

To Ben Hollister, Buddy said, "There's another hidden part of this. Sarah sent a message to me by a man named Tom Flannagan."

Hollister exchanged glances with his wife.

"Tom and I have been on a sort of race. Gilson is planning to force Sarah into marrying him when she turns eighteen. Tom and I are racing to get to her before he can do that. If she will agree to have one of us, marriage will block Gilson in whatever his scheme is. I don't know where Tom is. I'm here, but I'm not staying here. My leading is to get Sarah out of Gilson's clutches, and find a safe place for her until Tom gets here. Then we can let the Lord work out the details with Sarah. Tom and I have agreed that neither of us has the love for Sarah that would honor God's purpose in marriage. But, bringing Sarah here is not tied to Jo and Mary staying here if you will have them."

Hollister looked across the table at the girls, then looked to his wife. "Alice, would these two ease the pain in your heart, or add to it? They could not replace our littles that have gone on ahead of us, and I don't think they would try. Could you endure seeing Mary in Marty's things? Could you love these two who have lost loved ones as we have?"

Alice dropped her face on her arms on the table. Her shaking shoulders showed her anguish. Jo got up and walked around to stand behind the weeping woman. She began to rub her shoulders, then her neck, and her temples. The storm passed, and Alice rose, turned and embraced Jo. Cheek to cheek, their tears mingled. Alice reached toward Mary, who stood and ran around the table to be gathered into the hug.

Her voice steady, Alice said, "I can. I will. By God's grace, I will."

Hollister said, "You are next, Jo. You were on the trail for weeks with Buddy. I know you admire him. If he brings Sarah here, would you see her as a rival? Could you offer her support and comfort? Could you learn to love her? Would you be willing to share a home with her? Perhaps a room, or even a bed?"

Jo looked startled. Sarah had been a protective wall between her and Buddy. Would that wall be protective, or threatening? She whispered, "Not my will, but Yours..."

Jo looked at Mary, then at Buddy. "Give Sarah a home. I will embrace her as a sister. I will accept her, as Christ has accepted me."

Hollister looked across to Buddy. "Negotiations closed. We get girls. I get the use of a mammoth jack. You get the use of a mule. Come on out to the paddock area. Pick your ride. I've got a saddle that will fit any of them. They are like peas in a pod."

Beyond the barn, Buddy walked to the gate, and entered the paddock area. As he had done on the way to Independence, he stood quietly leaning against the fence.

He made eye contact with each animal, looking for personality as well as physical traits. All of them stood quietly, ears cocked forward. Then one detached himself from the herd, and walked across the paddock, nodding as he came. He walked up to Buddy, tipped his head, and waited for Buddy to scratch his ears.

Standing back from the paddock, Hollister voiced his amazement. "Well, I never... He's the pick of the bunch! I always need a rope. How in the world..."

"I just wait."

Hollister said, "All right, you wait. I'll get the tack. But, he's been the most reluctant one when it comes to giving up his freedom."

Hollister returned from the tack room in the barn, threw the saddle over the top rail of the fence, and handed Buddy the bridle.

"What's his name?

Hollister laughed. "I call him Ben. That's because I can be a bit mule headed myself."

It was Buddy's turn to laugh. "I had a mule back in Ohio named Ben. It was short for Benedict Arnold. He could turn traitor at a whim."

Hollister was dumbfounded as he watched Buddy slip the bridle over the mule's head.

"I have to fight him to get that thing in place. He just opened his mouth, and all but put the bit in by himself! You might want to tie him before you put the saddle on. And boy, does he ever dance when you try to mount!"

Buddy ground tied the mule, took the saddle and swung it into place, murmuring to the animal as he worked. The mule stood still as he reached under and fastened the cinch, adjusted it, and mounted.

Hollister laughed. "Well, make a liar of me! I wouldn't have believed it unless I had seen it. I guess he's your mount, all right. Want to ride him around the paddock before I open the gate?"

"No, go ahead and swing it open. He's ready." Buddy reached down and patted the mule's neck.

"I'm going to ride down to the Cascades, and check out the lay of the land. It'll likely be dark when I get back. Don't wait supper for me."

Hollister watched as Buddy led the mule across the front pasture and through the gate. As Buddy mounted and reined the animal down the trail, Hollister muttered, "There's something special about that kid. Lord, keep him safe where he's going." He was startled at his own unaccustomed prayer.

Ten miles west of the Hollister ranch, Buddy rode past the abandoned Wascopam Mission, and surveyed the scattered buildings that made up what was called Dalles City. The burgeoning population of stranded emigrants had disbursed with the completion of the Barlow Road around Mount Hood, and the people who remained stretched the meaning of the word city. The tents and wagons that had housed the temporary population had moved on to Oregon City and beyond.

According to what Ben Hollister had told him, he had at least another thirty miles to go, if not a little more. He set a pace that would get him to Gilson's place about dark, alternately trotting and walking the mule.

The roar of the Cascades of the Columbia reached his ears as a low rumble miles before he reached the point where the river narrowed and plunged into a curving staircase of destruction. It grew to a roar as the trail edged closer to the bluff above the point where the rapids seized everything in the water and tossed it into the forest of cabin-sized boulders.

Above the trail, he saw the lights of the derelict building Gilson passed off as an inn. He rode slowly past, memorizing the paths and obstacles between the hash house and the trail. Then, riding a hundred yards upstream from Gilson's, he tied the mule, and walked back down and hammered on the door.

The man who opened the door was about Buddy's stature, but soft and slovenly. He looked Buddy over, then said, "Hungry? Come in and set. It's venison steak tonight. And beans. Everybody gets beans. A dollar for dinner. Got it on you?"

Without smiling, Buddy said, "I've got it."

"Long way down river. Cost you a bunch, whichever way you go. Rafts cost, and the road around the mountain is a toll road. Got that?"

"Yeah, I've got it. I'll make it there, and see what I can find for farming. What's a room cost here? It's getting dark."

"Room and dinner, five dollars."

Buddy pulled gold coins from his pocket, and placed a five-dollar coin on the table. He watched Gilson's eyes narrow. A girl stood in the doorway to the lean-to that served as a kitchen. Seeing her, Gilson's voice hardened. "Get this man his dinner, and be quick about it."

Buddy scowled. "Take it easy on her. Who is she, anyway?"

"None of your business. She works here." Gilson snatched the coin from the table. "Why do you ask?"

"No reason. Just a point of honor."

The sound of breaking dishes came from the kitchen.

With an oath, Gilson kicked a chair aside, and strode through the kitchen door.

The sound of a slap, and a stifled yelp brought Buddy to his feet.

He heard Gilson yell, "Dishes and dinner, wasted! I'll fix you, but good!

Buddy reached the kitchen in time to catch the raised fist, grabbing Gilson's wrist. "No, you won't!" With a twist and shove, he sent Gilson stumbling back against the counter. "Run, Sarah! Head up the trail! I'll catch up!"

Sarah darted through the doorway and out into the darkness, as Gilson growled, "I'll kill you for that!" He had seized the knife Sarah used on the leg of venison that lay on the counter. As Gilson raised the knife to strike, Buddy seized his wrist with a grip that snapped the bones. The knife clattered to the floor. Buddy released Gilson's arm, and his fist found the side of the man's jaw, stunning him.

Buddy jumped over the prone man, and hurried out the front door. He did not see Gilson scramble to his feet, and slip out the back door.

Buddy felt his way through the gloom under the timber and found the trail. He stumbled as he went down the low bank, but caught himself. Turning right, he walked upstream, barely able to discern the shadow of the trail from the shadow of the abyss.

As the trail swung to the edge of the bluff, Buddy heard a branch crack above him. With a curse, Gilson leaped from the bank, intending to thrust Buddy over the edge.

Buddy threw himself flat on the ground. Gilson stumbled across the trail and plunged over the edge. His bellowed curse was abruptly silenced in the chasm below.

Shaking, Buddy scrambled up. He heard only the roar of the rapids. He stood a moment, waiting for his eyes to adjust to the darkness. Cautiously, he called, "Sarah?"

A shadow detached itself from the darkness, a pale face visible in the gloom. "Buddy? You came! I knew you would. Oh, thank You, Lord."

Buddy reached the girl, and caught her in an embrace as she collapsed in uncontrollable spasms of weeping.

Buddy held her close. "You're safe, now. He's dead. He did to himself what he has done to so many others."

When Sarah's emotions calmed, Buddy asked, "Is there anything you want from this place?"

"No. All I have are these rags. He did not spend money on me. Oh, wait. Let's go back a minute."

Buddy waited in the dining area. Sarah came back with a leather bag. "He owes me this for years of slavery."

Buddy asked, "Is that all? Are you sure?"

"Yes. Let's leave this place. I'm free! Free!" She threw her arms around Buddy. "You came! Point of honor!"

Buddy released himself, and said, "Here's another point of honor." He seized the oil lamp from the table, and hurled it against the wall. Oil spilled over the wall and floor, and the burning wick began to lick up the pool.

"Let's go! We don't want to get roasted!"

They found the trail by the light of the blazing building. Up the trail, Buddy called, "Ben, where are you?" The mule snorted. "Here you are. Let's head back. I know you are tired, and it will be morning before we arrive. Poor mule. You'll have to ride double this trip. Come here, Sarah."

Buddy lifted Sarah up behind the saddle, and then climbed up in front of her. "Hold on. We won't go fast, but I don't want you falling asleep and falling off. Ready?"

Sarah muttered, "More ready than you'll ever know."

The sun was rising as they rode through Dalles City. Sarah's hands were clasped in front of Buddy, and he clutched them with one hand so she would not topple off the donkey in her sleep. He held the reins with the other hand. Sarah's head lolled against his back. He had held the mule to a walk, conserving his waning energy.

"Ten more miles, Ben, then you'll get an extra measure of oats. Nearly a hundred miles in twenty-four hours is too much to ask of you. And carrying both of us for half of it!"

Behind him, he heard a sleepy voice. "Hmmm?"

"Wake up, Sleepyhead. You are missing the scenery!"

"It's all the same. Wake me up when it's over."

"Wake up, Sarah. I have to talk to you."

"Comferble..."

"Wake up, or I'll have to make you get down and

walk. Then you won't be so 'comferble'. You don't have any shoes."

He felt Sarah stretch behind him. "All right. I'm awake. What do you want?"

Buddy said, "I have about five miles to catch you up. I'm taking you to a place where you will be safe. I've arranged for you to stay with the Hollisters."

"Hollisters? Gilson hated them. Said he was looking for a chance to... He hated them. How can I stay there?"

"They are good people, Sarah. They already took in, well, two girls I found along the trail. Jo is your age, and her sister, Mary, is about ten.

"Gilson was my first mission. Well, you were, but I had to deal with Gilson to free you. Do you remember Tom Flannagan?"

"Tom? Yes. He was kind. He stuck up for me. Gilson was going to kill him, but he left to go east. He must have found you."

"He did. Now listen. He said that Gilson was going to force you to marry him, or sell you to somebody who wouldn't marry you. Tom proposed a solution. I would start west, and he would finish his business in the East, then head back here. Whoever got here first would marry you, if you agreed, to save you from Gilson. We agreed that neither of us had the love for you that would honor God, but we would pray that He would grow us into it.

"Gilson's dead. You don't have to marry, until you are ready. I don't know where Tom is, but I do know that he is a good man."

"So are you..."

"Now. I have another mission. Point of honor. The Hollisters lost three daughters coming west. I'm guessing it was cholera. They want you, along with Jo and Mary.

"I am going over the Barlow Road to the Willamette Valley. There's a skunk there that needs skinning. Rube Weston."

Sarah gasped. "Weston? He and Gilson were thick as thieves. Gilson talked about selling me to Weston if I didn't marry him. Weston is supposed to be coming back here next spring. He went to the Willamette Valley to do something for Gilson. I'm not sure what it was, because they always whispered. But it wasn't anything honest. It was that, and money, that Gilson wanted. But Weston is coming back to get me."

Sarah could not see the hardening of Buddy's face. She did, however, hear the terse, "I see."

The last mile passed in silence. Arriving at the gate, Buddy said, "Hop down, Sarah. We're here."

He dismounted, opened the gate, and led Ben inside. When he had fastened the gate, he led the mule across the field, his arm around Sarah's shoulders.

"A house! A real house! And I can stay here?"

Buddy squeezed her shoulders. "Yes. Come with me while I take care of Ben. He took care of us. He deserves a bit of rest." He stripped off the saddle, and hung it on the fence, then draped the bridle over a fence post.

A door slammed, and Mary's voice called, "Buddy! You got back!" Then Mary stopped. "Sarah?"

Sarah smiled at the younger girl. "You must be Mary. Buddy told me about you. Well, a little. He said you and Jo would fill me in. Is there breakfast? I'm hungry!"

"There is! We were just about to give up waiting for you. Jo thought something bad had happened and Buddy was hurted."

Ben Hollister walked slowly to the paddock, Jo beside him.

Buddy said, "Ben Hollister, this is Sarah. Gilson is dead. Sarah has only these rags, but she has a good heart. Jo, this is Sarah."

Jo smiled, and reached out for Sarah, who stood with her head bowed.

Sarah whispered, "I'm all dirty."

Jo held her anyway. "If your spirit is clean, you are clean enough for me. Welcome. Can I have you for a sister?"

"Will you? Do you really want me?"

"Come with me. I think I have a dress that is just your size. Which is it first? Wash and dress, or breakfast?"

Chapter 25

Ben Hollister gazed at the girls standing before him. Breakfast over, Jo had insisted on serving Sarah. She had carried water to the copper tub, then boiled kettle after kettle until it was comfortably hot. While Sarah bathed, Jo and Alice sorted necessary garments to clothe her.

Hollister said, "Sarah, I've seen you down at Gilson's pig sty. He treated you like the swine he was. Looks to me like Jo has made a right pretty silk purse."

Buddy entered, and stopped, staring at the change in Sarah. Her brown hair fell in waves to her shoulders. Jo had brushed her own hair out, and looking at Buddy, she said, "Twins! Well, almost."

Buddy looked to Ben, and said, "Get out the shotgun!"

Hollister laughed. "They come close, but they can't outshine my Alice!"

His wife was just coming down the stairs. "Oh, you! They're far more lovely than I am. You're just trying to butter me up."

"No Ma'am. I couldn't hold on to you then."

Sarah turned to Jo. "That bath was...glorious, as Grandma Wilson used to say. But you didn't have to wait on me. It was pleasant, though, to have somebody else fetch things. That always fell to me."

She glanced at Buddy, then said, "It was good to have a bath and get dressed without anybody spying on me. Gilson was always sneaking up and watching. Then he brought Weston. Even when I was dressed, Gilson was always undressing me with his eyes. Whenever he looked at me, I felt...well...violated."

Jo reached and touched Sarah's shoulder. "I know that feeling. Whenever Weston looked at me, I felt dirty all over. Buddy never looked, even when he found us with, um, nothing to wear."

Sarah looked at Buddy, catching a stern look on his face. "With Buddy, it would be a point of honor."

Buddy smiled at her. "It was. Grandma Wilson drummed respect for ladies into me. I don't think she ever got over us wading in No Name Creek, leaving our clothes on the rock."

Sarah said, "He never looked even when Grandma washed me in front of the cook stove. But Gilson..."

Buddy clipped his words. "It's a good thing he's washed down the river. I'd be tempted to go back and kill him again!"

"Buddy!"

"You're right, Mary. That was the desires of the flesh talking. Sorry. The Lord does not find delight in the death of the wicked. I shouldn't either."

"But Sarah, Jo, you both need to change your focus. What Weston and Gilson did, or might have done, is past. God will overshadow it over time, as you come to see what He has done for you. Where's the Bible I loaned you, Jo?"

Mary scampered up the stairs, and came running back down. "Here it is!"

Buddy opened it to Isaiah 61:3. "Girls, God has done for you what He plans to do for others. Read this. Out loud." He pointed to verse three.

Jo started to read, "To appoint unto them that mourn in Zion, to give unto them beauty for ashes, the oil of joy for mourning, the g-garment..of p-praise..."

Her voice faltered.

Buddy finished the verse. "...the garment of praise for the spirit of heaviness; that they might be called trees of righteousness, the planting of the LORD, that He might be glorified."

Both girls slowly smiled through tears. Jo said, "He has... Thank you, Buddy."

Ben Hollister asked, "What's next for you, Buddy?"

Buddy's voice was grim. "Weston."

Jo's eyes were wide and troubled as she looked at Buddy. "You're going after him? Like Gilson?"

"Jo, yes. I'm going after him. But know this. Gilson killed himself. I didn't do it. Sarah can tell you. What he did to others came back on his own head. I have an arrest warrant for Weston. I'll find him. Somebody else will hang him."

Sarah looked puzzled. "An arrest warrant? Are you a sheriff?"

"Deputy U. S. Marshal."

Hollister hid his smile behind his hand.

Buddy drew back his jacket. Inside, Sarah saw the badge. She looked at him with mingled fear and respect. "Were you going to arrest Gilson?"

Buddy nodded. "I was. I was baiting him."

Sarah's face clouded. "And me? He did all the killing and robbing. I didn't help him."

"No, Sarah, not you, point of honor. I came to arrest Gilson, and rescue you."

Sarah relaxed. "I really didn't do the bad stuff, Buddy. Honest. He beat me and locked me up when he went out. He would make flimsy rafts and sell them for a bunch of money, and send people down the rapids. Then he would go down and poke through the stuff at the bottom of the Cascades, and bring up what he thought he could sell to the next wagon train. He made me wash and dry what was useful. But I didn't help him."

Buddy crossed to Sarah, and held her close, looking over her head at Jo. When Sarah quieted, he signaled Jo to come, and eased Sarah into Jo's arms. Stepping back, he said, "Your hands are clean, Sarah. As clean as your heart. I wish I could bring back the lost years, and you could live them differently. But our Father can use even the hard things in making you more like His Son. He does not waste anything. Knowing what she knows, Jo can be a better comfort to you. She has had some rough patches in her own life."

With brimming eyes, Jo nodded, then rested her chin on Sarah's shoulder as the girl clung to her. "I have. I can, and I will."

Hollister asked, "What's your plan, Buddy?"

Glad to change his focus, Buddy said, "I used up that mule on this trip. I didn't push him, but it was a long grind, even for a mule. I'll rest him up a couple of days, feed him up for the next trip. I'll sort the stuff in the packs, and slim down the load to the necessary things. I don't think I'll need a map. The tracks should get me where I'm going.

"When I get to Oregon City, I'll start asking questions. Green wagon? Lop-eared mule? I'll run him down. I'll tell him about Jo and Mary."

At Jo's horrified expression, he said, "No, Jo, he won't come back here. That will just be to expose him. If he insisted on coming back here for you, I'd pull out Lieutenant Crawford's warrant. Joseph Meek would have to deal with him. He would not survive a trip back here to lay claim to you."

Anxiety faded from Jo's face. "I couldn't face him."

"You won't have to. Trust me."

Hollister said, "Buddy, let's you and me walk out to the barn." Outside, he faced Buddy. "Remember, my friend, that vengeance is in the hands of the Lord. Don't try to do His job."

Buddy nodded. "I know that. But when it comes to what the Gilsons and the Westons of this world do to the likes of these girls, well, my flesh wants to take over."

Hollister put both hands on Buddy's shoulders. "The Book says that whoever digs a pit will fall into it, and a stone will come back on whoever starts it rolling. Just be sure that man isn't you."

"You'd best pray for me. Weston as good as killed Jo and Mary, leaving them out there to die, and stealing their stuff."

"Yes, but the Lord used you to keep them alive. That was His work. So is this trip you are taking. I want you to come back here, and I want you to come back with clean hands. Got that?"

Buddy nodded. "We saw the reality of that verse you quoted in Gilson's end. The rock Weston rolled might get him at the end of a rope. I won't take that into my own hands, as much as I want to. Thanks."

In the barn, Hollister surveyed Buddy's supplies. "The jerky is good. That soup mix was a great idea. Think I'll try that myself. That would make a good winter supply to keep on hand. But will that be enough? It will, if you are not gone until spring.

"Guns are good, bedroll's good, especially those Hudson's Bay blankets. Eating supplies, fire makin's... Got a slicker for rain? It does get wet on the other side of the mountain."

"You don't need to tell me about rain!" Buddy recounted the torrential rains and floods back in Ohio. "But, no, I don't have a slicker."

"Take mine. I have a greatcoat that I can use if it gets rainy here. That does not happen often."

"Thanks." Buddy held his hands out to his sides.

"No rain today."

Hollister went on, "You and I are about the same size, like Sarah and Jo. I'll rustle you a change of clothes. You are here, so you know how to survive on the trail. You won't have hostiles on the Barlow Road, but you could run into bandits."

Buddy laughed, but there was no humor in it. "Ask Jo about bandits!"

Hollister laughed. "Yeah, she likely has enough stories to entertain us hours on end."

"Well, don't let her embellish them. Half of what she tells you just might be imagination."

"Well, Buddy, from what I've seen of you, I think I'll double whatever she says. If she holds back, I'll ask Mary."

Buddy groaned. "Oh, no. I'm in for it now!"

Three days later, Buddy rode out onto the trail again, headed for Dalles City, and the junction of the Barlow Road. Since the mule had worked long hours and miles to and from the Cascades, Buddy held him to a steady walk, and covered the often-hazardous Barlow Road in five days. The toll stops along the road were closed for the coming winter, but at the Oregon City end, he paid what was due.

He asked, "Did you have a short wagon train through here lately?"

At the positive answer, he continued. "Was there a green wagon in it? The off lead mule should have had only half an ear on the right side."

"Green with a half eared mule. Yeah, I remember that. Really stood out among all the traffic I've seen come through in the last several years. Potential buzzard bait driving?"

"You pegged it. Know where that wagon headed?"

"South. How far, I don't know. Looking for someone?"

Buddy turned back his coat, showing the badge. "Yeah."

The toll taker held out his hand, and gave Buddy's money back. "No charge for you. Hope you catch that guy before he causes somebody grief."

Grim-faced, Buddy said, "Too late. That wagon was stolen from a couple of orphaned girls he left to die on the trail."

The toll taker uttered an oath, and kicked a rock into the ditch. "Need some rope? Bring him back here, and I'll help. Poor kids. Did they die?"

"No. I found them. They were ready to, though."

Respect flooded the man's face. "I'm glad. But hang him anyway."

Buddy waved as he started forward. "I'll leave that to Joseph Meek."

"He'll do it, all right. Good luck finding the skunk."

As Buddy rode south, traces branched off the trail, but the main route was clear. The area was more settled. At Champoeg, he found a general store. He asked the storekeeper his usual questions.

"Green wagon, yes. Guy was heading down to Lee's Mission area. I even recall the mule."

Buddy recounted his conversation with the toll taker at Oregon City.

"Meek was through here day before yesterday. And, yeah, he has little patience with such as that."

Two days behind Meek, Buddy headed south.

The next day, Buddy stopped at a general store on Mill Creek. Tied at the rail, he saw Smokey. As he dismounted, the mule cocked his ear and a half at Buddy. "Too easy, my friend. I was supposed to have to search all over Salem for you."

He entered the store, and asked the storekeeper, "Where might I find Joseph Meek in this town?"

The man pointed. "Over there at the table. Dealing cards."

"Know who's riding that ear-and-a-half mule out there?"

"The guy across from Meek. Rusty hair. Why?"

"I have a bone to pick with him."

"Go easy. He's a rough customer."

Buddy walked over to the table, and stood looking at Weston, who finally looked up.

Buddy asked, "You riding that mule with half an ear?"

"Yeah. What's it to you?"

"Where'd you get it?"

"None of your business."

Meek looked up, interested in the direction of the conversation.

Buddy said, "I'm making it my business. Where'd you get it?"

Weston stood. His hand hovered near his belt.

Buddy said, "That mule belongs to Johanna Feeney."

"She's dead."

"She's waiting for you in Dalles City. You left her to die. I found her and Mary, and I took them as far as Dalles City. You arranged to marry her.

She's there."

Weston sneered. "You bedded her all the way to Dalles City, and now you want me to clean up your mess? I ain't taking on any of your whelps."

Behind the counter, the storekeeper shouted, "Take it outside, you two!"

Buddy backed toward the door. "I ought to blow the teeth out of your mouth for that."

Meek had risen, his narrowed eyes regarding Weston, who was inching toward Buddy. He said, "Go easy, Weston."

As Weston turned toward Meek, Buddy turned his coat back. Meek saw the badge, and gave a slight nod.

Buddy continued, "You outraged a young Indian girl out of Fort Hall, and knifed the kid who was saving the bride price for her. Lieutenant Crawford wants to talk to you."

A deep scowl clouded Meek's face.

Buddy had reached the door, and he turned to step outside.

Meek yelled, "Knife!"

Weston had pulled his knife, and rushed toward Buddy's back. At Meek's warning, Buddy dropped to the boardwalk. Weston's foot caught Buddy's hip. His momentum launched him across the walk, and into the street. His yell ended in a fluttering explosion of air. He rolled to his back, a blotch of crimson spreading across his shirt. His mouth was working silently, and his heels were drumming on the street. He arched his back, then fell limp.

Joseph Meek had followed Weston as he stumbled into the street. Now he kicked the closest foot. "Dead. Fell on his own knife."

"Like old King Saul."

"Who?"

"King Saul in the Bible. He didn't want to be taken, so he fell on his own sword."

"Well, he knew me well enough to know he was a dead man. I'd have hung him on account of the Indian girl. He wanted to take you with him."

Meek walked to where Buddy sat, and helped him to his feet. "Deputy? Deputy who?"

"Buddy Wilson, Sir."

Buddy showed him his badge again. "Know Jackson Wiggins in Ohio?"

"I do. Did he deputize you?"

"Yes. He said it should be good here. I have a warrant for Weston's arrest from Lieutenant Crawford here." He pulled the envelope from his pocket.

Meek nodded. "Won't need that, now. Come in the store, Wilson, and sit down. You look a bit shaky. We'll talk in there."

Seated, Meek said, "All right, spin me a tale. Who's Johanna Feeney? How does she tie in to this wagon and mule?"

At the end of the account, Meek sat silent. Then, he mused, "Weston came here in a green wagon. He had a team including that half-eared mule. An old timer east of town was ready to retire, and wanted to sell his claim. Weston paid him six hundred in gold, and took the fellow out to his cabin to get his stuff. If that money was stolen from the girls, I'll make the place over to them."

Buddy said, "They aren't old enough. Jo is only seventeen, and Mary is ten."

Meek said, "I'll add your name to make it legal. Here are your orders, Deputy. Ride out to the claim, and take the half-eared mule with you." He pulled the stub of a pencil out of his pocket, and a dirty scrap of paper. He drew a map, and handed it to Buddy. "This'll get you there. It's a good place. House, barn, the works. Come back and tell me what you find there."

He walked out to the street with Buddy. A wagon had pulled up in front of the store. Meek said, "Hold on a minute, Jake, before you haul this carrion away. I'll want to rummage through his pockets."

Meek found a key, and tossed it up to Buddy. "Front door. All right, Jake, I'll help you load. Just leave that knife sticking in him."

Buddy fished a coin out of his pocket. "Here, Jake. Take this. I'm the one who baited him into this. Don't leave his feet sticking out."

The two men loaded the corpse, and Jake trundled Weston to the burial ground, chuckling as he went. "Don't leave his feet sticking out." He shook his head.

Chapter 26

Buddy led Smokey out away from Mill Creek, and headed for the hills east of Salem. The map led him to a wagon trace that followed a stream, then turned to climb a gently-sloping ridge. Rounding a curve in the lane, he saw a point of the hill above a long valley. A house stood on the point, with a barn and another outbuilding lower in the valley. A green wagon stood by the barn. Three mules watched their arrival from the pasture below the barn.

"Well, mule, we're here. Let's get all of you together." He led Smokey and Ben to the barn, and let them drink at the trough. He tied Ben, removed the halter from Smokey, and turned him into the pasture. In the barn, he pulled the saddle from Ben, and removed the bridle. On a ledge, he found a curry brush, and gave the mule a rub down. He put him in a stall, and gave him oats and hay.

Having cared for the animals, Buddy turned to the house. The key worked the lock easily, and he entered. The house was not stale. He walked slowly through the rooms. On the chest in the big bedroom, he found a leather pouch. Emptying it, he counted six hundred dollars in gold. He stood gazing out the window. He gathered the gold and dropped it back into the bag.

In the trunk he found the clothing of a small-statured man, certainly not clothes that would fit Weston. Everything in the house indicated an elderly owner of long tenure.

Buddy went outside, and walked slowly around the house. All seemed in order. He went back to the barn, and as he passed Ben's stall, he rubbed the nose the mule extended, begging for a treat. "Next time, you mooch!"

In the back stall, Buddy saw a chest and other belongings, apparently taken from the wagon and stashed in haste. He opened the trunk, and found clothing for a man, a woman, and girls. He shook his head. "The Feeneys' stuff."

In the tray of the trunk was a Bible. On the family page, he read: "John Feeney and Elizabeth Martin, married December 25, 1831. Next was: "Johanna Ellen Feeney, born March 29, 1833." Below that, he read: "Mary Elizabeth Feeney, born March 14, 1841."

Buddy reverently closed and replaced the Bible. He started to examine the other things carelessly piled in the stall. Under hay behind the trunk, he found the body of an elderly man, wrapped in a blanket. Buddy pulled the blanket open. The old man had been stabbed.

Buddy shook his head. "He didn't even have the decency to bury you!"

Buddy dragged out the harness, and led the mules, one by one to the front of the wagon. When they were buckled in, he pulled the trunk aside, and carried the body out and laid the man in the wagon bed. He released the brake, and twitched the reins. "Let's go. 'Tis a dismal errand you have today!"

Meek was just leaving the store when Buddy drove up.

"Got something for you here. And for Jake." Buddy told the Marshal what he had found at the house. "He bought the place for six hundred, right?"

Meek nodded. "Yeah."

"Then he killed him for it. Hid the body in the barn. The bag of gold was on the trunk in the bedroom. He must have robbed somebody else, because I know he spent part of it on the trail. Everything in the house belonged to the old man. Where do I go with him? He needs a decent burial."

Meek said, "Wait here. I'll send for Jake. I think he's still planting Weston."

Buddy snorted. "He should toss Weston down by the stable, and bury him as he cleans out the stalls."

"I'd do just that." Joseph Meek grinned. It was not a pleasant smile. His eyes flashed as he said again, "I'll send for Jake."

Buddy hesitated, then asked, "Who owns that closed-up place next to this fellow's place?"

Meek smiled. "I do. Or Oregon does. Or the government does. The folks who developed it proved up, but did not pay up. Instead, they packed up and disappeared. The land and improvements reverted. Interested?"

"Maybe. What would it take to get my name on it?"

Meek scratched his chin, hidden beneath a forest of whiskers. "Well, the old man had a quarter section, and he sold it for six hundred. This is only an eighty, and the house is smaller. It does have a barn and a chicken coop. Oh, and an orchard. Those trees should be just about ready to start bearing. So, let's say, well, two fifty or three hundred... Two fifty, and it's yours. Gonna take it out of the girls' money? I'm thinking that it is theirs."

Buddy shook his head. "No. That's theirs. I won't rob them. They get all of it. Every dollar."

"Good. Glad to hear you say that. Make it two hundred even. Come in tomorrow, and I'll have all the papers ready. If you were going to use their money, you wouldn't have got anything. I like dealing with an honest man."

Buddy headed for the entrance to the store. "I'll do a bit of supply buying while you wait for Jake. Then I might load up the stuff that belongs to the girls. We have a bit of October left. I think I'll try to get back to Dalles City before the year gets much older. The road was open when I rode in. If I wait much longer, it might be June before I can get back over the mountain."

Joseph Meek said, "Or July. Or August. Might be you'll only get rain up on the top of the road through November. Or you might get twenty feet of snow. I'd try it.

Buddy thought a minute, then asked, "Could you keep an eye on those houses? Somebody might get here come summer. Don't know if you ever met Tom Flannagan. He might move into one of them."

"Flannagan? You know Tom? Be glad to watch things for a man like Tom."

Buddy pulled a twenty dollar gold coin from his pocket, and handed it to Meek. "Here. For your trouble."

Meek said, "You throw gold around like skipping stones on a pond. I'll take it, though. Thanks. Now go give some gold to Richardson. He's likely got everything you need, and a lot of what you don't need."

Buddy heard Jake drive up, and went out to meet him.

Jake said, "You again. You sure are keeping me busy!"

"Not me. This is on Weston, your last customer. But here. This man deserved better than he got. Put him in a box, not just in the dirt." He handed Jake more gold.

Jake said, "You hang around here, I'll die a rich man. Might not be much left of the town, though. Folks dropping like flies, they are."

Buddy wandered through the store, picking out things that might not be available in Dalles City. He picked out a bolt of calico, a bolt of gingham, and a bolt of plain linen. He added spools of thread, and the last three bricks of tea the store had. Tinned goods, large lumps of sugar, bags of flour and oats all disappeared into the wagon box. Lamp oil, candles and soap he tucked under the seat. The storekeeper looked wide eyed at the total. Buddy pulled the gold from his possible bag, and settled the account.

Back at the house, he rearranged the goods so he could load the girls' trunk. Jo had said the gold was in the tray. He retrieved the bag of gold coins from the bedroom, and laid it in the tray with the Bible.

Buddy was just tacking a canvas tarp over the wagon box when Joe Meek rode up, accompanied by another man.

"Park it in the barn, Wilson," Meek said. "You

won't be going over the mountain for a while. Tell him what you found, Jones."

The man named Jones said, "I made it over the Barlow Road, but barely. Storm came through, and there are hundreds of big trees blown down. I had to leave my horse up at the last toll station. Don't know how I'm going to get him. Road's closed. I did the last fifty miles or so on foot, climbing over tree trunks, sometimes trees on top of trees. There are maybe three or four places where there are trees down across the road between here and Oregon City. They're starting to work on clearing, but it is going to take months."

Meek said, "Park the wagon where it won't get wet. No need to unload it, if you still plan to go back. Barlow Road is one way, east to west. They built it so's wagons could come from Dalles City to Oregon City. They didn't figure on anybody heading the other way. There are places up above where two wagons can't pass. Maybe you'll be able to get through before the wagon trains try to come west. But you won't get through before spring. If it's a mild winter, you might try it in April. Thought I'd let you know before you took off. By the way, here's the key to the Roberts place."

"Roberts?" Buddy looked puzzled.

"The house and eighty you wanted. Look it over. I've got the papers ready. See you at the store.

Table there is my official desk. You'll need some supplies, seeing as you are going to be spending the winter here."

Buddy sighed as he walked around to the front of the wagon. He groaned as he lifted the wagon tongue and leaned it against the front of the driver's seat. Without turning, he said to Meek, "I'll be in tomorrow morning. I'll stay here, but I don't have to like it."

Meek chuckled. "Well, a winter here, and you might like it better than over the mountain. Gets right cold over on the other side. It's wet here, a bit, but we get supplies by ship, instead of by wagon train. Things cost less on this side, and there's more to choose from. Think about that. You might want to unload some of the supplies you loaded to take across, and leave them here. Bring Sarah over here. Tom, too, if he shows up. Think about that."

Buddy tended to the needs of the mules. He surveyed the hay supply with a critical eye. To Ben he said, "Looks like I can feed the lot of you until about May. Grass should come in before that, so I can save some hay for the trip over the mountain. There were places where you would have to scrape the moss off the rocks."

Buddy walked back to the house, and circled it, inspecting it like a denning bear. The roof was sound. Rain would drain away from the ground around it. Flagstones formed a walkway from the door to the barn where the mules were. Altogether, it was a well-built abode.

Inside, Buddy went to the kitchen to take inventory against tomorrow's shopping. In the cupboards, he saw an array of tinned goods, as well as jars of jam and preserves. One cupboard had cloth bags of dried beans, rice, cracked wheat and barley. There were jars with dried fruits of several kinds, and two large bottles of honey. Bins held sugar and flour.

"Well, whoever he was, he was well stocked." Buddy opened drawers, and discovered more utensils than he had seen in Grandma Wilson's kitchen. Pots and pans hung on hooks above the cook stove. "Guess I'd better learn to cook. Too bad Sarah can't see all of this."

The thought of Sarah brought him back to his disappointment. "Lord, I'm rebelling against what You have ordained. I'm wanting my will, not Yours. I need Your wisdom and grace in this trial. Or, maybe it isn't a trial. Could You help me see the blessing here, and the path ahead? Is this consistent with all Your Son is? I know that is what He meant when He said to ask in His name."

Buddy turned to the kitchen counter. He had never seen a sink and faucets. The Wilsons did not have such things, nor had the Hollisters. Intrigued, he twisted the handle on one faucet. Water gushed into the sink. Looking under the counter, he saw pipes. One turned toward the cook stove.

At the stove, Buddy took the lifter from the wall. Opening lids, he found the firebox under four of them. On the right side, a fifth lid concealed a water reservoir. There was a valve on the side of the stove. When Buddy turned it, water gushed into the reservoir. "Hot water! I wonder where that pipe goes?"

A door opened off the kitchen. Opening it, Buddy saw an enameled tub with faucets at one end. "A bath tub? Boy, if Sarah could see that! Jo wouldn't have to carry water!"

A wooden tank hung on the wall, with a chain hanging from it. A stool stood beneath it. Buddy pulled the chain, and water gurgled down the pipe to the stool. He opened the lid in time to see water swirl out of the bowl. "I know what that's for. I've never seen one, but it sure will beat running to the back house all winter!"

In the fading afternoon light, Buddy went outside to find where the water was sourced. In a grove up behind the house, he found a spring with a pipe running from its pool toward the house. The spring overflowed the berm that trapped the pool, and the extra water flowed down toward the barn and into the valley. Looking at the house, Buddy saw a tank he had missed seeing on his earlier inspection. The spring was higher than the tank, and gravity pushed the water through the pipe on the wall, filling the tank. An overflow pipe ran down the wall, and apparently filled the trough by the barn.

"The man thought of everything! Water in the house and the barn. Hot water, and an indoor privy. He bought it, then the girls' money bought it." He stopped. "All this belongs to Jo and Mary! And they even got the money back. The farm, and the money! They are back in Dalles City, paupers, with riches laid up for them here in the valley. And I can't get to them to let them know."

Light rain fell the next morning as Buddy saddled the mule to ride to town. He shrugged into his slicker, mounted Ben, and rode out of the barn. The mule was reluctant. "I know, Ben, but at least the saddle will keep part of you dry. Someone should invent a tent you could wear, so your shelter would keep up with you."

He tethered the mule, then flung the water from his hat. Entering the store, he hung his slicker on a peg near the door. Meek sat at his table.

"Well, Deputy, any more carcasses to plant today?"

"Not that I've found. But say, who was that last one yesterday? I don't even know whose house I'm living in."

"Simon was the name. Walter Simon. Smart man with an eye for convenience, he was. He built well, and he put stuff in that house very few in this valley have. He had the sweetest water in that spring. He had the money to do things really well. His wife died last year. Old age, I guess. She wasn't sick a day, far as I know. Once she was gone, he kinda gave up. That's why he sold. Might have been a relief for him when he got stabbed. Look around that house. I think he had a coin or two stashed somewhere."

Buddy mused, "Walter Simon. English, I'd say. I looked at his supplies. He had enough to keep me going until spring. I'll have to look for tea, though. He must have had some. He even rigged hot water in the house! In the kitchen, and in a bathtub. I'm going to get soft. No more cold baths in the river or creek!"

Meek laughed. "That was for Eldora. She was a mousy woman, and he wanted everything comfortable for her. Good woman." Joseph Meek's voice trailed off. "My wife was a good woman. My girls..."

Buddy looked away. The hard, gruff Joseph Meek had a soft spot, after all.

"They were killed back in forty-seven at the Whitman massacre." It was as if there had been no break in Meek's account. "My wife died, too. Not there. She was a girl from the tribe. That's why I said I'd hang Weston on account of the Indian girl."

Buddy nodded. "Men ought to take care of girls,

not abuse them. But some men are without honor."

Meek suddenly straightened, and gathered the scattered papers before him. "Here are the documents we need to sign and record. You sign here on this one. That gives the Simon place to you. I put it in your name, but we can change that if you have somebody else to add. On this other one, for the Roberts place, I forgot who you wanted on it, so it is in your name, too. You are not filing a homestead claim, so there is no problem with you having so many acres. You bought the existing claims." He looked at Buddy. "You are of age though, aren't you?"

"I'm twenty-one."

"Good enough. Sign those papers, and give me a couple of those gold coins for filing them. Then be on your way. The rain is going to get heavier. I have a barometer in my joints."

Buddy bought matches and candles, and a couple of extra oil lamps. He added a slab of bacon, some butter, and a smoked ham. Richardson said, "I have two brined chickens. Want one of them?" Buddy added the bird to his supply. The chicken he would cook today, and the ham would keep. He wondered if Simon had a built-in springhouse. He would have to look. With all the other things in the house, there just might be a place to cool the perishables.

Back in the house, Buddy placed his supplies on the kitchen counter. The back door led to an enclosed back porch that housed a large sink with hot and cold water. A washboard hung on the wall above the sink. To the side, another door revealed a pantry. Buddy saw a trap door in the floor, and underneath, discovered a double-walled tin box with a fitted lid. The overflow water from the tank outside gurgled between the walls of the box. The interior was almost ice cold. "Good place for the ham and bacon. Butter too. I can put the rest of the chicken in here, and it should be good for a few days. I'll have to see if anybody has eggs. They would keep in here, too."

Buddy came to view his forced confinement in the valley as a stewardship of the girls' property. Recalling the bitter cold in Ohio, he acted on the idea of boxing in the pipes on the outside wall of the house.

November and December were wet. Heavy rains soaked the Willamette Valley. Rivers and creeks topped their banks, but did not flood. Snow mantled the hills to the east and west of the valley, but only reached the low part once in December.

January brought a change. Snow covered the farms, and Buddy only ventured out to care for the mules. February brought color. The sun came out, and daffodils sprouted. Crocus blossoms were gems on both sides of the flagstones. March filled the sprouting grass with patches of gold, the daffodils trumpeting the arrival of new life.

The last week of March, Meek rode out to the farm. "Pack up, Deputy. The road's open. Man came down from Dalles City yesterday. Said they had the trees cut, and crossings doable. Give it a week for the water levels to go down, and you should be able to go over. Coming back?"

"I don't know. I'll know more when I get over the mountain."

Chapter 27

Buddy wandered out to the barn. He lowered the wagon tongue, then raised it again. Opening the canvas he had tacked over the wagon box, he began sorting the goods he had purchased. The oats would stay for the journey. He pondered over the foodstuffs. The Hollisters could use it. He knew he would need to load hay for the mules for the barren stretches along the road. As he debated the various items, some made their way into the house. Lamp oil could stay on this side of the mountain.

Flour and tinned goods went into the cupboards in the kitchen. The more he debated with himself, the less remained in the wagon. Eventually, he had the load reduced to oats, hay, and the girls' trunk.

For himself, he threw his soogan in the back. He could sleep on the hay. The mules could eat it even after he slept on it. If they did not like his smell, he would keep his mattress all the way to Dalles City, then sweep the wagon box clean.

Uncertainty agitated him. Could the mules handle

that steep climb along the trail? Had the girls survived the winter? Were Jo and Sarah able to be friends? Where was Tom Flannagan? Would late-season snow close the road? Should he have left immediately?

Buddy pulled out the bags he had used on the trail. From the possible bag, he took the gold from the wagon on Deer Creek, and laid it on the table. Two hundred dollars remained. His money belt still held the six hundred from Uncle Jack. He muttered, "More than enough."

He got out the cape gun, cleaned and oiled it, and wrapped it in oilskin. He cleaned and oiled the revolver, and checked his supply of caps and bullets. "Not that I'll need them, but then..."

He began to plan the trip over. Two days to Oregon City. He'd better allow five or six days to cover the eighty-some miles of the Barlow Road. Figure another day to reach Hollisters' place. His mind started playing the 'what if' game.

"That is not faith, Father. I need to set my thoughts on You, and on my Savior. Looking at things here, I get to wanting what I want, not what You want. Give me the grace to see Your hand in all You do."

Unable to concentrate on things in the house, Buddy went to the barn, and dragged the harnesses out of the far stall. He arranged the straps, oiled the leather and the hardware, and laid them out to be ready for the mules. He decided to pony Ben behind the wagon, and threw the mule's saddle and saddle blanket under the driver's seat.

The thought occurred to him, "What if trees come down?" He hung a crosscut saw and an ax on the sides of the wagon box, then threw a shovel and pick in for good measure, hiding them under the driver's seat. He tucked the bundle of papers Meek had drawn up in the tray of the girls' trunk.

Impatience dogged his every move. He had headed west for Dalles City, not knowing what he would find or find out. He had found Sarah, but knew no more than he knew when he left Ohio. Now here he was, heading again for Dalles City, not knowing what he would find. It was the not knowing that agitated him, that irritated him. Meek had said to wait a week. Five days had dragged by. Tomorrow would be close to a week. He was leaving!

By nine the next morning, Buddy had the mules harnessed, and Ben tied to the back of the wagon. He pulled out of the barn, and jumped down to close the door. Back on the driver's seat, he twitched the reins, setting the mules in motion. Clouds hung over the hills, but no rain was falling.

He pulled the wagon to a stop in front of the store on Mill Creek. From the wagon seat, he looked through the window. Meek was again sitting at his table. He rose as Buddy entered. "Leaving today, are you? I figured you would. Can't sit still, can you?"

"Nope. Gotta get going. I have to get over the hill before the wagons start coming this way. Here. Take this." Buddy held out the key to the Simon place.

Meek said, "I'll check on things for you. Hold the key for you, too. Mighty rainy this winter, but I'll expect you back anyway. Keep your eyes open."

With that admonition, Buddy left the store. Meek watched him climb to the seat, and start the mules north. "Good stuff in that kid," Meek muttered.

The clatter of hooves and the rumble of wheels lulled Buddy into drowsy endurance as the wagon rolled north past Champoeg, and scattered farms and clustered houses. Late the second day, He reached Oregon City, and turned to go the wrong way over the Barlow Road, built for wagons headed west. The road crossed rivers and creeks, then began the long climb along ridges, upward, ever upward. Laurel Hill was a challenge for the mules. Buddy led Ben to the front of the wagon, and tied a rope from his saddle to the tongue of the wagon. With the five pulling, the wagon crept to the top of the hill.

Buddy decided if he came the other way with the wagon, he would need to bring a lot of rope to let the wagon down the slope. The brakes would never hold on that steep pitch.

The road flattened out a bit at the top of the grade. It still climbed, but at a manageable degree. Ben was behind the wagon again, at the end of his lead rope. The ridge spread out, and the road led through dense timber on each side. Fallen trees slowly decayed on the forest floor, victims of the relentless pioneer axes as they built the road around Mount Hood. Back in the timber, Buddy saw a large black bear, recently awakened, lolloping away from the trail. The breeze brought the scent of the bear to the mules. They snorted, but did not shy.

The next day, Buddy guided the wagon onto the downward stretch of road that led to the creek that marked the final eastward portion of the Barlow Road. It would follow the creek out into the Deschutes Valley, where he would turn north toward Dalles City.

"We're getting there," Buddy called to the mules. "Keep it up, Smokey! Twenty-five miles down this valley, then we turn left for another twenty-five. Then at Dalles City, it's right for another twelve or so, and you get to rest! But we can't make it in one day. We'll stop at the end of this valley."

Where the Barlow Road turned north, Buddy saw diverging wagon traces. One led toward the Deschutes, and two more angled south into the valley of the Deschutes. He drove half a mile toward the river, and stopped in a broad meadow. "Settlers must be taking claims up here," Buddy muttered. "Not bad, but really rocky." Basalt outcroppings and stacks broke the grassland, with benches of soil stair-stepping up from the river somewhere south of the turning of the road. The creek he had been following sang its way eastward toward the river. "By God's direction." Buddy talked to the mules as he picketed them. "The creek runs to the Deschutes, the Deschutes runs to the Columbia, and the Columbia runs to the ocean. I wonder if the creek knows where it's going."

The mules turned to cropping the fresh spring grass, ignoring the musings of the one they served. As he prepared a meager supper, Buddy talked to the campfire. "I guess I'm like the creek. Something lies ahead, and like the creek, I suppose whatever it is will carry me." Looking up, he prayed, "Isn't that how You work sometimes, Lord? You don't show us what lies ahead, but You order our steps. Sometimes You use delays or events we don't see coming. When this creek reaches the ocean, the rain comes back to the mountains, and the creek runs down the valley. Is life like that? Do I go back to where I started? To the farm in Ohio? If that's what You have for me, I'll go. I need Your light."

Next morning, as he harnessed the mules, Buddy told them, "The hardest part is over. You get good road today. We should reach Hollister's place by evening."

The sun was settling toward the peak of Mount Hood when he pulled the team to a stop at the gate to Hollister's front pasture. There were no horses there to greet him. When he had fastened the gate, he drove to the barn, and pulled the mules to a stop. There were no mules in the corral.

Buddy heard the house door close. Turning, he saw a man walking toward where he had stopped the wagon. It was not Hollister.

Buddy climbed down from the wagon, and stood waiting, confusion lining his brow. The man reached out his hand. "Beckwith. Ed Beckwith. Hollister said I was to watch for a green wagon. You must be Wilson."

"I'm Buddy Wilson. Where's Hollister?"

"Gone east. He sold out. Gave up when Alice died. Said this part of the country had taken everything he had. He was going home."

"Alice died?" Buddy pictured the big-hearted woman who had embraced the three girls, even in the midst of her own sorrow. "What happened?"

"Pneumonia. They had a bit of a wedding here. Fellow named Tom Flannagan showed up first of December, and in February, he married a girl staying with the Hollisters. Sarah, it was. A week later, Alice was dead.

"I ran into Hollister two weeks ago in Dalles City. I was looking for a place to locate, and he sold me his claim. He had already sold off his stock. He lit out over the trail a week ago, riding a mule and leading three more mules that he had loaded with harness, and a donkey that carried his stuff. A mammoth jack, it was. Said he'd find a wagon somewhere. Maybe Fort Bridger."

Buddy surveyed the farm, now devoid of livestock. Beckwith said, "Sally's got supper on the stove. Pot of stew. There's plenty, if I can get you to share our table. Simple fare. She baked biscuits, too."

"I'll stay for supper, but I'll be moving along. Got a wagon to deliver."

As they entered the house, Buddy was met by memories of the girls, and the Hollisters. He closed his eyes, then opened them to see a young wife who could pass for Sarah's twin.

Ed Beckwith said, "Sally, this is the fellow we were to watch for. Buddy Wilson. He came looking for the Hollisters, and found us instead. Go ahead and set another place at the table. He's had a long haul today, and isn't done yet."

Sally smiled at Buddy as she turned to the kitchen.

"When Ben Hollister left, Tom and Sarah took the

other girls with them. Tom said if you got here I was to give you this." He reached for a paper on the mantle over the fireplace, and handed Buddy a map. "He took a place down from the elbow of the Barlow Road, where it heads out of the Deschutes Valley. You might have seen wagon tracks where people didn't go to Oregon City. A fellow named Oswald Shaw built a double cabin just above the Deschutes, but he's gone over the hill to Oregon City to meet a steamer. Seems there's a girl coming he's hoping to marry. Sally will be tickled if there's another young bride here.

"Tom's there for a short time. Said he's waiting for you."

Buddy frowned. "I camped on the wagon trace that headed toward the river. I must have stopped too soon."

After supper, Buddy said, "I appreciate your hospitality. But really, I have to get going. Maybe I'll stop by again."

A handshake, and he was on his way. Back on the trail, he headed toward Dalles City. "Sorry, mules. You thought you were done, but we have to go back. It'll be morning before you get to rest. In the fading light, Buddy wrote a message on the back of Tom's map:

"Tom, permit me to offer my best wishes to you and Sarah. She married a good man. You won, Tom. I'm leaving, so I won't cause Sarah to wonder. If you are ever in Ohio, I expect you to stop by the farm. God keep you both. Oh, and tell Jo to be sure to go through the trunk. It has personal things and her money."

Darkness ended his writing. The road was plain, even though night had fallen. The mules plodded through the gloom.

Buddy reined onto the Barlow Road, heading south up the Deschutes. In the half light of morning, Buddy passed his previous camp. It was a mile later that he made out the ghosts of the cabin and barn through the fog that clung to the valley floor. He took the fork that led to the barn. He unharnessed the mules, and tied them to the fence. He saddled Ben, and hung his bags and soogan behind the saddle. Ready for the trail, he picked up a rock and walked quietly to the porch. He laid the note on the top step, and weighted it down with the rock.

He led his mule back up the wagon trace to where he could mount without awakening anybody in the cabin, then rode back toward the Barlow Road. He turned in the saddle, and waved, although he knew nobody would see. "Good-bye, Sarah, Jo. And you, Mary." Misty-eyed, he headed out on a long journey into yesterday.

Chapter 28

The fog held back the dawn at the double cabin above the Deschutes. Beams of spring sunlight swept the last wisps from the valley, and awakened the cabin dwellers. Jo was the first to emerge, and froze mid-stretch. Her look swept from the green wagon to the four mules. "Oh! Smokey!" She started for the barn, but saw the paper on the step. She grabbed it and read the message.

The morning chill was torn by a drawn-out wail, "Oh, No-o-o-o." Tom emerged from the other cabin to find Jo seated on the step, staring blankly at the wagon. She held the paper out to Tom. "He's gone. He c-came sometime...in the n-night. He's gone..." Jo collapsed into spasms of grief.

Tom read the note, then strode into the house. He showed the note to Sarah, and said, "He can't be too far ahead. I'll catch him. I'll bring him back if I have to hogtie him!"

^ ^ ^

Buddy camped near the Deschutes Crossing. "I won't bother the ferryman tonight. Tomorrow is soon enough." Buddy chewed jerky, and gnawed the last biscuit Sally had pressed upon him.

He sat gazing into the dying embers of his campfire. Tiny tongues of flame took on shapes that danced before him, memories that appeared and faded. Sarah on the farm in Ohio. Jo and Mary in their make-shift clothes along the North Platte. The trail. The long endless trail. Now he faced it again, without interest or enthusiasm.

"Hello, the camp!"

Buddy shook his head in despair. He had not seen Tom's ghost in the embers.

"Wilson, is that you?"

No, it was Tom himself. "Come on, and pull up a rock, Tom. How'd you find me?"

"I just followed the scent of despair you've been trailing." He came up on the other side of the embers, and all the ghosts that had danced before Buddy vanished.

Tom sat on a rock next to Buddy. "Where do you think you are headed, my friend?"

"Did you see my note? I'm going back to the farm in Ohio."

"You're on a fool's errand, then. Wiggins sold the farm. There's nothing there for you."

"Sold the farm? It's gone?"

"It's still there, but for you, it's gone. Remember the couple he let it to? Jennings, it was. They bought it. Went partners with Joe Simmons. Wiggins sent you the money. He got a thousand for the farm. The potato crop brought five hundred, and with the rest of the money for the years of crops, it came to three thousand. In that chest at the foot of the bed, your grandparents had another thousand. I dragged all that gold across the country. I left it back at the cabin. You should have stopped."

"I did, but I left. I didn't think I could see Sarah, now she's your wife."

Tom shook his head. "Buddy, you could never have married her. She's your sister."

Buddy sat in stunned silence. Then, "My sister? As in, same parents?"

"Right. Remember that trunk in the Wilsons' bedroom that you never dealt with? Wiggins searched it, and there was a family Bible in it. Remember he told you your mother died in childbirth? Well, Sarah was that child. Your mother died, but the baby lived. But she didn't get a name. She was just Baby. The neighbors who took you had a cousin across in Kentucky who had just had a baby boy. That cousin wet nursed Sarah until she was weaned, then took her to her own grandmother, Grandma Wilson.

Your mother's name was Sarah Wilson Logan. Joseph and Edna Wilson were your grandparents. They knew Sarah was their granddaughter, and gave her her mother's name. You just appeared, and they did not know who you were. The people you knew as Aunt Sarah and Uncle Hank were the neighbors of Michael and Sarah Logan. Your father had Logan's Crossing at the mouth of Raccoon Creek. When your parents died, those neighbors did the best they could for you. Then they moved on. As they were headed down river, they let you off at your grandparents home.

"Little Sarah took you up to the house, and the Wilsons took you in, never knowing you were Sarah's brother. I married Sarah, because you couldn't.

"We had to wait for someone to marry us. Sarah turned eighteen on February first. Daniel Lee came to check on something to do with the mission, and while he was here, he married us there at Hollister's. Daniel is the nephew of Jason Lee. Jason started the mission in the Willamette Valley."

"The Wilsons were my own family? But I'm not a Wilson. I'm a Logan?"

"Right. The Bible has you as James Joseph Logan. You got your grandpa's name for your middle name."

"That explains the Seamas. That's Irish for

James. That's why my mother always corrected me by saying 'Don't shame us'."

Tom laughed. "That's a good one. But, yes. You are a Logan, son of Michael Logan, grandson of Joseph Wilson. So the money I brought is to share between you and your sister."

Buddy mused, "When Gilson took her, Sarah's note mentioned an estate. Did Jackson Wiggins find out anything about that?"

Tom coughed, then said, "Aye, Sir Buddy, and ye're the rightful Laird o' the hoose o' Gilson. A gr-r-rand estate it was, tae."

"Be serious."

"I am serious. In Scotland, there was a manor house with townlands and farm lands and a fortune to support the estate. The House of Gilson. And you are the rightful laird of the estate."

"Impossible!"

"Not only possible, but true. Savor that bit of prestige a moment before I shatter your fantasy. Wiggins found out the trail of descent."

"How do I figure into that? Is it related to Elmer Gilson? Am I?"

"In a way. He got wind of the rumored estate in some papers from his family archives. He was not Sarah's Uncle George. He was a distant cousin.

Do you want the story from front to back, or in order?"

Buddy shook his head in amazement. "Start at the back and work down to how I come in."

Tom chuckled. "All right, we'll start with the next to the last laird. Charles Gilson, it was. He inherited the House of Gilson from his father. At that time, the estate was sound, tidy, and well funded. Rents came in, as well as shares from the farms. Sir Charles thought more highly of himself than he ought to. His ego was inflated by his position. But, he was a fool. He was a drunkard and a gambler. Alcohol makes a gambler reckless. Charles ran up enormous debts, and to satisfy them, he gradually sold off the townlands and farmlands. The estate was stripped of the income that would keep it solvent.

"The next laird was his son, Malcolm. He followed in his father's footsteps. He was a fool, a drunkard and a gambler."

Buddy muttered, "The sins of the fathers..."

Tom shook his head. "No, that's not it. Don't misunderstand that Scripture. Malcolm chose his sin. It was not inevitable because his father did the same things. We all choose our own sins."

Buddy said, "But doesn't the Bible say God visits the sins of the fathers on the descendants to the third and fourth generation?"

"It does, but that has to do with God's mercy. He said that to the Children of Israel, and in dealing with them, He withheld the consequences of their sin for three or four generations, to give them space to repent.

"They didn't. Then He said he would not hold the sons accountable for the sins of the fathers. Everyone would bear the consequences of his own sins. It was not that God changed his mind. He emphasizes different aspects of His character at different times. They despised His mercy, so he dealt with them in his justice.

"Malcolm saw the consequences of the sins of his father. He could have chosen different sins, but without Christ, he could only choose sin. His idea was that he could do a better job of sinning than Charles did. He determined to win back the manor house lands. The only resources he had to use in his gamble were the funds in the estate's account. He was no better at gambling than his father had been. When the financial estate was squandered, he set the manor house afire, and shot himself inside the burning building. If Elmer Gilson wanted the estate, all he would have found was ashes, ashes of the manor house and of his ancestor."

Buddy was stunned by the fall of the house of Gilson. "So, there is no estate?"

"No. The land was taken by the Crown. I suppose the title is still hanging out there somewhere.

There's more. This is where you come in. Malcolm had a son named Thomas. The son was in school in London when the collapse occurred. With no means of support, he moved to Ireland, and then came to the Colonies for a fresh start. To get out from under the stigma of failure, he changed his name to Wilson. A generation later, his cousin Wilfred Gilson came over, and kept the name. Elmer Gilson was Wilfred's great-grandson.

"Thomas Wilson was with George Washington when he surveyed the Ohio Valley. Thomas Wilson's great grandson Joseph moved to the Ohio Valley after the war, and built the cabin and farm on Brush Creek. His daughter Sarah, your mother, married Michael Logan, who had the ferry at Raccoon Creek. So, by right of primogeniture, you are the rightful Laird of the House of Gilson."

Buddy frowned. "And that is what led Elmer Gilson to, in effect, kidnap Sarah?"

"Yes. He did not know about you, the first born. He figured that by line of descent, if he married Sarah, he would have a claim to the title and the estate. He did not know you were Sarah's older brother. You would have to deny any claim to the estate before he could strut around as a laird."

Buddy laughed. "I don't want a title. It would mean nothing on this side of the ocean. I have a better inheritance waiting for me in the heavenlies, anyway. Joint heirs with Jesus, the Book tells us. I've been adopted."

"Better, indeed! The one Elmer Gilson craved has been devoured by moths and rust, and stolen by thieves. Sarah has a better guardian of her estate. She is being kept by God's power, and so is her estate. Elmer Gilson missed out all around."

Buddy chuckled. "You married Sarah, so if I die with no heir, that would make you the laird, wouldn't it?"

Tom laughed. "I suppose it would. Oh, the honor of position! But seriously, what's next for you?"

"I don't know. There's really nothing here for me."

"And do you disdain God's precious gift to you? Do you count it as nothing? I'm taking you back with me, if I have to tie your ankles together under that mule of yours. And I mean it."

"God's gift? What do you mean by that?"

"I mean Jo. She loves you with a deep and abiding love. You left her in a pool of despair as deep as your own this morning."

"Jo hates me. She told me so."

Tom smacked his hand with his fist. "Listen, you! You kept Mary between the two of you on the trail, but you held Sarah between you in your mind. Jo kept a wall of animosity between the two of you. She couldn't trust you, or any other man, after what Weston did. But you knocked that wall down. With kindness. With something as little as a hair brush.

"When you rescued Sarah, and asked Jo to accept her, Alice heard Jo whisper, 'Not my will, but Yours...' After the rescue, she hugged Sarah. Jo has loved you for hundreds of miles, but hid it on Sarah's account. At that moment, Jo sacrificed all her dreams on the altar. Now she had hope again, and you dashed those hopes when you dropped the wagon without so much as waving."

Buddy muttered, "I waved. At the cabin, anyway."

"Doesn't count."

"I don't love her in the right way."

"Buddy, you have done nothing but seek her best interest since you found her. You sacrificed your own interests all along the trail. You guarded her, and guarded her purity. She told me. Everything. That's the way God loves us. He has always sought our best interest, even if we did not think so. He has guarded us. He is making us pure in His Son. That is His love for us. That is the love He pours into our hearts, so we can share that love. By His Spirit, that love is in you, if you will only let it flow through you. To Jo. She's waiting, Buddy. You don't have to wait like we did.

Remember, I'm ordained. Sarah can be a witness, and I'm sure we can find another. That's all you need."

"I can't just go and tell her, 'Well, Tom married Sarah. How about you marrying me?' That would make her a consolation prize."

"Don't look at it that way. Jo doesn't. It was never a choice between the two girls. The Lord himself delayed your return until I came with what Wiggins had found out. Look at it that way. See Jo as the treasure God has been trying to give you since you found her on the Platte."

"You know how I found her, don't you?"

"I do. Naked as a newborn baby, and at the point of death. You rescued her, covered her nakedness, and nursed her back to strength. She held it against you that you saw her as you did, and that you held Sarah between you. But the Lord softened her heart. Your loyalty to Sarah, and your constant kind treatment of Mary softened her heart. No, it wasn't that. It was you sharing the Gospel with Mary, and indirectly with her, that the Lord used to soften her heart and turn her animosity toward you to love. You might have missed it. The seeds of trust sprouted when she said to Mary, 'No, he won't look.' But she loved you behind your back from the moment you placed that bag with the comb and hair brush in her lap. Trust led to confidence, and dependence. You fed her physical hunger, and her spiritual hunger. I honor you for that. I also honor you for saving Sarah, and sheltering her from what she perceived as her shame. Now, load up, and let's go. It'll take all night, but Jo will be sitting on the porch, waiting for you, even if it is just before dawn. She will be waiting for the dawn of love to brighten her day. Load up. I left my horse down on the trail."

Buddy scattered the embers, and drizzled water from his canteen over the place where his memories had danced. The water sizzled and steamed, and in the cloud of steam, he imagined Jo.

Ghosts in the gloom, the horse and mule turned onto the Barlow Road. Hoof beats drummed in the darkness. Once more, in the pre-dawn shadows, Buddy rode down the wagon trace toward the Deschutes. They approached the cabin. As Tom had predicted, two figures huddled on the porch, sitting, waiting.

"Tom? Buddy?" Sarah's voice called out to them.

Tom answered, "We're here!" The two men dismounted, and stood together. The two girls ran to meet them, both embracing Buddy. Sarah's voice was tinged with rebuke. "That was naughty of you, to drop the wagon and run. Where have you been?"

Hearing voices, Mary came out on the porch. "Did Buddy come?"

Sarah said, "Yes, Mary. He's here. Come get a hug."

"I'm in my night dress."

Jo's quavery voice said, "He won't look, Mary."

Tom said, "Inside, all of you. Sarah, Honey, light the lamp. Buddy might fall asleep at the table, but we'd better feed him, and Jo will want to see him in the light, just to know he's really here."

Jo's giggle was soggy.

Inside, Sarah said, "All right, Brother. It sounds funny to say that. But, out with it. Where have you been?"

"Brother. It does sound funny, Sister. Say, how's your back?"

Sarah blushed, looking downward.

Tom answered, "Smooth as silk!

Sarah's blush deepened. To cover her embarrassment, she repeated, "Where have you been?"

Tom winked at Sarah and said, "Later, Wife. Feed the man. He hasn't slept in ages. He drove to Beckwiths, and found out we were married and were living here. Then he turned around and drove all night to get back here. He actually camped a mile from us before he went to Beckwiths. Then he traveled all day. I found him camping just this side of the Deschutes Crossing, planning to take the ferry in the morning. But we rode all night to get here this morning. That is too long without sleep. He plans to unroll his soogan in the hay, and not talk to anybody until he wakes up, today, tomorrow or next week. But, feed the man, first. I'll eat the crumbs that fall from the table."

Sarah smiled at him. "You will not. I'll fix enough for all of us. And if he does not wake up in time for supper, I'll get a bucket of water from the river to help him."

During breakfast, Jo sat with her eyes downcast, throwing Buddy an occasional shy glance. He did not notice. Breakfast over, he stumbled to the barn, burrowed into his blankets, and fell into a dreamless sleep. It was indeed nearly dinner time when he finally stirred. He stretched, and sat looking around himself at unfamiliar objects. Finally, his glance fell on Jo, who sat at the foot of his bed.

"Is it morning?"

Jo tossed her head, laughing. "No, but it was. Suppertime, Sleepyhead!" She jumped up and ran to the cabin. Buddy stretched, crawled out of his blankets, and stretched again. Tired joints and muscles cracked and popped. He was so slow in coming out of the barn that Jo had come running back. She threw her arms around him, and said, "I love you, Buddy, or Jimmy, or

James, or whatever you want to be called! I may be a shameless hussy, but I mean it. I love you with all of me, all my heart."

Freeing himself, and holding her at arm's length, Buddy said, "You're no hussy. But I'll wait to say it, Jo, until I'm sure. I have to digest all the news." Pulling her back to himself, he said, "I do like you, though. I just have to be sure it's God's kind of love. Wanting you isn't enough."

Jo closed her eyes, but nodded. "I understand. I kept pushing you away. I'm sorry."

Buddy crushed her to himself, then released her. "It isn't you, Jo. It's me. There's more than you know, and more than I can understand right now. Did you get into the stuff in the wagon?"

Walking beside him, Jo said, "No. I couldn't. I was too..."

"Hurt? I'm sorry, Jo. You knew more than I did, and what I did not know sent me away. But we'll talk about what lies ahead over supper."

Over dinner, Buddy recounted the delays caused by the storm, and the struggle to get back over Laurel Hill. "It is steep! So steep that heading for Oregon City, a wagon would slide to the bottom and crash, if it was not held back by ropes. Coming this way, I had to add my riding mule to the team, and lead him as he led the team that pulled the wagon."

Looking to Tom, he asked, "What are your plans, Tom? Beckwith said you are not here permanently."

Tom paused, and looked at Sarah. "I was thinking of trying to locate a place where I might be able to make a home for Sarah. Then maybe do some ministry. We don't know where, though."

Buddy got up and headed for the door. "I'll be right back. There are some things I have to get from the wagon." He returned with the girls' family Bible, their pouch of gold, and a packet of papers which he placed on the table. Opening the Bible to the family record, he pushed it across to Jo and Mary. "There you both are, with your mother and father. You just had a birthday, Mary. You're eleven now."

Jo looked up and said, "I did, too. I'm eighteen."

Buddy shook his head. "I missed all three birthdays. Did anyone have a party?"

Sarah laughed. "I did, if you could call a wedding a party. But that was not for my birthday."

Jo and Mary pretended to pout. Mary said, "We forgot. We were waiting and waiting, and forgot."

Jo and Mary looked with hungry eyes at the names on the page, then at each other. Jo said, "They were married on Christmas Day."

Their foreheads bumped together as they bowed over the page. Jo's voice was unsteady as she said, "Thank you for this, Buddy. I have longed for this more than anything else Weston stole."

All that he said at dinner was small talk. As Sarah cleared away the dishes, Buddy looked across at Jo. "Weston's dead. I didn't do it. He tried to stab me in the back, but Joseph Meek warned me. I dropped flat, and Weston fell on his own knife."

Horror lined Jo's face. "He tried to kill you?"

"He did. But Ben Hollister told me there's a verse in the Bible that says that whoever digs a pit will fall into it, and a stone will come back on the one who starts it rolling. Gilson and Weston were alike in that. What they did to others, well, the Lord brought onto their own heads."

Jo said, "If you have nine lives like a cat, you're down to five. The Indians took one, the bandits took one, and Gilson and Weston each took one. The rest are mine!"

Buddy smiled, and went on. "There's more to that story. Weston had spent your money to buy the home and land of a man who had lost his wife. The man was in grief, and wanted to leave the area. Weston took him out to the house, to help him gather his stuff, as he said. But Weston killed him, and took back your gold. Since it was your money that bought the place, Joseph Meek said it is yours if you want it. Yours and Mary's.

It's a quarter section, with a house and two barns. Since I could not get back here last fall, I lived in the house all winter.

"There's another house and barn with eighty acres next to it. It has an orchard with it that Joe Meek says is ready to start bearing fruit. I have not been in that house, but I used some of the money from the wagon on Deer Creek to secure it. Sarah, it's yours if you want it."

He laid the papers on the table. "Here are the papers for the Simon place. It's the big one, that belongs to Jo and Mary. This other bundle is for the Roberts place, the eighty acres with a house and barn.

Jo and Mary asked together, "We could live there?"

Buddy smiled. "Comfortably. More comfortably than you can imagine."

Tom looked to Sarah. "A home all ready for you, Honey. It's not here, but we could get there. Soon."

Sarah's eyes brimmed with tears. "Let's!"

Buddy looked up to see Jo watching him, dreams of home and family kindling in her eyes.

"Tom, I don't know what the Roberts house is like. It was close to the girls' house, so I just...bought it. Both are in my name, but Joe

Meek said it would just take a recording fee to change that. Simon included things in the girls' house you would not believe. He captured water at a spring above the house. Gravity fills a tank, and then gravity sends the water into the house. In the kitchen, there's a tub in the counter with gizmos that when you twist the knob, water runs into the tub. Water also goes through pipes into a hot water reservoir in the cook stove. From there you get hot water in the kitchen, and there's a room with an indoor privy with a tank where you pull the chain and it washes out the privy. There's an enamel bath tub, and hot and cold water run into that. I don't know if you have those things in the Roberts house, but there's money to put in whatever you want to add."

Tom just sat shaking his head. "God is good, Sarah girl. God is good. I'll take you."

Buddy looked across at Jo, who sat dreaming. "While you are dreaming, Jo, when I left, the house was surrounded by crocuses and daffodils. I'm guessing Simon planted them for the missus."

Called back from her dreamland, Jo asked, "Did you say the house is furnished? Beds and everything?"

"Furnished? I should say. It has three bedrooms, and beds in all of them. The kitchen has everything you could need, and more. There's a table with chairs, and a rocking chair and a really long chair in the front room. And a soft chair. There's even a swing on the porch."

Jo was off in her dream world again.

Mary said, "I could have one bedroom, Jo could have one, and you could have one."

Buddy shook his head. "Not so fast, Kiddo. I can't live in the house with you unless Jo and I got married!"

Mary's solution was simple. "Then get married."

"Mary!" Jo's smile softened her reprimand.

"Well, he should! You cry when you think I'm asleep, but I know. 'Sides, you told me that you love him."

"Mary, that's not supposed to be shared."

Mary retreated into a silent pout.

Buddy looked at Jo. Mentally, he faded her out. He thought, "What would life be like without her?" He gazed down the corridor of time, imagining the empty years. The word came to mind, 'Bleak.' In that moment, he knew. He thought, "Thank You, Lord, for this precious gift!"

He said, "Jo, come out to the wagon with me." He took her hand and pulled her up from her chair.

When he got to the parked wagon, he felt his

way to the front, and reached under the driver's seat.

Jo asked, "What are you looking for?"

"My possible bag."

"Why do you call it that?"

"Fitzpatrick at Fort Laramie said mountain men carried them, and put whatever it might be possible to need in them. I carry my tinder box, powder flask, bullets and caps." He groped in the bottom of the bag. "I even put the money from the Deer Creek wagon in here." He felt the silk jewelry bag, and pulled it out, fingering the rings through the fabric, then slipped it into his pocket.

He turned Jo to face him, and said simply, "Jo, I'm sure. Will you..." His words were cut short by hungry lips on his.

ABOUT THE AUTHOR

Raised on a farm in rural Oregon, Michael Leamy knows the endless quietness of isolation found in nature. Quietness is an odd word to choose, as the wind rustles the leaves, and the creek burbles over stones, accompanied by a choir of birds. And yet, in the midst of the business of modern life, it is in this oasis of peace that leaden ears can finally perceive the quiet voice of God's Spirit.

Michael Leamy and his wife, Lynda, enjoy life on a peaceful knoll overlooking Young's Bay, on the way to the Pacific Ocean. Psalm 23 says "He leads me beside the still waters…" Still waters are the waters of quietness. Whatever the waters are doing, they quiet the tumult of the mind. The crashing waves of the Pacific ocean can be heard from miles away, but even the roar of the ocean brings peace.

Tucked within these pages, please find the words of truth that speak peace to the troubled soul. May they guide you to the Book, and a fuller knowledge of the Prince of Peace.

Other Books By This Author:

Higher Ground / Quest for the White Robin / PulsePoint

Among the Stones / Between the Dates

A Handful of Quietness / Today's Thought

Clay Baby (With Rowlanda Leamy)

All Available on Amazon

Made in the USA
Middletown, DE
04 August 2024

58503458R00212